Louis Joseph Vance

Nobody

Outlook

Louis Joseph Vance

Nobody

1. Auflage | ISBN: 978-3-73262-245-0

Erscheinungsort: Frankfurt am Main, Deutschland

Erscheinungsjahr: 2018

Outlook Verlag GmbH, Frankfurt.

NOBODY

LOUIS JOSEPH VANCE

"Miss Manwaring! For the Love of Mike—"
Page 326 Nobody.

1

NOBODY

By LOUIS JOSEPH VANCE

AUTHOR OF "The Lone Wolf,"
"The Brass Bowl,"
"Cynthia of the Minute,"
"The Destroying Angel,"
Etc.

With Frontispiece
By W. L. JACOBS

A. L. BURT COMPANY

Publishers
New York
Published by Arrangement. with GEORGE H. DORAN COMPANY
Copyright, 1914,
By LOUIS JOSEPH VANCE
Copyright, 1915,
By GEORGE H. DORAN COMPANY

*This novel was originally published serially,
under the title of "An Outsider."*

CHAPTER

NOBODY

CHAPTER I

ANARCHY

"What you gonna have?"

To this inquiry the patron made no response; head bent, nose between the pages of the magazine, she pored sedulously over a legend attached to one of the illustrations.

After a decent pause in waiting the waitress renewed her demand with a sharper accent:

"Say, lis'en; what you want?"

"White satin, veiled with *point d' Angleterre*,'" Miss Manvers replied distinctly, if without looking up, aware simply of something imperative in the starched but humid presence at her elbow.

Pardonably startled, the waitress demanded with the rising inflection: "*Wha-a-at?*"

"'The court train,'" Miss Manvers pursued in abstraction, "'is lined with lace and dotted with bouquets of orange-blossoms—'"

She checked herself suddenly, looked up shyly, and essayed a pale, apologetic smile.

"I'm sorry; I didn't realise—"

But now the waitress had caught a glimpse of the illustration and was bending over the patron's shoulder for a better look.

"Gee!" she commented sincerely. "Ain't that a dream?"

"Yes," Miss Manvers admitted wistfully, "it's a dream, right enough!"

"That's so, too." Deftly, with a large, moist, red hand, the waitress arranged knife, fork, spoon, and paper serviette on the unclothed brown board before

Miss Manvers. "That's the worst of them fashion mag'zines," she complained; "they get your goat. Sometimes after readin' some of that dope I can't hardly remember orders right, just for wishin' somebody'd come along and hang some of them joyful rags onto me!"

Then, catching the eye of the manager, she straightway resumed her professional habit of slightly wilted hauteur—compounded in equal parts of discontent, tired feet, heat-fag and that profound disdain for food-consuming animals which inevitably informs the mind of every quick-lunch waitress.

"What you gonna have?" she demanded dispassionately.

"Ham-and, please."

"Plate of ham-and. Cawfy?"

"Yes, iced coffee and"—Miss Manvers hesitated briefly—"and a napoleon."

Reciting the amended order, the waitress withdrew.

For the next few moments the customer neglected the fashion magazine which she had found—apparently a souvenir of some other absent-minded patron—on the seat of the chair next that one of her own casual choice.

She stared blankly at the smudged and spotted bill of fare propped up, in its wooden frame, against an armour-plate-china sugar-bowl. She was deeply intrigued by the mystery of human frailty as exemplified by her reckless extravagance in ordering that superfluous bit of pastry. Miss Manvers's purse contained a single coin of silver, the quarter of a dollar; being precisely the sum of her entire fortune. Her ham and beans would cost fifteen cents, the coffee and the napoleon five cents each. In other words, she would be penniless when she had paid her score—and Heaven only knew for how long afterward.

Her lips moved without sound in her worn and pallid face. "What's the difference?" she bully-ragged her conscience. "I might as well be broke as the way I am!"

The argument was painfully reasonable; that inmate of New York who has but five cents has nothing.

On the other hand, there was nothing whatever to be advanced in extenuation of her folly in thus inviting indigestion—a passion for pastry is its own punishment no less than any other infatuation to which mortal flesh is prone. Sally was morally certain she would suffer, and that severely, before nightfall.

"Well, what of it?" she grumbled sullenly. "If I die for it, it's cheap at the price! And, no matter what happens, it can't be any hotter afterward than it is now."

Somehow soothed by this cynical reflection, she sat up, mopped her flushed forehead with a handkerchief of which she was not proud, and drank thirstily of her tumbler of ice-water.

The grateful draft reminded her that she had actually been athirst ever since noon. It was now almost three o'clock—thanks to which fact she might eat in the comparative comfort of a lunchroom which boasted no patron other than herself. But she was little appreciative of this boon; she comprehended her surroundings with just a little languid resentment of their smug cleanliness and their atmosphere impregnated with effluvia of cheap edibles. But if these seemed offensive she would have been willing to overlook them on certain conditions—as she proved when the waitress reappeared with her order.

"I don't suppose—" Miss Manvers began, but hesitated.

"What say?"

"I don't suppose you need any more girls here?"

"Lookin' for a job?" the waitress inquired brilliantly. "I dunno—I'll ask the manager, if you want."

Miss Manvers nodded a barely audible "Please!" She munched drearily for a few minutes, staring out through the front windows wherein, from dawn till dark, a white-clad chef industriously browned the wheats and cast sinkers; beyond their wide expanse of plate-glass, stenciled with the name of the establishment in reverse, a vista of sun-smitten street danced drunkenly through the reek from the sheet-iron griddles. Miss Manvers wondered dully if the sidewalks were really less hot than those same griddles.

"The manager says nothin' doin'," the waitress reported. "But you can leave your name and add-ress if you wanta."

"Thanks," said Miss Manvers; "but what's the use?"

"That's right, all right," the other sympathised. "Besides, take it from me, this ain't the kind of a job you could make good at. You gotta be a horse like me to stand it, 'specially days like this."

"Yes, I was thinking of that—"

"Believe me or not, nobody ain't got no idear what hot is without they've juggled hash in one of these joints on a summer day. The kitchen back there is honest' somethin' fierce. Three of our girls fainted dead away in the noon rush."

"Oh, I know," Miss Manvers sighed; "I've tried it before—and failed."

The entrance of another customer prevented further confidences, and Miss

Manvers was left to resume her scanning of the fashion magazine.

If its distracting quality was unquestionable, it hardly contributed comfort to her mood.

"In selecting her personal apparel," she read, "the bride-to-be must, of necessity, be guided by individual requirements and the social position which she is to assume. Although much has been said about the advisability of purchasing only what is really needed and can be worn before the styles change, it is a common fault of brides to buy too much.... It is assumed that the June bride will have already on hand a suit or two, a one-piece frock of serge or similar material, a top-coat, an afternoon coat or one of the new capes, evening gowns, and an evening wrap, one or two afternoon and luncheon frocks, and hats, shoes, and similar accessories...."

Here Miss Manvers withdrew from the printed page long enough mentally to inventory her own wardrobe.

"That lets me out," she said, and turned a page.

The caption, "A Feudal Aristocracy," caught her attention. "Long Island," she learned, "is a poem itself to-day, even if it is suffering from cheap developments, the encroachment of tenantry, and the swarming of the commuters. It is too bad that this garden spot must be overrun, and indeed there has been a movement to stay the tide of immigration from the city. In one section our best people are buying up vast stretches of property to add to their private estates...."

Fascinated, Miss Manvers thrust aside a garnished plate, took a gulp of the decoction called coffee, and attacked her napoleon.

"I am so glad," she continued to read, "to see that we are adding to our estates and fast forming an aristocracy of the countryside; we really live at our country places now for over half the year. Even the large weddings are no longer town affairs. If one has an estate it is so much smarter now to marry off one's daughters from the country place. Yet there is always one difficulty about this method of procedure: can such weddings be afforded the prominence necessary? Weddings, of course, must be given a certain amount of advertisement, through the proper channels, because each of us stands for a representative house, which must not drop into oblivion...."

At this point Miss Manvers wrinkled her nose indignantly. "Just for that," she informed the unknown author of this artless screed, "just for that now, I've a great mind not to go to Long Island at all this summer—not even once to Coney!"

She turned impatiently back to the advertising pages and reviewed the "classified wants" listlessly, forewarned by experience that they would offer no invitation to one of her singularly modest accomplishments; none of these advertisers desired the services of a saleswoman, a typist, or even a lady's-maid. Not that Miss Manvers imagined she would score a success in the role of lady's-maid, though it was almost the only means open to her of earning a livelihood which, thus far, she had not essayed.

Such work was hardly calculated to suit a girl with a mind of independent cast and what is known as a temper of her own: prohibitive barriers between her and such bread as may be earned in the sweat of domestic servitude.

Little disappointed, then, she turned attention to "Chat of the Social World," gossip which exercised potent fascination upon the girl's intelligence. She devoured with more avidity than she had her food those pretentiously phrased chronicles of the snobocracy—trite announcements of post-season luncheons, dinners, dances, and bridge parties; of departures for Europe and for American country homes, of engagements and of weddings—distilling therefrom an acid envy that robbed her napoleon of all its savour.

Such was the life for which she yearned with every famished aspiration of her being. And why not? Who were these whose half-tone portraits smirked complacence or scowled disdain to her inspection—who were these that they should enjoy every good thing in life while she must go hungering all her days for a little pleasure? Scarce one betrayed by feature or expression either breeding or intelligence superior to that of Sally Manvers, late of the hardware notions in Huckster's Bargain Basement!

Regarding the full-page reproduction of a photograph showing a jibber-jawed June bride in full regalia, Miss Manvers was moved enviously to paraphrase an epigram of moot origin: "There, but for the grace of God, stands Sally Manvers!"

There was enough truth in that to excuse a little gulp of emotion; which, however, was craftily dissembled.

In due course, rising, Miss Manvers stood and delivered at the desk of the blond cashier, then, penniless, wandered forth into the brutal sunshine.

Her homeward way took her up Sixth Avenue, through Thirty-Fourth Street, and northward on Park Avenue.

She went slowly, wearily, as suited a drudge to whom respite from drudgery brought no earnest of ease or pleasure. The burning air beat up into her downcast face from sun-baked stones that scorched through the soles of her shoddy shoes, and she gulped down acrid mouthfuls of it rather than breathed.

June was still young, but already summer, like some burly ruffian shouldering spring aside with her work half done, held the city in the hollow of a hot and humid hand.

In the mid-afternoon glow, lower Park Avenue owned its personal atmosphere of somnolent isolation, in strong contrast with the bustle of proletarian Fourth Avenue at its one extreme and the roar at the other of traffic-galled Forty-Second Street. Of the residences a few, whose awninged windows resembled heavy-lidded eyes, overlooked wayfaring folk with drowsy arrogance; the greater number, with boarded doors and blinded windows, like mouths and eyes tight shut in seasonable slumber, ignored the world entirely.

Though she had passed that way twice a day for years on end—always in consciousness of that aloof spirit informing the inanimate, and in such resentment thereof as properly rewarded a studied insolence—never before to-day had Sarah Manvers found the genius of the neighbourhood so unmitigatedly intolerable. It was with downright relief that presently she turned from the avenue eastward and accomplished in the span of one short cross-town block a transit of the most violent contrasts, from the dull dignity of the socially eligible, if somewhat *passé*, through a stratum of shabby gentility, to a region of late years dedicated to the uses of adversity undisguised.

A few doors short of Lexington Avenue she paused, sighed, turned, climbed weather-bitten steps to a brownstone entrance, and addressed herself to three long flights of naked stairs.

She left behind, at the entrance, the dingy parlours of "Mme. Levin, Modes et Toilettes," on the first landing the wailing-rooms of a hag-ridden teacher of vocal culture, on the next several dusty chambers perennially unrented, and gained at the top an open door whose panels sported a simple rectangle of cardboard advertising the tenancy of (in engraved script) *Miss Lucy Spode*, (in ink) *M. A. Warden*, and (in pencil, a scrawl) *Manvers*.

Through this the girl walked into a back room of generous size, which boasted a top-light together with the generic name of studio, and was furnished with an ill-assorted company of lame and dismal pieces. The several vocations of its tenants were indicated by a typewriting-machine beneath a rubber hood thick with dust, a folding metal music-stand and a violin-case, and a large studio easel supplemented by a number of scrubby canvases. A door in the partition wall communicated with a small bedchamber of the kind commonly termed "hall room." And in one corner a stationary wash-stand and a gas-stove for morbid cookery lurked behind a Japanese screen of dilapidated panels.

Near the windows, on the end of a box-couch, a young woman was perched, thin shoulders rounded over the ink-stained drawing-board resting on her knees. She had a large, self-willed mouth and dark Bohemian hair, and wore a dreary cotton kimono over a silk petticoat whose past had been lurid. One hand clutched gingerly a bottle of India ink, the other wielded a scratchy steel drafting-pen.

Interrupted, she looked up with a start that all but spilled the ink and cried in a voice heavily coloured with the enervating brogue of the Southern born:

"My land, Sally! *What* time is it?"

In the act of unpinning her hat (a straw that even a drowning woman would have hesitated to grasp at) Miss Manvers paused to consult an invalid alarm-clock which was suffering palpitations on an adjacent shelf.

"Twenty past three," she reported, sententious.

The artist cocked her head, squinted malevolently at her drawing, dipped, and busily scratched once more.

"Scared me," she explained: "coming home so early!"

Sally removed her collar with a wrench and a grunt: "Got a date?"

"Sure; with Sammy—four o'clock."

"Salamander stuff, eh?"

"What do you want—a day like this? I'm half-cooked already, and I guess I can go through a little fire for the sake of a sixty-cent *table d'hôte* and a trip to Coney. But you needn't worry; it'll be hotter than this before Sammy warms up enough to singe anything. His intentions are so praiseworthy they pain him; he blushes every time he has to recognise the sex question long enough to discuss the delights of monogamy in a two-family house within commuting distance of Prospect Park South."

"You don't mean to say you've got that far along—already!"

"That's the reward of a year's steady angling, honey."

"Heavens, but how you must carry on with Sammy!"

"Believe me, it's something scandalous," sighed Lucy Spode.

"But why—" Sally began in a tone of expostulation.

The other quickened with a flash of temper. "Don't ask me! I came No'th to study art and mingle with the world of intellect and fashion, and after three years I'm drawing heads for fashion magazines at a dollar per, and I know a minor poet who's acquainted with the assistant editor of *The Scrap-Book*, and the one man I know who owns a dress-suit gets fifty cents an hour for posing in it. If that isn't enough to make me welcome even the prospect of married life with Sammy Myerick and a woman to do the washing, I don't know—"

"Well, if you aren't crazy about Sammy, why not chuck him? Marriage isn't the last resource for a girl like you. You've got just as many wits to live on as the next one. This town's full of young women no better-looking than either of us, and with even less intelligence, who manage pretty comfortably, thank you, on the living the world owes them."

"Sally Manvers!" cried the Southern girl, scandalised, "what a way to talk!"

"Oh, *all* right," said the other indifferently. "Where's Mary Warden?"

"Lyric Hall-rehearsing."

"Lucky Mary!"

Lucy Spode looked up in astonishment. "Lucky!" she protested; "dancing till she's ready to drop, in this awful heat, and no pay for rehearsals!"

"All the same," Sally contended, "she's got some chance, some right to hope for better things. She's an understudy, and her principal might fall ill—or something. That's better than marrying a man you don't care for—or clerking at Huckster's for seven dollars a week."

"Cat," said Miss Spode dispassionately. "Who's been mussing your fur?"

"Life."

The steel pen was poised again while Lucy Spode surveyed Sally Manvers suspiciously.

"What do you mean—life?" she demanded.

"This sort of thing." Sally waved a comprehensive hand. "Living here, in this hole, and most of the time not even able to pay my share of the rent; slaving for a dollar a day, and losing part of that in unjust fines; walking to and from the store to save car fare; eating the sort of food we do eat; never having pretty clothes or pleasures of any sort. I don't call this a life!"

"You've got indigestion," Miss Spade diagnosed shrewdly. "I'll bet two bits you've been eating napoleons again."

"I have got indigestion, but it's thanks only to being fed up with existence— the kind we lead, at least. I want something better."

"The vote, perhaps?"

"For two cents I'd throw something at you."

The artist uncoiled her legs, stuck the pen in her hair, set the ink-bottle down on the floor, sighed, and, lifting the drawing-board, held it at arm's length, studying her work through narrowed eyelids.

"Then it must be a man," she concluded absently. "When a woman of twenty-seven wants something and doesn't know what it is, it's either the vote or a man."

"Oh, shut up."

"With man an odds-on favourite in the betting." Miss Spode laid the board aside with a "Thank goodness, that's finished!" and, rising, stretched her cramped limbs. "What I'd like to know," she persisted, "is whether it's man abstract or a man concrete."

Sally laughed bitterly. "Take a good look at me, dear—as an exhibit, not as a friend—and tell me honestly whether any man worth having would glance twice at me."

"You can be pretty enough," Miss Spade returned seriously, "when you want to take the trouble—"

"But I don't—ever."

"The more fool you."

"What's the use—on seven a week? What's the good of being pretty in rags like these? It only gets a girl in wrong. I don't care how fetching I might make myself seem—"

"But you ought to."

"Look here; do you know how a reporter would describe me?"

"Of course; 'respectable working girl.'"

"Well, then, men worth while don't run after 'respectable working girls'; they leave that to things who wear 'Modish Men's Clothing'—with braided cuffs and pockets slashed on the bias!—and stand smirking on corners we have to pass going home. Do you think I'd do my hair becomingly, and—and all that —to attract such creatures?"

"So it's abstract man. Thought so!"

"It's starvation, that's what it is. I'm sick for want of what other girls get without asking—pretty clothes and—and all that sort of thing."

"Meaning," the artist interpreted gravely, "love."

"Well," Sally demanded, defiant, "why not?"

"Why not indeed?" Lucy returned obliquely, wandering round the studio and collecting various articles of wearing-apparel toward her appearance in public.

"I'm twenty-seven," Miss Manvers declared mutinously. "I'll never be younger—I want to be loved before I'm old!"

She paused, viewed with reassuring amusement Lucy's countenance of perplexity, and laughed again.

"I've had ten years of independence; and what has it brought me? The reward of virtue: that swaybacked couch for my bed, Uneeda biscuit for my bread, and for salt—tears of envy!"

"Virtue is its own reward," Lucy enunciated severely.

"Virtue is its only reward, you mean!"

"You don't talk fit to eat."

"You know what I mean. Only mental bankrupts go to the devil because they're hungry. I'm less bothered about keeping body and soul together — Huckster's seven a week does that after a fashion—than about keeping soul and mind together."

"It sounds reasonable."

"I'm desperate, I tell you! And there's more than one resort of desperation for a girl of intelligence."

"As, for instance-" "Well—

you've named one." "Man?"

"That's the animal's first name."

"But you've just pointed out, a successful campaign demands a wardrobe."

"Even that can be had if one's unscrupulous enough."

"Whatever do you mean?"

"To seek happiness where I can find it. I'm game for anything. I'm 'north of fifty-three'!"

"You're *what*?"

"Have you forgotten the 'Rhyme of the Three Sealers'? 'There's never a law of God or man runs north of fifty-three'! Well, the age of twenty-seven is a woman's fifty-three, north latitude—at least, it is if she's unmarried—time to jettison scruples, morals, regard for the conventions, and hoist the black flag of social piracy!"

"In plain language, you think the hour has struck to doll yourself up like a man-trap. What?"

"Yes—and hang the expense!"

"By all means, hang it. But where? It's a case of cash or credit; the first you haven't got, and I don't see your visible means of supporting a charge-account at Altman's."

"There are ways," Sally insisted darkly.

"You can't mean you'd do anything dishonest—"

"I'd do *anything*. Look at all the people in high places who began as nothing more nor less than adventurers. Nobody's fussing about how they got their money. It's a sin to be poor nowadays, but the sin of sins is to stay poor!"

A moment of silence followed this pronouncement; then Miss Spode observed pensively:

"Something's happened to you to-day, Sally. What is it? You haven't been—"

"Fired again'? Not exactly. Just laid off indefinitely—that's all. With good luck I may get my job back next September."

"Oh, but honey!" Lucy exclaimed, crossing to drop a hand on Sally's shoulder: "I am sorry!"

"Of course you are," Sally returned stonily. "But you needn't be. I'm not going to let this make things any harder for you and Mary Warden."

"How perfectly mean! You know I wasn't thinking anything like that!"

"Yes, dear, I do know it." In sudden contrition, Sally caught the other girl's hand and laid her cheek transiently against it. "What I meant to make clear was"—she faltered momentarily—"I've made up my mind I'm a Jonah, and the only decent thing for me to do is to quit you both, Lucy, my dear!"

She ended on a round note of determination rather than of defiance, and endured calmly, if with a slightly self-conscious smile, the distressed look of her companion.

"Don't be silly!" this last retorted, pulling herself together. "You know you're welcome—"

"Of course I do. All the same, I'm not taking any more, thanks."

"But it's only a question of time. If you can't wait for Huckster's to take you on again, Mary and I can easily keep things going until you find another job."

"But that wouldn't be fair!"

"What wouldn't be fair?"

"To sponge on you two under false pretences." "False pretences!" Lucy iterated blankly.

"I was laid off last Saturday. I didn't say anything, but I've been looking for something else ever since—and this is Wednesday, and I'm through. I'm sick and tired. I've got just as much right as anybody to live on society, and that's what I'm going to do from now on!"

Miss Spode lowered a cloth skirt over her head and blouse before pursuing. "But what I can't understand is how—assuming you're in earnest—"

"Deadly earnest!" Sally declared.

"—and mean to go through with this—how you think you'll get a start without doing something downright wrong."

"It wouldn't be fair to tempt me the way I feel to-day."

"There's only one thing," Miss Spode announced, adjusting her hat, "that prevents me from speaking to a cop about you: I know you're a fraud. You couldn't do anything dishonourable to save you."

"Oh, couldn't I!" Sally returned ominously. "You wait and see!"

"Well, well," said the other indulgently, "have it your own way. Hooray for crime! But if I stop here listening to you preach anarchy I'll be late for Sammy. So I'm off." Pausing in the doorway, she looked back with just a trace of doubt colouring her regard. "Do try to brace up and be sensible, honey. I'm worried about leaving you alone with all these blue devils."

"You needn't be. I can take care of myself—"

"Well, promise to do nothing rash before I come home."

"Promises made for keeps are specifically prohibited by article nine of the Social Pirate's Letters of Marque. But I don't mind telling you the chances are you'll find me on the roof when you get back, unless this heat lets up. I'm going up now; this place is simply suffocating!"

But her smile grew dim as she resigned herself to an evening whose loneliness promised to be unbroken; that faint flush faded which had crept into her cheeks in the course of her half-whimsical, half-serious harangue; she looked once more what life had made her—a work-worn shop-girl, of lack- lustre charm, on the verge of prematurely middle-aged, hopeless spinsterhood.

Another six months of this life would break her, body and spirit, beyond repair.

Her eyes, that ranged the confines of those mean quarters, darkened quickly with their expression of jaded discontent.

Another six months? She felt as if she could not suffer another six hours... .

After a time she rose and moved languidly out into the hall, from which an iron ladder led up through a scuttle to the roof, the refuge and retreat of the studio's tenants on those breathless, interminable summer nights when their quarters were unendurably stuffy. Here they were free to lounge at ease, *en déshabillé*; neither the dressmaker nor the teacher of voice-production ever troubled their privacy, and seldom did other figures appear on any of the roofs which ran to the Park Avenue corner on an exact plane broken only by low dividing walls and chimney-stacks.

Three chairs of the steamer type, all maimed, comprised the furniture of this roof-garden, with (by way of local colour) on one of the copings a row of four red clay flower-pots filled with sun-baked dust from which gnarled and rusty stalks thrust themselves up like withered elfin limbs.

Selecting the soundest chair, Sally dragged it into the shadow cast by the hood of the studio top-light, and settling down with her feet on the adjacent coping, closed her eyes and sought to relax from her temper of high, almost hysterical nervous tension.

Thoughts bred of her talk with Lucy for a time distracted her, blending into incoherent essays at imaginative adventures staged in the homes and parks of the wealthy, as pictured by the sycophantic fashion magazine and cast with the people of its gallery of photographs—sublimely smart women in frocks of marvellous inspiration, and polo-playing, motor-driving, clothes-mad men of an insouciance appalling.

On the edge of unconsciousness she said aloud, but without knowing that she spoke, three words.

These were: "Charmeuse ... Paquin ... Bride ..."

And then she slept; her pallid face upturned to that high-arched sky of brass, from which light and heat beat down in brutal waves, she slept the sleep of exhaustion, deep and heavy; dark and stupefying sleep possessed her utterly, as overpowering and obliterating as though induced by drugs.

CHAPTER II

BURGLARY

She wakened in sharp panic, bewildered by the grotesquerie of some half-remembered dream in contrast with the harshness of inclement fact, drowsily realising that since she had fallen asleep it had come on to rain smartly out of a shrouded sky.

Without the least warning a blinding violet glare cut the gloom, the atmosphere quaked with a terrific shock of thunder, and the downpour became heavier.

Appalled, the girl sprang from her chair and groped her way to the scuttle through a crepuscle resembling late twilight.

It was closed.

Somebody, presumably the janitor, had shut it against the impending storm without troubling to make sure there was no one on the roof, for her chair had been invisible behind the shoulder of the top-light.

With a cry of dismay the girl knelt and, digging fingers beneath the cover, tugged with all her might. But it was securely hooked beneath and held fast.

Then, driven half frantic less by the lashing rain than by a dread of lightning which she had never outgrown, she stumbled back to the glass face of the top-light and pounded it with her fists, screaming to Mary Warden to come and let her in. But no lights showed in the studio, and no one answered; reluctantly she was persuaded that Mary was not yet home from rehearsals.

The long rolling, grinding broadsides of thunder made almost continuous accompaniment—broken only by the briefest intermissions—to the fiery sword-play that slashed incessantly through and through that grim tilt of swollen black cloud.

Half-stunned and wholly terrified, dazzled and deafened as well, the girl dashed the rain from her eyes and strove to recollect her wits and grapple sanely with her plight.

Already she was wet to her skin—water could no more harm her—but the mad elemental tumult confounded all her senses; her sole conscious impulse was to gain shelter of some sort from the sound and fury of the tempest.

It was a bare chance that a scuttle on some one of the adjacent roofs might be, at least, not fastened down.

18

Fighting the buffeting wind, the scourging rain, and her panic fright, she gained the scuttle of the roof to the west, but found it immovable.

She tried the next roof, with no better fortune.

Panting, even sobbing a little in her terror, she scrambled on through a sort of nightmarish progress to the next roof, and on and on to the next and the next.

She kept on reckoning, and couldn't have said how many roofs she had crossed, when at length she discovered a scuttle that was actually ajar, propped wide to the pounding flood; and without pause to wonder at this circumstance, or what might be her reception and how to account for herself, she swung down into that hospitable black hole, found footing on the ladder, let herself farther down—and by mischance dislodged the iron arm supporting the cover.

It fell with a bang and a click, and Sally barely escaped crushed fingers by releasing the rim and tumbling incontinently to the floor.

Happily she hadn't far to fall, wasn't hurt, and hastily picking herself up, stood half-dazed, listening for sounds of alarm within the house.

Coincidently the storm sounded a crisis in a series of tremendous, shattering crashes, so heavy and so prolonged that all the world seemed to rock and vibrate, echoing the uproar like a gigantic sounding-board.

This passed; but from the body of the house Sally heard nothing—only the crepitation of rain on the roof and the sibilant splatter of drops trickling from her saturated skirts into the puddle that had formed beneath the scuttle.

She stood in what at first seemed unrelieved darkness—but for glimpses revealed by the incessant slash and flare of lightning—at one end of a short hallway, by the rail of a staircase well. Three or four doors opened upon this hall; but she detected no sign of any movement in the shadows, and still heard no sound.

Wondering—and now, as she began to appreciate her position, almost as unhappy in her refuge as she had been in the storm—Sally crept to the rail and peered down. But her straining senses detected nothing below more than shadows, solitude, and silence; which, however, failed to convey reassurance; the fact of the open scuttle would seem to indicate that she hadn't stumbled into an uninhabited house.

Stealthily she proceeded to investigate the several rooms of that topmost story —servants' quarters, comfortably furnished, but tenantless.

Then step by timid step she descended to the next floor, which she found devoted to three handsomely appointed bedchambers, also empty. And slowly, as her courage served, another flight took her down to a story given over wholly to two bedchambers with baths, dressing-rooms and boudoirs adjoining, all very luxurious to a hasty survey.

Below this again was an entrance hall, giving access to a drawing-room, a library, and, at the back of the house, a dining-room, each apartment in its way deepening the impression of a home toward whose making wealth and good taste had worked in rarely harmonious collaboration.

And finally the basement proved to be as deserted as any room above; this though the kitchen clock still ticked on stertorously, though the fire in the range had been banked rather than drawn, though one had but to touch the boiler to learn it still held water piping-hot.

It required, however, only a moment's sober thought, once satisfied she was alone, to suggest as one reasonable solution to the puzzle that the owners had fled town for the week-end, leaving the establishment in care of untrustworthy servants, who had promptly elected to seek their own pleasure elsewhere.

Content with this theory, Sally chose one of the windows of the servants' dining-room from which to spy out stealthily, between the shade and the sill, over a flooded area and street; first remarking a sensible modification of the gloom in spite of an unabated downpour, then that the house was near the Park Avenue corner, finally a policeman sheltered in the tradesman's entrance of the dwelling across the way.

At this last disquieting discovery Sally retreated expeditiously from the window, for the first time realising that her presence in that house, however adventitious and innocent, wouldn't be easy to explain to one of a policeman's incredulous idiosyncrasy; the legal definition of burglar, strictly applied, fitted Sarah Manvers with disconcerting neatness.

But nobody knew; it was only half past six by the clock in the kitchen; it was reasonably improbable that the faithless servants would come back much before midnight; and she need only wait for the storm to pass to return across the roofs, or, for that matter, to leave circumspectly by the front door. For it would certainly be dark by the time the storm uttered its last surly growl and trailed its bedraggled skirts off across Long Island.

For an instant finely thrilled with a delicious sense of the wild adventure of being alone in a strange house, free to range and pry at will, she found the full piquancy a bit difficult to relish with sodden clothing clinging clammily to her body and limbs.

None the less it was quite without definite design that Sally retraced her way to that suite of rooms in the second story which seemed to be the quarters of the mistress of the establishment; and it was no more than common-sense precaution (prompted, it's true, by sheer, idle curiosity) which moved her to darken windows already shuttered by drawing their draperies of heavy, rose-coloured silk before switching on the lights.

It may have been merely the reflection of rose-tinted walls that lent the face of the girl unwonted colour, but the glow that informed her eyes as she looked about was unquestionably kindled by envy as much as by excitement.

Nothing, indeed, lacked to excite envy in that hungry heart of hers. The bedchamber and its boudoir and bath were not only exquisitely appointed, but stood prepared for use at a moment's notice; the bed itself was beautifully dressed; the dressing-table was decked with all manner of scent-bottles, mirrors, and trays, together with every conceivable toilet implement in tortoise-shell with a silver-inlay monogram—apparently A-M-S; the rugs were silken, princely, priceless; elusive wraiths of seductive perfumes haunted the air like memories of lost caresses.

And when the girl pursued her investigations to the point of opening closed doors she found clothes-presses containing a wardrobe to cope with every imaginable emergency—frocks of silk, of lace, of satin, of linen; gowns for dinner, the theatre, the street, the opera; boudoir-robes and negligees without end; wraps innumerable, hats, shoes, slippers, mules—and a treasure of lingerie to ravish any woman's heart.

And against all this sybaritic store the intruder had to set the figure mirrored by a great cheval-glass—the counterfeit of a jaded shop-girl in shabby, shapeless, sodden garments, her damp, dark hair framing stringily a pinched and haggard face with wistful, care-worn eyes.

Her heart ached with a reawakened sense of the cruel unfairness of life. Her flesh crept with the touch of her rain-soaked clothing. And in her thoughts temptation stirred like a whispering serpent.

Beyond dispute it was wrong, what she contemplated, utterly wrong, and wild to madness; but the girl was ripe for such temptation and frail with a weakness due to long years of deprivation. Full half of her heart's desire was here, free to her covetous fingers, a queen's trousseau of beautiful belongings.

"It's only for an hour. No one need ever know. I'll leave everything just as I found it. And I'm so uncomfortable!"

She hesitated a moment longer, but only a moment; of a sudden smouldering embers of jealousy and desire broke into devastating flame, consuming doubts and scruples in a trice. Swift action ensued; this was no more an affair of

21

conscience, but of persuasion and resistless impulse. She flew about like one possessed—as, indeed, she was, no less.

Her first move was to turn on hot water in the shining porcelain tub. Then, instinctively closing and locking the hall door, she slipped from her despised garments and, hanging them up to dry in a tiled corner where their dampness could harm, nothing, slipped into the bath... .

Half an hour later, deliciously caressed by garments of soft white silk beneath a feather-weight *robe-de-chambre*, she sat before the dressing-table, drying her hair in the warm draft of an electric fan and anointing face, hands, and arms with creams and delicately scented lotions.

A faint smile touched lips now guiltless of any hint of sullenness; she hummed softly to herself, whose heart had almost forgotten its birthright of song and laughter; never the least pang of conscience flawed the serene surface of her content.

Properly dressed, her hair was beautiful, soft, fine and plentiful, with a natural wave that lent an accent to its brownish lustre. When she finished arranging it to her complete satisfaction she hardly knew the face that smiled back at her from the mirror's depths. Miraculously it seemed to have gained new lines of charm; its very thinness was now attractive, its colour unquestionably intrinsic; and her eyes were as the eyes of a happy child, exulting in the attainment of long-coveted possessions.

It wasn't in human nature to contemplate this transformation and feel contrition for whatever steps had been necessary to bring it about.

And when she could do no more to beautify her person Sally turned again to the clothes-press, by now so far gone in self-indulgence, her moral sense so insidiously sapped by the sheer sensual delight she had of all this pilfered luxury, that she could contemplate without a qualm less venial experiments with the law of *meum et tuum*.

She entertained, in short, a project whose lawless daring enchanted her imagination, if one as yet of vague detail. But with command of the resources of this wonderful wardrobe, what was to prevent her from appropriating a suitable costume and stealing forth, when the storm had passed, to seek adventure, perhaps to taste for a night those joys she had read about and dreamed about, longed for and coveted, all her life long? Nothing could be more mad; there was no telling what might not happen; there was every warrant for believing that the outcome might be most unpleasant. But adventures are to the adventurous; and surely this one had started off propitiously enough!

"And what I need she'll never miss. Besides, I can send back everything in the morning, anonymously, by parcel-post. It's only borrowing."

Already she had passed from contemplation to purpose and stood committed to the enterprise, reckless of its consequence.

But she found it far from easy to make her selection; it wouldn't do to fare forth *en décolletée* without an escort—a consideration that sadly complicated the search for just the right thing, at once simple and extravagant, modish and becoming. Moreover, any number of captivating garments positively demanded to be tried on, then clung tenaciously to her pretty shoulders, refusing to be rejected.

She wasted many a sigh over her choice, which was ultimately something darkish, a frock (I think) of dark-blue *crépe-de-chine*, designed primarily for afternoon wear, but, supplemented by a light silk wrap, quite presentable for evening; and it fitted to admiration.

This question once settled, she experienced little trouble finding slippers and a hat to her taste.

The testimony of a small gilt clock startled her when at length she stood ready for the next step in her nefarious career: the hour-hand was passing ten. That seemed almost incredible.

Running into the unlighted boudoir, she caught back the window-draperies, raised the sash, and peered cautiously out through the slanted slats of the wooden blinds.

The sky that now shone down upon the city was a fair shield of stars unblurred by cloud; the storm had passed without her knowledge.

Closing the window, Sally delayed for one last, rapturous survey of herself in the cheval-glass, then put out the lights and went to the door.

She hardly knew why it was that she opened it so gently and waited so long upon the threshold, every nerve tensed to detect alien sound in the stillness of the empty house. But it was as if with darkness those vacant rooms and passages had become populous with strange, hostile spirits. She heard nothing whatever, yet it was with an effect of peril strong upon her senses that she stole forth through the hallway and up the stairs to the topmost floor, where, perched precariously upon the iron ladder, she tried her patience sorely with a stubborn scuttle-cover before recalling the click that had accompanied its closing—the click of a spring-latch.

And this last, when gropingly located, proved equally obdurate; she fumbled doggedly until back and limbs ached with the strain of her position; but her fingers lacked cunning to solve the secret; and in the end, when on the point of climbing down to fetch matches, she heard a sound that chilled her heart and checked her breath in a twinkling—an odd, scuffling noise on the roof.

At first remote and confused, it drew nearer and grew more clear—a sound of light footfalls on the sheet-tin.

Her self-confidence and satisfaction measurably dashed, she climbed down, so fearful of betraying herself to the person on the roof that she went to the absurd extreme of gathering her skirts up tightly to still their silken murmur.

Now she must leave by the street. And now she remembered the policeman who kept nightly vigil at the avenue crossing!

She was beginning to be definitely frightened, vividly picturing to herself the punishment that must follow detection.

And as she crept down-stairs, guided only by the banister-rail, the sense of her loneliness and helplessness there in that strange, dark place worked upon the temper of the girl until her plight, however real, was exaggerated hideously and endued with terrors so frightful that she was ready to scream at the least alarm.

CHAPTER III

ACCESSARY AFTER THE FACT

At the foot of the stairs Sally paused in the entry-hall, thoughtfully considering the front door, the pale rectangle of whose plate-glass was stenciled black with the pattern of a lace panel. But she decided against risking that avenue of escape; it would be far less foolhardy to steal away *via* the basement, unostentatiously, that the always-possible passer-by might more readily take her for a servant.

Turning back, then, toward the basement staircase, she began to grope her way through blinding darkness, but had taken only a few uncertain steps when, of a sudden, she stopped short and for a little stood like a stricken thing, quite motionless save that she quaked to her very marrow in the grasp of a great and enervating fear.

If she could not have said what precisely it was that she feared, her fright was no less desperately real. She could see nothing; she had heard no sound; her hands had touched nothing more startling than the banister-rail, and yet ...

It was as if sensitive filaments of perceptions even finer than sight, touch, and hearing had found and recoiled from something strange and terrible skulking there, masked by the encompassing murk.

Probably less than twenty seconds elapsed, but it seemed a long minute before her heart stirred anew, leaping into action with a quickened beat, and she was able to reassert command of her reason and— reassured, persuaded her fright lacked any real foundation—move on.

Five paces more brought her to the elbow of the rail; here, in the very act of turning to follow it down to the basement, she halted involuntarily, again transfixed with terror.

But this time her alarm had visible excuse; that there was something wrong in that strange house, so strangely deserted, was evident beyond dispute.

She stood facing the dining-room door, the door to the library on her left; if not in any way evident to her senses, she could fix its position only approximately by an effort of memory. But through the former opening her vision, ranging at random, instinctively seeking relief from the oppression of blank darkness, detected a slender beam of artificial light no thicker than a lead-pencil—a golden blade that lanced the obscurity, gleaming dull upon a rug, more bright on naked parquetry, vivid athwart the dust-cloth shrouding the dining-table.

For a moment or two the girl lingered, unstirring, fascinated by that slender, swerveless ray; then, slowly, holding her breath, urged against her will by importunate curiosity, she crossed the threshold of the dining-room, following the light back to its source—a narrow crack in the folding doors communicating with the library.

Now Sally remembered clearly that the folding doors had been wide open at the time of her first tour of investigation; as, indeed, had the door between the library and hall—now tight shut, else this light would have been perceptible in the hall as well.

It was undeniable, then, that since she had closeted herself up-stairs another person had entered the house—some one who had shut himself up there in the library for a purpose apparently as clandestine as her own. Or why such pains to mask the light, and why such care not to disturb the silence of the house?

To have gone on and made good an escape without trying to read this riddle would have been hardly human of the girl, for all her misgivings; she stole on to the folding doors with less noise than a mouse had made and put an eye to the crack, which, proving somewhat wider than she had imagined, afforded a fair view of the best part of the other room.

An electric chandelier was on full-blaze above the broad and heavy centre-table of mahogany, beyond which, against the farther wall, stood on the one hand a bookcase, on the other a desk of the roll-top type—closed. Above each of these the wall was decorated with trophies of ancient armour; between them hung a huge canvas in a massive gilt frame—the portrait of a beautiful woman beautifully painted. And immediately beneath the portrait stood a young man, posed in profound abstraction, staring at the desk.

He rested lightly against the table, his back square to Sally's view, revealing a well-turned head thatched with dark hair, clipped snugly by well-formed ears, and the salient line of one lean, brown cheek. But even so, with his countenance hidden, something conveyed a strong impression to the girl of a perplexed and disconcerted humour.

She was frankly disappointed. For some reason she had thought to discover a burglar of one or another accepted type—either a dashing cracksman in full-blown evening dress, lithe, polished, pantherish, or a common yegg, a red-eyed, unshaven burly brute in the rags and tatters of a tramp. But this man wore unromantic blue serge upon a person neither fascinating nor repellent. She could hardly imagine him either stealing a diamond tiara or hopping a freight.

But that he was of a truly criminal disposition she was not permitted long to doubt; for in another moment he started from his pensive pose with the animation of one inspired, strode alertly to the wall, stepped up on the seat of a chair beside the desk, and straining on tiptoes (though tolerably tall) contrived to grasp the handle of a short-bladed Roman sword which formed part of one of the trophies.

With some difficulty and, in the end, a grunt of satisfaction, he worked the weapon loose and, jumping down, turned to the desk, thrust the point of the sword between the writing-pad and the edge of the roll-top, forced the blade well in, and bore all his weight upon the haft of this improvised jimmy. Promptly, with a sound of rending wood, the top flew half-way up.

At this the man released the sword, which fell with a thump to the rug at his feet, pushed the top as far back as it would go, and, bending over the desk, explored its rack of pigeonholes and drawers. One of the latter eventually yielded the object of his search; he took from it first a small automatic pistol, which he placed carelessly to one side, then a small leather-bound book whose pages he thumbed in nervous haste, evidently seeking some memorandum essential to his ends. This found, he paused, conned it attentively for an instant, then turned and took the book with him across the room beyond the bookcase, thus vanishing from the field of Sally's vision.

Now was her chance to slip down-stairs and, undetected, away. But, surprisingly enough, she proved of two minds about advantaging herself of the opportunity. To begin with, she was no more afraid—at least, not to any great extent. What, she argued scornfully, was one man, after all?—especially one who had no more lawful business than she upon those premises! She wasn't afraid of men; and even were this one to catch her watching him (something Sally meant to take good care he shouldn't) he could hardly denounce her to the police. Besides, what *was* he up to, anyhow, over there in that corner, out of sight? She simply had to know the meaning of those noises he was making.

They were difficult to diagnose—an odd whirring sound broken by repeated muffled clanks and by several others as baffling, notably a muted metallic knocking and rattling.

She experienced an exasperating effect of trying to see round a corner.

But in the end she identified those sounds beyond mistake: the man was fretting the combination of a safe, pausing now and again to try the handle. For what, indeed, had he forced that desk if not to find the combination?

In due course the noises ceased and the malefactor re-appeared, bringing with him a morocco-bound box of good size. She made no doubt whatever that this was a jewel-case, and took his smile for confirmation of her surmise, though it was really less a smile than satisfaction twitching the full lips beneath his dark little moustache (one of those modishly flat affairs so widely advertised by collarmakers).

For now the miscreant was facing Sally as he bent over the table and fumbled with the lock of the jewel-case, and she made good use of this chance to memorise a countenance of mildly sardonic cast, not unhandsome—the face of a conventional modern voluptuary, self-conscious, self-satisfied, selfish—rather attractive withal in the eyes of an excited young woman.

But a moment later, finding the case to be fast-locked, the burglar gave utterance to an exclamation that very nearly cost him his appeal to her admiration. She couldn't hear distinctly, for the impatient monosyllable was breathed rather than spoken, but at that distance it sounded damnably like "*Pshaw!*"

And immediately the man turned back to the desk to renew his rummaging—in search of a key to fit the case, she guessed. But his business there was surprisingly abbreviated—interrupted in a fashion certainly as startling to him as to her who skulked and spied on the dark side of the foldingdoors.

Neither received the least intimation that the door from the library to the hall had been opened. Sally, for one, remained firmly persuaded that they two were alone in the silent house until the instant when she saw a second man hurl himself upon the back of the first—a swift-moving shape of darkness, something almost feline in his grim, violent fury that afforded the victim no time either to turn or to lift a hand in self-defence. In a twinkling the two went headlong to the floor and disappeared, screened by the broad top of the table.

There, presumably, Blue Serge recovered sufficiently from the shock of surprise to make some show of fighting back. Confused sounds of scuffling and hard breathing became audible, with a thump or two deadened by the rug; but more than that, nothing—never a word from either combatant. There was something uncanny in the silence of it all.

For an instant Sally remained where she was, rooted in fright and wonder; but the next, and without in the least understanding how she had come there, she found herself by the open door in the entry-hall, just beyond the threshold of the library, commanding an unobstructed view of the conflict.

Apparently this neared its culmination. Though he had gone down face forward, Blue Serge had contrived to turn over on his back, in which position he now lay, still struggling, but helpless, beneath the bulk of his assailant—a burly, blackavised scoundrel who straddled the chest of his prey, a knee pinning down either arm, both hands busy with efforts to make an unappetising bandana serve as a gag.

Pardonably rewarded for this inconsiderate treatment, the fat one suddenly snatched one hand away, conveyed a bitten finger to his mouth, instantly spat it out together with a gust of masterful profanity and, the other taking advantage of the opportunity to renew his struggles, shifted his grip to Blue Serge's throat and, bending forward, strove with purpose undoubtedly murderous to get possession of the short Roman sword.

It lay just an inch beyond his reach. He strained his utmost toward it, almost touched its haft with eager finger-tips.

At this a strange thing happened—strangest of all to Sally. For she, who never in her life had touched firearm or viewed scene of violence more desperate than a schoolboy squabble, discovered herself inside the library, standing beside the desk and levelling at the head of the heavy villain the automatic pistol that had rested there.

Simultaneously she was aware of the sound of her own voice, its accents perhaps a bit shaky, but none the less sharp, crying: "Stop! Don't you dare! Drop that sword and put up your hands! I say, put up your hands!"

The stout assassin started back and turned up to the amazing apparition of her a ludicrous mask of astonishment, eyes agoggle, mouth agape, pendulous beard-rusty chin aquiver like some unsavoury sort of jelly. Then slowly— thanks to something convincing in the manner of this young woman, aflame as she was with indignant championship of the under dog—he elevated two grimy hands to a point of conspicuous futility; and a husky whisper; like a stifled roar, rustled past his lips:

"Well, can yuh beat it?"

A thrill of self-confidence galvanised the person of Miss Manvers, steadying at once her hand and her voice.

"Get up!" she snapped. "No—keep your hands in sight. Get up somehow, and be quick about it!"

Without visible reluctance, if with some difficulty, like a clumsy automaton animated by unwilling springs, the fat scoundrel lurched awkwardly to his feet and paused.

"Very good." She was surprised at the cold, level menace of her tone. "Now stand back—to the wall! Quick!"

She was abruptly interrupted by a vast, discordant bellow: "Look out, lady! Look out! That gun might go off!"

And as if hoping by that sudden and deafening roar to startle her off guard, the man started toward her, but pulled up as quickly, dashed and sullen. For she did not flinch an inch.

"That's your lookout!" she retorted incisively. "If you're afraid of it—stand back and keep your hands up!"

With a flicker of a sheepish grin the rogue obeyed, falling back until his shoulders touched the wall and keeping his hands level with his ears.

Still holding the pistol ready, the girl shifted her glance to Blue Serge.

He had already picked himself up, and now stood surveying his ally with a regard which wavered between amaze and admiration, suspicion and surprise. Meanwhile he felt gingerly of his throat, as if it were still sore, and nervously endeavoured to readjust a collar which had broken from its moorings. Catching her inquiring eye, he bowed jerkily.

"Thanks!" he panted. "I—ah—good of you, I'm sure—"

She checked him coolly. "Take your time—plenty of it, you know—get your breath and pull yourself together."

He laughed uncertainly. "Ah—thanks again. Just a minute. I'm—ah—as dumfounded as grateful, you know."

She nodded with a curtness due to disillusionment; the man was palpably frightened; and, whatever his excuse, a timid Raffles was a sorry object in her esteem at that instant. She had anticipated of him—she hardly knew what—something brilliant, bold, and dashing, something as romantic as one has every right to expect of a hero of romantic fiction. But this one stood panting, trembling, "sparring for wind," for all the world like any commonplace person fresh from rough handling!

It was most disappointing, so much so that she conceded grudgingly the testimony of her senses to the rapidity with which he regained his normal poise and command of resource; for one evidence of which last she noted that he backed up to the centre-table with a casual air, as if needing its support, and with a deft, certain, swift gesture slipped the jewel-case into his coatpocket. And she noted, too, a flash of anxiety in his eyes, as if he were wondering whether she had noticed.

At this she lost patience. "Well?" she said briskly. "If you've had time to think —"

"To be sure," Blue Serge returned easily. "You mean, about this gentleman? If you ask me, I think he'd be far less potentially mischievous facing the wall."

"All right," Sally agreed, and added with a fine flourish of the pistol: "Face about, you!"

With flattering docility the fat rascal faced about. "And now," Blue Serge suggested, "by your leave—"

Drawing near the girl, he held out his hand for the pistol, and to her own surprise she surrendered it without demur, suddenly conscious that he was no more afraid, that he was rapidly assuming comprehensive command of the situation beyond her to gainsay, and that he knew, and knew that she knew he knew, that she had never entertained any real intention of pulling the trigger, however desperate the emergency.

And incontinently, as though he had taken away all her courage, together with that nickel-plated symbol, she started back, almost cringing in a panic of sadly jangled nerves.

Happily for her conceit, once he had disarmed her, Blue Serge transferred his interest exclusively to his late assailant.

Calmly showing the girl his back, he stepped over, poked the pistol's nose significantly into the folds of the ruffian's neck, and with a sharp word of warning slapped smartly his two hips; in consequence of which singular performance he thrust a hand beneath the tail of the fellow's coat and brought away a bull-dog revolver of heavy calibre.

And then he stepped back, smiling, with a sidelong glance of triumph for Sally's benefit—a glance that spent itself on emptiness.

For Sally was no more there; her uninstructed fingers were already fumbling with the fastenings of the front door when Blue Serge discovered her defection.

CHAPTER IV

BLACKMAIL

There was a breathless instant while the combination of knobs, bolts, and locks defied her importunity so obstinately that Sally was tempted to despair.

She dared not look behind her; but momentarily, as she groped, fumbled, and trembled at the front door, she was aware that a man had backed out of the library into the hall and paused there in the gush of light, staring after her.

And when the door suddenly yielded she heard—or fancied that she heard—his voice, its accent peremptory: "Stop!" Or perhaps it was: "Wait!"

She did neither; the door slammed behind her with a crash that threatened its glass; she was at the foot of the front steps before that sound had fairly registered on her consciousness; and her panic-winged heels had carried the young woman well round the corner and into Park Avenue before she appreciated how interesting her tempestuous flight from that rather thoroughly burglarised mansion would be apt to seem to a peg-post policeman. And then she pulled up short, as if reckoning to divert suspicion with a semblance of nonchalance—now that she had escaped.

But a covert glance aside brought prompt reassurance; after all, the gods were not unkind; the policeman was just then busy on the far side of the avenue, hectoring humility into the heart of an unhappy taxicab operator who had, presumably, violated some minor municipal ordinance.

Inconsistently enough—so strong is the habit of a law-abiding mind—the sight of that broad, belted, self-sufficient back, symbolic of the power and sanity of the law, affected Sally with a mad impulse to turn, hail the officer, and inform him of the conditions she had just quitted. And she actually swerved aside, as if to cross the avenue, before she realised how difficult it would be to invoke the law without implicating herself most damningly.

Recognition of that truth was like receiving a dash of ice-water in her face; she gasped, cringed, and scurried on up Park Avenue as if hoping to outdistance thought. A forlorn hope, that: refreshed from its long rest (for since the storm she had been little better than the puppet of emotions, appetites, and inarticulate impulses) her mind had resumed its normal functioning.

Inexorably it analysed her plight and proved that what she had conceived in an hour of discontent and executed on the spur of an envious instant could nevermore be undone. What had been planned to be mere temporary appropriation of an outfit of clothing—"to be returned in good order, reasonable wear and tear excepted"—was one thing; safe-breaking, with the theft of Heaven only knew what treasure, was quite another. As to that, had she not been guilty of active complicity in the greater crime? How could she be sure (come to think of it) that the stout man had not been the lawful caretaker rather than a rival housebreaker?

She had indeed commenced adventures with a vengeance!

The police were bound to learn of the affair all too soon; her part in it was as certain to become known; too late she was reminded that the name "Manvers" indelibly identified every garment abandoned in the bath-room. Before morning certainly, before midnight probably, Sarah Manvers would be the quarry of a clamorous hue-and-cry.

Appalled, she hurried on aimlessly, now and again breaking into desperate little jog-trots, with many a furtive glance over shoulder, with as many questing roundabout for refuge or resource.

But the city of that night wore a visage new and strange to her, and terrifying. The very quietness of those few residential blocks, marooned amid ever-rising tides of trade, had an ominous accent. All the houses seemed to have drawn together, cheek by jowl, in secret conference on her case, sloughing their disdainful daytime pose and following her fugitive, guilty figure with open amusement and contempt. Some (she thought) leered horribly at her, others scowled, others again assumed a scornful cast; one and all pretended to a hideous intelligence, as though they knew and, if they would, could say what and why she fled.

It was as if the storm had been a supernatural visitation upon the city, robbing it of every intimate, homely aspect, leaving it inhumanly distorted in an obsession of abominable enchantment.

With the start of one suddenly delivered from dream-haunted sleep, she found herself arrived at Forty-Second Street, and safe; none pursued her, nothing in her manner proclaimed the new-fledged malefactor; she need only observe ordinary circumspection to escape notice altogether. And for several moments she remained at a complete standstill there on the corner, blocking the fairway of foot traffic and blindly surveying the splendid facade of Grand Central Station, spellbound in wonder at the amazing discovery that Providence did not always visit incontinent retribution upon the heads of sinners—since it appeared that she who had sinned was to escape scot-free.

With this she was conscious of a flooding spirit of exultant impenitence; the deadly monotony of her days was done with once and for all. It mattered little that—since it were suicidal to return to the studio, the first place the police would search for her—she was homeless, friendless, penniless; it mattered little that she was hungry (now that she remembered it) and had not even a change of clothing for the morrow; these things would somehow be arranged —whether by luck or by virtue of her wit—they *must!*

All that really mattered was that the commonplace was banished from her ways, that she was alive, foot-loose and fancy-free, finally and definitely committed to the career of an adventuress.

Paradoxically, she was appalled by contemplation of her amazing callousness; outlawed, *declassée*, she was indifferent to her degradation, and alive only to the joy of freedom from the bondage of any certain social status.

Now as she lingered on the corner, people were passing her continually on their way over to the terminal; and one of these presently caught her attention —a man who, carrying a small oxford hand-bag, came up hastily from behind, started to cross the street, drew back barely in time to escape annihilation at the wheels of a flying squadron of taxicabs, and so for a moment waited, in impatient preoccupation with his own concerns, only a foot or two in advance but wholly heedless of the girl.

Sally caught her breath sharply, and her wits seemed to knit together with a sort of mental click; the man was Blue Serge, identified unmistakably to her eyes by the poise of his blue-clad person—the same Blue Serge who owed his life to Sally Manvers!

In another instant the way cleared and the man moved smartly on again, with every indication of one spurred on by an urgent errand—but went no more alone. Now a pertinacious shadow dogged him to the farther sidewalk, into the yawning vestibule of the railway station, on (at a trot) through its stupendous lobbies, even to the platform gates that were rudely slammed in his face by implacable destiny in the guise and livery of a gateman.

At this, pausing a little to one side, Sally watched Blue Serge accost the guardian, argue, protest, exhibit tickets, and finally endeavour to bribe a way past the barrier. But the train was already pulling out; with a shake of his stubborn head the uniformed official moved on; and ruminating on a power of pent profanity, Blue Serge turned and strode back into the waiting-room, passing so near to Sally that their elbows almost touched without his rousing to the least recognition of her existence.

But that in itself was nothing to dismay or check the girl in her purpose, and when Blue Serge a minute later addressed himself to the Pullman bureau she was still his shadow—an all but open eavesdropper upon his communications with the authority of the brass-barred wicket.

"I've just missed the eleven ten for Boston," she heard him explain as he displayed tickets on the marble ledge, "and, of course, I'm out my berth reservation. Can you give me a lower on the midnight express?"

"No," Authority averred with becoming sententiousness.

"An upper, then?"

"Nothing left an the midnight."

"Not even a stateroom?"

"I told you nothing doing."

"Well, then, perhaps you can fix me up for the Owl train?"

"Wait a minute."

A pause ensued while Authority consulted his records; not a long pause, but one long enough to permit a wild, mad inspiration to flash like lightning athwart the clouded horizon of Sally's doubt and perplexity. Surely it were strangely inconsistent with her role of adventuress to permit this man to escape, now that destiny had delivered him into her unscrupulous hands!

"Owl train? De luxe room or ordinary stateroom—all I got left."

"Good enough. I'll take—"

If Blue Serge failed promptly to nominate his choice, it was only because Miss Manvers chose that juncture to furnish him—and incidentally herself, when she had time to think things over—with what was unquestionably for both of them the most staggering surprise of that most surprising night.

Peremptorily plucking a blue-serge sleeve with the brazenest impudence imaginable, she advised her victim:

"Take both, if you please!"

Had she schemed deliberately to strike him dumb in consternation, her success must have afforded Sally intense satisfaction. Since she hadn't, her personal consternation was momentarily so overpowering as to numb her sense of appreciation. So that for the period of a long minute neither of them moved nor spoke; but remained each with a blank countenance reflecting a witless mind, hypnotised by the stupefaction of the other.

Then, perhaps a shade the quicker to recover, Sally fancied that her victim's jaw had slackened a bit and his colour faded perceptibly; and with this encouragement she became herself again, collected, aggressive, confronting him undismayed before recognition dawned upon Blue Serge, and, with it, some amused appreciation of her effrontery. Even so, his first essay at response was nothing more formidable than a stammered "I beg your pardon?"

She explained with absolute composure: "I said, take both rooms, please. I'm going to Boston, too."

"Oh!" he replied stupidly.

She nodded with determination and glanced significantly aside, with a little toss of her head, toward the middle of the lobby.

"There's a Central Office man over there," she observed obliquely, dissembling considerable uncertainty as to what a Central Office man really was, and why.

"There is!"

"If you go to Boston, I go," she persisted stolidly. His countenance darkened transiently with distrust or temper. Then of a sudden the man was shaken by a spasm of some strange sort—the corners of his mouth twitched, his eyes twinkled, he lifted a quizzical eyebrow, his lips parted.

But whatever retort he may have contemplated was checked by the accents of Authority and the tapping of an imperative pencil on the window-ledge.

"Say, I'm busy. Which are you going to take now, de luxe room or—"

"Both!" With the dexterity of a stage conjurer Blue Serge whipped a bill from his pocket and thrust it beneath the wicket, not for an instant detaching his gaze from Sally. "And quick," said he; "I'm in a hurry!"

Grunting resentfully, Authority proceeded to issue the reservations, thus affording Sally, constrained to return without a tremor the steadfast regard of her burglar, time to appreciate the lengths to which bravado had committed her. And though she stood her ground without flinching, her cheeks had taken on a hue of bright crimson before Blue Serge, without troubling to verify them, seized tickets and change and turned squarely to her.

"Now that's settled," he inquired amiably, "what next?"

The better to cover her lack of a ready answer, she made believe to consult the mellow orb of the four-faced clock that crowns the bureau of information.

"The Owl train leaves when?" she asked with a finely speculative air.

"One o'clock."

"Then we've got over an hour and a half to wait!"

"How about a bite of supper? The station restaurant is just down-stairs—"

"Thank you," she agreed with a severe little nod.

Lugging his bag, he led the way with the air of one receiving rather than conferring a favour.

"Curious how things fall out," he observed cheerfully; "isn't it?"

"Yes—"

"I mean, your popping up like this just when I was thinking of you. Coincidence, you know."

"Coincidences," Sally informed him consciously, "are caviar only to book critics. There's nothing more common in real life."

He suffered this instruction with a mildly anguished smile.

"That's true, I presume, if one knows anything about real life. I don't go in for realistic novels you see, so can't say. But you're right one way: it isn't anything extraordinary, come to consider it, that you and I, both headed for Boston, should run into each other here. By the way," he added with a casual air, "speaking of coincidences, it sort of triple-plated this one to have your friend from Central Office hanging round so handy, didn't it? If he's in sight, why not be a sport and tip me off?"

"I don't see the necessity," Sally returned, biting her lip—"yet."

"Not from your point of view, perhaps—from mine, yes. Forewarned is fortunate, you know."

"I dare say."

"You won't put me wise?"

"Certainly not."

"Well, of course, one can guess why."

"Can one?"

"Why, forgive me for calling your bluff, it wouldn't be safe, would it? Of course, I'm a sure-enough bad man—and all that. But you must be a bird of my feather, or you wouldn't flock together so spontaneously."

Sally opened her eyes wide and adopted a wondering drawl known to have been of great service to Miss Lucy Spode: "Why, whatever do you mean?"

"Good!" Blue Serge applauded. "Now I *know* where I stand. That baby stare is the high sign of our fraternity—of blackbirds. Only the guilty ever succeed in looking as transparently innocent. Too bad you didn't think of that in time."

"I don't follow you," she said truthfully, beginning to feel that she wasn't figuring to great advantage in this passage of repartee.

"I mean, your give-away is calculated to cramp your style; now you can't very well cramp mine, threatening to squeal."

"Oh, can't I?"

"No. I know you won't go through with it; not, that is, unless you're willing to face Sing Sing yourself. For that matter, I don't see how you're going to make Boston at all to-night, after that break, unless you go on your own; I don't believe I'm scared enough to stand for being shaken down for your transportation."

He was gaining the whip-hand much too easily. She averted her face to mask a growing trepidation and muttered sullenly: "What makes you think I'm afraid—?"

"Oh, come!" he chuckled. "I know you hadn't any lawful business in that house, don't I?"

"How do you know it?"

"Because if you had, I would now be going peaceful, with the kind policeman instead of being a willing victim of a very pleasant form of blackmail."

Burning with indignation and shivering a bit with fear of the man, she stopped short, midway down the ramp to the "lower level," and momentarily contemplated throwing herself upon his mercy and crawling out of it all with whatever grace she might; but his ironic and skeptical smile provoked her beyond discretion.

"Oh, very well!" she said ominously, turning, "if that's the way you feel about it, we may as well have this thing out here and now."

And she made as if to go back the way she had come; but his hand fell upon her arm with a touch at once light and imperative.

"Steady!" he counselled quietly. "This is no place for either bickering or barefaced confidences. Besides, you mustn't take things so much to heart. I was only making fun, and you deserved as much for your cheek, you know. Otherwise, there's no harm done. If you hanker to go to Boston, go you shall, and no thanks to me. Even if I do pay the bill, I owe you a heap more than I'll ever be able to repay, chances are. So take it easy; and I say, do brace up and make a bluff, at least, of being on speaking terms. I'm not a bad sort, but I'm going to stick to you like grim death to a sick nigger's bedside until we know each other better. That's flat, and you may as well resign yourself to it. And here we are."

Unwillingly, almost unaware, she had permitted herself to be drawn through the labyrinth of ramps to the very threshold of the restaurant, where, before she could devise any effectual means of reasserting herself, a bland head waiter took them in tow and, at Blue Serge's direction, allotted them a table well over to one side of the room, out of earshot of their nearest neighbours.

Temporarily too fagged and flustered to react either to the danger or to the novelty of this experience, or even to think to any good purpose, Sally dropped mechanically into the chair held for her, wondering as much at herself for accepting the situation as at the masterful creature opposite, earnestly but amiably conferring with the head waiter over the bill of fare.

Surely a strange sort of criminal, she thought, with his humour and ready address, his sudden shifts from slang of the street to phrases chosen with a discriminating taste in English, his cool indifference to her threatening attitude, and his paradoxical pose of warm—it seemed—personal interest in and consideration for a complete and, to say the least, very questionable stranger.

She even went so far as to admit that she might find him very likable, if only it were not for that affected little moustache and that semi-occasional trick he practised of looking down his nose when he talked.

On the other hand, one assumed, all criminals must seem strange types to the amateur observer. Come to think of it, she had no standard to measure this man by, and knew no law that prescribed for his kind either dress clothing with an inverness and a mask of polished imperturbability, or else a pea-jacket, a pug-nose, a cauliflower ear, with bow legs and a rolling gait... .

"There, I fancy that will do. But hurry it along, please."

"Very good, sir—immediately."

The head waiter ambled off, and Blue Serge faced Sally with an odd, illegible smile.

"At last!" he hissed in the approved manner of melodrama, "we are alone!"

She wasn't able to rise to his irresponsible humour. Thus far her audacity seemed to have earned her nothing but his derision. He was not in the least afraid of her—and *he* was a desperate criminal. Then what was she in his esteem?

Such thoughts drove home a fresh painful realisation of her ambiguous personal status. It began to seem that she had been perhaps a little hasty in assuming she was to be spared punishment for her sin, however venial that might in charity be reckoned. Chance had, indeed, offered what was apparently a broad and easy avenue of escape; but her own voluntary folly has chosen the wrong turning.

Her hands were twisted tight together in her lap as she demanded with tense directness:

"What have you done with them?"

He lifted the ironic eyebrow. " *Them?* "

"The jewels. I saw you steal them—watched you from the dining-room, through the folding doors—"

"The deuce you did!"

"I saw you break open the desk—and everything."

"Well," he admitted fairly, "I'm jiggered!"

"What have you done with them?"

"Oh, the jewels?" he said with curious intonation. "Ah—yes, to be sure; the jewels, of course. You're anxious to know what I've done with them?"

"Oh, no," she countered irritably; "I only ask out of politeness."

"Thoughtful of you!" he laughed. "Why, they're outside, of course—in my bag."

"Outside?"

"Didn't you notice? I checked it with my hat, rather than have a row. I ought to be ashamed of myself, I know, but I'm a moral coward before a coat-room attendant. I remember keeping tabs one summer, and—will you believe me?—a common, ordinary, every-day three-dollar straw lid set me back twenty-two dollars and thirty cents in tips. But I hope I'm not boring you."

"Oh, how can you?" she protested, lips tremulous with indignation.

"Don't flatter; I bore even myself at times."

"I don't mean that, and you know I don't. How can you sit there joking when you—when you've just—"

"Come off the job?" he caught her up as she faltered. "But why not? I feel anything but sad about it. It was a good job—wasn't it?—a clean haul, a clear getaway. Thanks, of course, to you."

She responded, not without some difficulty: "Please! I wouldn't have dared if he hadn't tried to get at that sword."

"Just like him, too!" Blue Serge observed with a flash of indignation: "his kind, I mean—less burglars than bunglers, with no professional pride, no decent instincts, no human consideration. *They* never stop to think it's tough enough for a householder to come home to a cracked crib without finding a total stranger to boot—a man he's never even *seen* before, like as not—ah—weltering on the premises—"

"Oh, do be serious!"

"Must I? If you wish."

The man composed his features to a mask of whimsical attention.

"What—what did you do with him?" the girl stammered after a pause during which consciousness of her disadvantage became only more acute.

"Our active little friend, the yegg? Why, I didn't do anything with him."

"You didn't leave him there'?"

"Oh, no; he went away, considerately enough—up-stairs and out through the scuttle—the way he broke in, you know. Surprisingly spry on his feet for a man of his weight and age—had all I could do to keep up. He did stop once, true, as if he'd forgotten something, but the sword ran into him—I happened thoughtlessly to be carrying it—only a quarter of an inch or so—and he changed his mind, and by the time I got my head through the scuttle he was gone—vanished utterly from human ken!"

"He had broken the scuttle open, you say?"

"Pried it up with a jimmy."

"And you left it so? He'll go back."

"No, he won't. I found hammer and nails and made all fast before I left."

"But," she demanded, wide-eyed with wonder, "why did you take that trouble?"

"My silly conceit, I presume. I couldn't bear the thought of having that roughneck return and muss up one of my neatest jobs."

"I don't understand you at all," she murmured, utterly confounded.

"Nor I you, if it matters. Still, I'm sure you won't keep me much longer in suspense, considering how open-faced I've been. But here's that animal of a waiter again."

She was willingly silent, though she exerted herself to seem at ease with indifferent success. The voice of her companion was like a distant, hollow echo in her hearing; her wits were all awhirl, her nerves as taut and vibrant as banjo-strings; before her vision the face of Blue Serge swam, a flesh-tinted moon now and again traversed by a flash of white when he smiled.

"Come!" the man rallied her sharply, if in an undertone, "this will never do. You're as white as a sheet, trembling and staring as if I were a leper—or a relation by marriage or—something repulsive!"

She sat forward mechanically and mustered an uncertain smile. "Forgive me. I'm a little overwrought—the heat and—everything."

"Not another word, then, till you've finished. I'll do the talking, if it's all the same to you. But you needn't answer—needn't listen, for that matter. I've no pride in my conversational powers, and you mustn't risk losing your appetite."

He seemed to find it easy enough to make talk; but Sally spared him little attention, being at first exclusively preoccupied with the demands of her hunger, and later—as the meal progressed, renewing her physical strength and turning the ebbing tide of her spirits—thoroughly engaged with the problem of how to extricate herself from this embarrassing association or, if extrication proved impossible, how to turn it to her own advantage. For if the affair went on this way—his way—she were a sorry adventuress indeed.

Small cups of black coffee stood before them, steaming, when a question roused her, and she shook herself together and faced her burglar across the cloth, once more full mistress of her faculties.

"You're feeling better'?"

"Very much," she smiled, "and thank you!"

"Don't make me uncomfortable; remember, this is all your fault.

"That I'm here, alive and whole, able to enjoy a most unique situation. *Who are you?*"

But she wasn't to be caught by any such simple stratagem as a question plumped suddenly at her with all the weight of a rightful demand; she smiled again and shook her head.

"Shan't tell."

"But if I insist?"

"Why don't you, then?"

"Meaning insistence won't get me anything?"

Sensitive to the hint of a hidden trump, she stiffened slightly.

"I haven't asked you to commit yourself. I've got a right to my own privacy."

There fell a small pause. Lounging, an elbow on the table, a cigarette fuming idly between his fingers, the man favoured her with a steady look of speculation whose challenge was modified only by the inextinguishable humour smouldering in his eyes—a look that Sally met squarely, dissembling her excitement. For with all her fears and perplexity she could never quite forget that, whatever its sequel, this was verily an adventure after her own heart, that she was looking her best in a wonderful frock and pitting her wits against those of an engaging rogue, that she who had twelve hours ago thought herself better dead was now living intensely an hour of vital emergency.

"But," the man said suddenly, and yet deliberately, "surely you won't dispute my right to know who makes free with my own home?"

Her bravado was extinguished as suddenly as a candle-flame in a gust of wind.

"*Your* home?" she parroted witlessly.

"Mine, yes. If you can forgive me." He fumbled for his card-case. "It has been amusing to play the part you assigned me of amateur cracksman, but really, I'm afraid, it can't be done without a better make-up."

He produced and placed before her on the cloth a small white card; and as soon as its neat black script ceased to writhe and run together beneath her gaze she comprehended the name of *Mr. Walter Arden Savage*, with a residence address identical with that of the house wherein her great adventure had begun.

"You!" she breathed aghast, "you're not *really* Mr. Savage?"

He smiled indulgently. "I rather think I am."

"But—"

Sally's voice failed her entirely, and he laughed a tolerant little laugh as he bent forward to explain.

"I don't wonder you are surprised—or at your mistake. The fact is, the circumstances are peculiar. It's my sister's fault, really; she's such a flighty little thing—unpardonably careless. I must have warned her a hundred times, if once, never to leave valuables in that silly old tin safe. But she won't listen to reason—never would. And it's her house—her safe. I've got no right to install a better one. And that is why we're here."

He smiled thoughtfully down his nose. "It's really a chapter of accidents to which I'm indebted for this charming adventure," he pursued with a suavely personal nod, "beginning with the blow-out of the taxicab tire that made us five minutes late for this evening's boat. We were bound up the Sound, you understand, to spend a fortnight with a maternal aunt. And our luggage is well on its way there now. So when we missed the boat there was nothing for it but go by train. We taxied back here through that abominable storm, booked for Boston by the eleven ten, and ducked across the way to dine at the Biltmore. No good going home, of course, with the servants out—and everything. And just as we were finishing dinner this amiable sister of mine gave a whoop and let it out that she'd forgotten her jewels. Well, there was plenty of time. I put her aboard the train as soon as the sleepers were open—ten o'clock, you know—and trotted back home to fetch the loot."

A reminiscent chuckle punctuated his account, but struck no echo from Sally's humour. Moveless and mute, the girl sat unconsciously clutching the edge of the table as if it were the one stable fact in her whirling world; all her bravado dissipating as her daze of wonder yielded successively to doubt, suspicion, consternation.

"I said there was plenty of time, and so there was, barring accidents. But the same wouldn't be barred. I manufactured the first delay for myself, forgetting to ask Adele for the combination. I knew where to find it, in a little book locked up in the desk; but I hadn't a key to the desk, so felt obliged to break it open, and managed that so famously I was beginning to fancy myself a bit as a Raffles when, all of a sudden—*Pow!*" he laughed—"that fat devil landed on my devoted neck with all the force and fury of two hundredweight of professional jealousy!

"And then," he added, "in you walked from God knows where—"

His eyes affixed a point of interrogation to the simple declarative.

She started nervously in response, divided between impulses which she had no longer sufficient wit to weigh. Should she confess, or try to lie out of it?

Must she believe this glibly simple and adequate account or reject it on grounds of pardonable skepticism?

If this man were what he professed to be, surely he must recognise her borrowed plumage as his sister's property. True, that did not of necessity follow; men have so little understanding of women's clothing; it pleases them or it displeases, if thrust upon their attention, but once withdrawn it is forgotten utterly. Such might well be the case in this present instance; the man gave Sally, indeed, every reason to believe him as much bewildered and mystified by her as she was by him.

On the other hand, and even so ...

The infatuate impulse prevailed, to confess and take the consequences.

"I'm afraid—" she began in a quaver.

"No need to be—none I know of, at least," he volunteered promptly, if without moderating his exacting stare.

"You don't understand—"

She hesitated, sighed, plunged in desperation. "It's no use; there's nothing for me to do but own up. What you were not to-night, Mr. Savage, I was."

"Sounds like a riddle to me. What is the answer?"

"You were just make-believe. I was the real thing—a real thief. No, let me go on; it's easier if you don't interrupt. Yes, I'll tell you my name, but it won't mean anything. I'm nobody. I'm Sarah Manvers. I'm a shop-girl out of work."

"Still I don't see ..."

"I'm coming to that. I live on your block—the Lexington Avenue end, of course—with two other girls. And this afternoon—the studio was so hot and stuffy and lonesome, with both my friends away—I went up on the roof for better air, and fell asleep there and got caught by the storm. Somebody had closed the scuttle, and I ran across roofs looking for another that wasn't fastened down, and when I found one—it was your house—I was so frightened by the lightning I hardly knew what I was doing. I just tumbled in

44

—"

"And welcome, I'm sure," Blue Serge interpolated.

She blundered on, unheeding: "I went all through the house, but there wasn't anybody, and—I was so wet and miserable that I—made myself at home—decided to take a bath and—and borrow some things to wear until my own were dry. And then I thought ..."

She halted, confused, realising how impossible it would be to convince anybody with the tale of her intention merely to borrow the clothing for a single night of arabesque adventure, finding it difficult now to believe in on her own part, and hurried breathlessly on to cover the hiatus.

"And then I heard a noise on the roof. I had closed the scuttle, but I was frightened. And I crept down-stairs and—saw the light in the library and ... That's all." And when he didn't reply promptly, she added with a trace of challenge: "So now you know!"

He started as from deep reverie.

"But why call yourself a thief—for that?"

"Because ... because ..." Overstrung nerves betrayed her in gusty confession. "Because it's no good blinking facts: that's what I was in my heart of hearts. Oh, it's all very well for you to be generous, and for me to pretend I meant only to borrow, and—and all that! But the truth is, I did steal—and I never honestly meant to send the things back. At first—yes; then I meant to return them, but never once they were on my back. I told myself I did, I believed I did; but deep down, all along, I didn't, I didn't, I didn't! I'm a liar as well as a thief."

"Oh, come now!" Blue Serge interjected in a tone of mild remonstrance, lounging back and eying the girl intently. "Don't be so down on yourself."

"Well, everything I've said was true except that one word 'borrow'; but that in itself was a lie big enough to eclipse every word of truth... . But you'll never understand—never! Men can't. They simply can't know what it is to be clothes-hungry—starving for something fit to wear—as I have been for years and years and years, as most of us in the shops are all our lives long."

"Perhaps I understand, though," he argued with an odd look. "I know what you mean, at any rate, even if I'm not ready to admit that shop-girls are the only people who ever know what it is to desire the unattainable. Other people want things, at times, just as hard as you do clothes."

"Well, but ..." She stammered, unable to refute this reasonable contention, but, womanlike, persistent to try: "It's different—when you've never had anything. Try to think what it must be to work from eight till six—sometimes later—six days a week, for just enough to keep alive on, if you call such an existence being alive! Why, in ten years I haven't seen the country or the sea —unless you count trips to Coney on crowded trolley-cars, and mighty few of them. I never could afford a vacation, though I've been idle often enough— never earned more than ten dollars a week, and that not for many weeks together. I've lived on as little as five—on as little as charity, on nothing but the goodness of my friends at times. That's why, when I saw myself prettily dressed for once, and thought nothing could stop my getting away, I couldn't resist the temptation. I didn't know where I was going, dressed like this, and not a cent; but I was going some place, and I wasn't ever coming back!"

"Good Lord!" the man said gently. "Who'd blame you?"

"Don't sympathise with me," she protested, humanly quite unconscious of her inconsistency. "I don't deserve it. I'm caught with the goods on, literally, figuratively, and I've got to pay the penalty. Oh, I don't mean what you mean. I'm no such idiot as to think you'll have me sent to jail; you've been too kind already and—and, after all, I did do you a considerable service, I did help you out of a pretty dangerous fix. But the penalty I'll pay is worse than jail: it's giving up these pretty things and all my silly, sinful dreams, and going back to that scrubby studio—and no job—"

She pulled up short, mystified by a sudden change in the man's expression, perceiving that she was no longer holding his attention as completely as she had. She remarked his look of embarrassment, that his eyes winced from something descried beyond and unknown to her. But he was as ready as ever to recover and demonstrate that, if his attention had wandered, he hadn't missed the substance of her harangue; for when she paused he replied:

"Oh, perhaps not. Don't let's jump at conclusions. I've a premonition you won't have to go back. Here comes some one who'll have a word to say about that—or I don't know!"

And he was up before Sally had grasped his meaning—on his feet and bowing civilly, if with a twinkling countenance, to a woman who swooped down upon him in a sudden, wild flutter of words and gestures:

"Walter! Thank God I've found you! I've been so upset—hardly knew what to do—when you didn't show up... ."

What more she might have said dried instantly on the newcomer's lips as her gaze embraced Sally. She stiffened slightly and drew back, elevating her eyebrows to the frost-line.

"Who is this woman? What does this mean?" Without awaiting an answer to either question, she observed in accents that had all the chilling force and cutting edge of a winter wind:

"*My* dress! *My* hat!"

CHAPTER V

CONSPIRACY

"My dear sister!" interposed Mr. Savage with an imitation so exact of the woman's tone that he nearly wrung a smile even from Sally. "Do calm yourself—don't make a scene. The matter is quite easy to explain—"

"But what—"

"Oh, give us a chance. But permit me!" He bowed with his easy laugh. "Adele, this is Miss Manvers—Miss Manvers, my sister Mrs. Standish. And now"—as Sally half started from her chair and Mrs. Standish acknowledged her existence by an embittered nod—"do sit down, Adele!"

With the manner of one whose amazement has paralysed her parts of speech, the woman sank mechanically into the chair which Savage (having thoughtfully waved away the hovering waiter) placed beside the table, between himself and his guest. But once seated, precisely as if that position were a charm to break the spell that sealed them, promptly her lips reformed the opening syllables of "*What does this mean?*"

Mr. Savage, however, diplomatically gave her no chance to utter more than the first word.

"Do hold your tongue," he pleaded with a rudeness convincingly fraternal, "and listen to me. I am deeply indebted to Miss Manvers—for my very life, in fact. Oh, don't look so blamed incredulous; I'm perfectly sober. Now *will* you please give me a show?"

And, the lady executing a gesture that matched well her look of blank resignation, her brother addressed himself to a terse summing up of the affair which, while it stressed the gravity of the adventure with the fat burglar, did not seem to extenuate Sally's offence in the least and so had the agreeable upshot of leaving the sister in a much-placated humour and regarding the girl with a far more indulgent countenance than Sally had found any reason at first to hope for.

As for that young woman, the circumstance that she was inwardly all a-shudder didn't in the least hinder her exercise of that feminine trick of mentally photographing, classifying, and cataloguing the other woman's outward aspects in detail and, at the same time, distilling her more subtle phases of personality in the retort of instinct and minutely analysing the precipitate.

The result laid the last lingering ghost of suspicion that all was not as it should be between these two, that Blue Serge had not been altogether frank with her.

She had from the first appreciated the positive likeness between Mrs. Standish and the portrait in the library, even though her observation of the latter had been limited to the most casual inspection through the crack of the folding doors; there wasn't any excuse for questioning the identification. The woman before her, like the woman of the picture, was of the slender, blonde class— intelligent, neurotic, quick-tempered, inclined to suffer spasmodically from exaltation of the ego. And if she had not always been pampered with every luxury that money has induced modern civilisation to invent, the fact was not apparent; she dressed with such exquisite taste as only money can purchase, if it be not innate; she carried herself with the ease of affluence founded upon a rock, while her nervousness was manifestly due rather to impatience than to the vice of worrying.

"And now," Mr. Savage wound up with a graceless grin, "if you'll be good enough to explain what the dickens you're doing here instead of being on the way to Boston by the eleven-ten, I'll be grateful; Miss Manvers will quit doubting my veracity—secretly, if not openly; and we can proceed to consider something I have to suggest with respect to the obligations of a woman who has been saved the loss of a world of gewgaws as well as those of a man who is alive and whole exclusively, thanks to ... Well, I think you know what I mean."

"Oh, as for that," said Mrs. Standish absently, "when you turned up missing on the train I stopped it at the Hundred and Twenty-Fifth Street station and came back to find out what was the matter. I've been all through this blessed place looking for you—"

"Pardon!" Mr. Savage interrupted. "Did I understand you to say you had stopped the train?"

"Certainly. Why not? You don't imagine I was going to let myself be carried all the way to Boston in ignorance—"

"Then, one infers, the eleven-ten doesn't normally stop at One Hundred and Twenty-Fifth Street?"

"No. I had to speak to the conductor. Do be quiet. It doesn't matter. What were you going to say?"

"Nothing much, except that the clothes Miss Manvers stands in are hardly to be considered an adequate reward."

"True. But you mentioned some suggestion or other—"

"Without being downright about it, thereby sparing Miss Manvers any embarrassment, she might feel should you disapprove, as I'm confident you won't—"

This was the woman's turn; she silenced him with a gesture of infinite ennui. "Why is it," she complained, "that you *never* get anywhere without talking all around Robin Hood's barn?"

"Objection," Mr. Savage offered promptly, "on the ground of mixed metaphor."

"Objection sustained," his sister conceded. "But do come to the point."

"I wish only to remind you of the news imparted by our respected aunt in her letter of recent date."

The woman frowned slightly, as with mental effort; then a flash of comprehension lightened her blue eyes. Immediately her brows mutely circumflexed a question. A look of profound but illegible significance passed between the two. Mr. Savage nodded. Mrs. Standish pursed speculatively her thin, well-made-up lips and visibly took thought, according to the habit of her sex, by means of a series of intuitive explosions. Then she nodded vigorously and turned upon Miss Manvers a bewildering smile, for the first time addressing her directly.

"My dear," she said pleasantly enough—though, of course, the term had no accent whatever of affection—"this half-witted brother of mine once in a while stumbles upon the most brilliant inspiration imaginable. I'm sure he has seen enough of you in this last hour to be making no mistake in offering you as one answer to a very delicate question which has been distressing us both for a long time. If you're not overscrupulous …"

She paused with a receptive air.

"I'm sure I don't know what you're driving at," Sally said bluntly; "but I'm hardly in a position to be nice-minded about trifles."

"It's this way," Savage interposed; "we're offering you a chance to get away, to enjoy a summer by the seashore, to mix with a lot of mighty interesting people, and all that sort of thing—everything you tell me you've been pining for—if you'll consent to sail under false colours."

"Please!" Sally begged with a confused and excited little laugh.

"He simply can't help it; indirection is Walter's long suit," Mrs. Standish took up the tale. "First of all, you must know this aunt of ours is rather an eccentric —frightfully well off, spoiled, self-willed, and quite blind to her best interests. She's been a widow so long she doesn't know the meaning of wholesome restraint. She's got all the high knee-action of a thoroughbred never properly broken to harness. She sets her own pace—and Heaven help the hindermost! All in all, I think Aunt Abby's the most devil-may-care person I've ever met."

"You're too modest," Mr. Savage commented abstractedly.

"Be quiet, Walter. Aunt Abby's passionately fond of two things—cards and what she calls 'interesting people.' Neither would matter much but for the other. She gambles for sheer love of it, and doesn't care a rap whether she wins or loses. And her notion of an interesting person is anybody fortunate or misfortunate enough to be noticed by the newspapers. A bit of a scandal is sure bait for her regard ..."

Pausing, Mrs. Standish smiled coolly. "Take me, for example. Until I found it necessary to get unmarried, my aunt never could find time to waste on me. But now, in spite of the fact that the decree was in my favour, I'm the object of her mad attachment. And if Walter hadn't come into the limelight through a Senatorial inquiry into high finance, and made such a sick witness, and got so deservedly roasted by the newspapers—well, nothing is now too good for him. So, you see, the people Aunt Abby insists on entertaining are apt to be a rather dubious lot. I don't mean she'd pick up with anybody openly immoral, you know; but she certainly manages to fill her houses—she's got several— with a wild crew of adventurers and—esses—to call 'em by their first names.

"They're smart enough, God knows, and they do make things hum, but they charge her—some of them—fat fees for the privilege of entertaining them. Funny things have happened at her card tables. So Walter and I have been scheming to find some way to protect her without rousing her resentment by seeming to interfere. If we could only get evidence enough to talk privately to some of her friends—about time-tables, for instance—it would be all right. And only recently she herself showed us the way—wrote me that she had quarrelled with her corresponding secretary, a spinster of acid maturity, and discharged her; and would we please look round for somebody to replace Miss. Matring. Do you see?"

"You mean," Sally faltered, dumfounded—"you can't mean you'll recommend *me* for the position?"

"I'll do more. I'll see that you get it; I'll take you with me to-night, and by to-morrow noon you'll be engaged. But you must understand we're giving you the chance solely that you may serve us as well as Aunt Abby, by keeping your eyes and ears wide open and reporting to us in strictest confidence and secrecy anything that doesn't look right to you."

"But—but I—but how—why do you think you can trust me?" the girl stammered. "Knowing what you do—"

"That's just the point. Don't you see'? We can trust you because you won't dare betray us."

"But—but after I've stolen—"

"Don't say it!" Savage cut in. "You stole nothing, if you please; you merely anticipated a reward for a service not yet rendered."

"But … Oh, it's kind of you, but don't you see it's impossible?"

"Nothing is impossible except your refusal," said Mrs. Standish. "Do be sensible, my dear, and realise that we—that I intend you shall have this chance. What can you possibly find to object to? The deceit? Surely an innocent deception, practised upon a dear old lady for her own good!"

"Deceit," Mr. Savage propounded very sagely, "is like any other sin, it's only sinful when it is. That's elementary sophistry, but I invented it, and I'm strong for it. Besides, we've got just twenty minutes now to get aboard the Owl—and I've got to beg, borrow, or buy transportation on it, because there wasn't a room left but the two I bought for you and me—and now Adele will have to have one of the rooms—"

"But I've nothing to wear but these things!" "Don't worry about that," Mrs. Standish reassured her. "I've got nine trunks on the way—and you unquestionably fill my things out like another perfect figure."

"But how will you explain? Who am I to be? You can't introduce me as a shop-girl out of work whom you caught stealing your clothes."

"*La nuit porte conseil*," Mr. Savage announced sagely, and with what was no doubt an excellent accent. "Let Adele sleep on it, and if she doesn't come through in the morning with a good, old-fashioned, all wool, yard-wide lie that will blanket every possible contingency, I don't know my little sister."

"An elder brother, let me tell you, Miss Manvers, is the best possible preceptor in prevarication."

"Elder!" exclaimed the outraged young man. "Well, of all—" He turned appealingly to Sally. "*What* did I tell you?"

CHAPTER VI

ALIAS MANWARING

Fickle-minded fortune favoured Mr. Savage's belated application for additional sleeping-car accommodation: somebody turned back a reservation only ten minutes or so before train-time, in consequence of which Mrs. Standish and Miss Manvers enjoyed adjoining compartments of luxury, while Mr. Savage contented himself with less pretentious quarters farther aft.

Thus it was that at one minute past one o'clock, when a preternaturally self-respecting porter dispassionately ascertained that nothing more would be required of him till morning and shut himself out of her presence, the girl subsided upon the edge of a bed of such sybaritic character as amply to warrant the designation *de luxe*, and, flushed and trembling with excitement (now that she dared once again to be her natural self) and with all incredulity appropriate to the circumstances, stared at the young woman who blankly stared back from a long mirror framed in the door.

It was truly a bit difficult to identify that modishly dressed and brilliantly animated young person with S. Manvers of the Hardware Notions in Huckster's Bargain Basement, while reason tottered and common sense tittered when invited to credit the chain of accidents responsible for the transformation.

Strange world of magic romance, this, into which she had stumbled over the threshold of a venial misdemeanour! Who now would dare contend that life was ever sordid, grim, and cruel, indigestible from soup to savoury? Who would have the hardihood to uphold such contention when made acquainted with the case of Sarah Manvers, yesterday's drudge, unlovely and unloved, to-day's child of fortune, chosen of a golden destiny?

Sally's jubilation was shadowed by a pensive moment; dare she assume that the winters of her discontent had been forever banished by one wave of Chance's wand?

She shook a confounded head, smiled an uncertain smile, sighed a little, broken sigh, and with determination bade adieu to misgivings, turning a deaf ear to the dull growls of mother-wit arguing that the Board of Health ought to be advised about the State of Denmark. Sufficient unto the night its room de luxe; she found her couch no less comfortable for the sword that conceivably swayed above it, suspended by a thread of casual favour.

For a time she rested serenely in the dark—only half undressed in view of the ever-possible accident—cheek to pillow, face turned to the window that endlessly screened the sweeping mysteries of that dark glimmering countryside, quite resigned so to while away the night, persuaded it was inevitable that one with so much to ponder should be unable to sleep a wink.

Deliberately, to prove this point, she closed her eyes... .

And immediately opened them to broad daylight, revealing, through that magic casement, the outskirts of a considerable city, street after suburban street wheeling away like spokes from a restless hub.

A simultaneous pounding on the door warned her she had but ten minutes in which to dress; no time to grasp the substance of a dream come true, no time even to prepare a confident attitude with which to salute the fairy godparents of her social debut—time only to struggle into her outer garments and muster a half-timid, deprecatory smile for those whom she was to find awaiting her in the corridor, impatient to be off, none too amiably conscious of foregone beauty sleep, accepting their protegee with a matter-of-course manner almost disillusioning.

"Got to hurry, you know," Savage informed her brusquely; "only twenty minutes to snatch a bite before our train leaves for the Island."

They hurried down a platform thronged with fellow passengers similarly haunted by the seven devils of haste, beneath a high glazed but opaque vault penning an unappetizing atmosphere composed in equal parts of a stagnant warm air and stale steam, into a restaurant that had patently been up all night, through the motions of swallowing alternate mouthfuls of denatured coffee and dejected rolls, up again and out and down another platform—at last into the hot and dusty haven of a parlour-car.

Then impressions found time for readjustment. The journey promised, and turned out, to be by no means one of unalloyed delights. The early morning temper discovered by Mrs. Standish offered chill comfort to one like Sally, saturate with all the emotions of a stray puppy hankering for a friendly pat. Ensconced in the chair beside her charge, the patroness swung it coolly aside until little of her was visible but the salient curve of a pastel-tinted cheek and buried her nose in a best-selling novel, ignoring overtures analogous to the wagging of a propitiatory tail. While Savage, in the chair beyond his sister, betrayed every evidence of being heartily grateful for a distance that precluded conversation and to a Providence that tolerated *Town Topics*. Sally was left to improve her mind with a copy of *Vanity Fair*, from contemplation of whose text and pictures she emerged an amateur adventuress sadly wanting in the indispensable quality of assurance. It wasn't that she feared to measure wits, intelligence, or even lineage with the elect. But in how many mysterious ways might she not fall short of the ideal of Good Form?

What—she pondered gloomily, chin in hand, eyes vacantly reviewing a countryside of notable charms adrowse in the lethargic peace of a mid-summer morning—what the dickens was Good Form, anyway?

Nothing, not even her own normally keen power of observation, offered any real enlightenment.

She summed up an hour's studious reflection in the dubious conclusion that Good Form had something subtly to do with being able to sit cross-kneed and look arrogantly into the impertinent lens of a camp-follower's camera—to be impudently self-conscious, that is—to pose and pose and get away with it.

The train came to a definite stop, and Sally startled up to find Mrs. Standish, afoot, smiling down at her with all her pretty features except her eyes, and Mr. Savage smiling in precisely the reverse fashion.

"All out," he announced. "Change here for the boat. Another hour, and—as somebody says Henry James says—there, in a manner of speaking, we all are."

They straggled across a wharf to a fussy small steamer, Mrs. Standish leading the way with an apprehensive eye for possible acquaintances and, once established with her brother and Sally in a secluded corner of the boat's upper deck, uttering her relief in a candid sigh.

"Nobody we know aboard," she added, smiling less tensely at Sally.

"Eh—what say'?" Mr. Savage inquired from a phase of hypnosis induced by a glimpse of Good Form in a tailored skirt of white corduroy.

"Nobody of any consequence in this mob," his sister paraphrased, yawning delicately.

"Oh," he responded with an accent of doubt. But the white corduroy vanished round a shoulder of the deck-house, and he bestirred himself to pay a little attention to Sally.

"There's the Island," he said, languidly waving a hand. "That white-pillared place there among the trees—left of the lighthouse—that's Aunt Abby's."

Sally essayed a smile of intelligent response. Not that the Island failed to enchant her; seen across a fast diminishing breadth of wind-darkened blue water, bathed in golden mid-morning light, its villas of delicious grey half buried in billows of delicious green, its lawns and terraces crowning fluted grey-stone cliffs from whose feet a broad beach shelved gently into the sea, it seemed more beautiful to Miss Manvers than anything she had ever dreamed of.

But what was to be her reception there, what her status, what her fortunes?

"I've been thinking," Mrs. Standish announced when a sidelong glance had reassured her as to their practical privacy, "about Miss Manvers."

"I hope to Heaven you've doped out a good one," Savage interrupted fervently. "In the cold grey dawn it doesn't look so good to me. But then I'm only a duffer. Perhaps it's just as well; if I'd been a good liar I might have married to keep my hand in. As it is, I never forget to give thanks, in my evening prayers, for my talented little sister."

"Are you finished?" Mrs. Standish inquired frigidly.

"I'd better be."

"Then, please pay close attention, Miss Manvers. To begin with, I'm going to change your name. From now on it's Sara Manwaring—Sara without the *h*."

"Manwaring with the *w* silent, as in wrapper and wretch?" Savage asked politely.

For Sally's benefit Mrs. Standish spelled the word patiently.

"And the record of the fair impostor?" Savage prompted.

"That's very simple. Miss Manwaring came to me yesterday with a letter of introduction from Edna English. Edna sailed for Italy last Saturday, and by the time she's back Aunt Abby will have forgotten to question Miss Manwaring's credentials."

"What did I tell you?" Mr. Savage wagged a solemn head at Sally. "There's Art for you!"

"She comes from a family prominent socially in"—Mrs. Standish paused a fraction of a second—"Massillon, Ohio—"

"Is there any such place?"

"Of course—"

"What a lot you do know, Adele!"

"But through a series of unhappy accidents involving the family fortunes was obliged to earn her own living."

"Is that all?"

"Isn't it enough?"

55

"Plenty. Simple, succinct, stupendous! It has only one flaw."

"And that, if you please?" Mrs. Standish demanded, bristling a trifle.

"It ain't possible for anyone to be prominent socially in a place named Massillon, Ohio. It can't be done—not in a place I never heard of before."

"Do you understand, Miss Manwaring?" the woman asked, turning an impatient shoulder to her brother.

"Perfectly," Sally assented eagerly; "only—who is Edna English?"

"Mrs. Cornwallis English. You must have heard of her."

"Oh, yes, in the newspapers …"

"Social uplift's her fad. She's done a lot of work among department-store girls."

"To their infinite annoyance," interpolated Savage.

"At all events, that's how she came to notice you."

"I see," said Sally humbly.

"You may fill in the outlines at your discretion," Mrs. Standish pursued sweetly. "That's all I know about you. You called at the house with the letter from Mrs. English yesterday afternoon, and I took a fancy to you and, knowing that Aunt Abby needed a secretary, brought you along."

"Thank you," said Sally. "I hope you understand how grate—"

"That's quite understood. Let us say no more about it."

"Considerable story," Savage approved. "But what became of the letter of introduction?"

"I mislaid it," his sister explained complacently. "Don't I mislay everything?"

For once the young man was dumb with admiration. But his look was eloquent.

Deep thought held the amateur adventuress spellbound for some minutes. "There's only one thing," she said suddenly, with a puzzled frown.

"And that?" Mrs. Standish prompted.

"What about the burglary? Your servants, when they came home last night, must have noticed and notified the police."

"Oh, I say!" Savage exclaimed blankly.

"Don't let's worry about that," Mrs. Standish interrupted. "We can easily let it be understood that what was stolen was later recovered from—whatever they call the places where thieves dispose of their stealings."

"That covers everything," Savage insisted impatiently. "Do come along. There's the car waiting."

Coincident with this announcement a series of slight jars shook the steamer, and with surprise Sally discovered that, without her knowledge in the preoccupation of being fitted with a completely new identity, the vessel had rounded a wooded headland, opening up a deep harbour dotted with pleasure craft, and was already nuzzling the town wharf of a sizable community.

She rose and followed her fellow conspirators aft and below to the gangway, her mind registering fresh impressions with the rapidity of a cinema film.

The grey cliff had given place to green-clad bluffs sown thick with cottages of all sorts, from the quaintly hideous and the obviously inexpensive to the bewitchingly pretty and the pretentiously ornate —a haphazard arrangement that ran suddenly into a plot of streets linking a clutter of utilitarian buildings, all converging upon the focal point of the village wharf.

Upon this last a cloud of natives and summer folk swarmed and buzzed. At its head a cluster of vehicles, horse-drawn as well as motor-driven, waited. In the shadow beneath it, and upon the crescent beach that glistened on its either side, a multitude of children, young and old, paddled and splashed in shallows and the wash of the steamer.

Obviously the less decorative and exclusive side of the island, it was none the less enchanting in Sally's vision. A measure of confidence reinfused her mood. She surrendered absolutely to fatalistic enjoyment of the gifts the gods had sent. Half closing her eyes, she drank deep of salt-sweet air vibrant with the living warmth of a perfect day.

A man whose common face was as impassive as a mask shouldered through the mob and burdened himself with the hand-luggage of the party. Sally gathered that he was valet to Mr. Savage. And they were pushing through the gantlet of several hundred curious eyes and making toward the head of the pier.

"Trying," Mrs. Standish observed in an aside to the girl. "I always say that everything about the Island is charming but the getting here."

Sally murmured an inarticulate response and wondered. Disdain of the commonalty was implicit in that speech; it was contact with the herd, subjection to its stares, that Mrs. Standish found so trying. How, then, had she brought herself so readily to accept association on almost equal terms with a shop-girl misdemeanant—out of gratitude, or sheer goodness of heart, or something less superficial?

The shadow of an intimation that something was wrong again came between Sally and the sun, but passed as swiftly as a wind-sped cloud.

The valet led to a heavy, seven-seated touring-car, put their luggage in the rear, shut the door on the three, and swung up to the seat beside the chauffeur. The machine threaded a cautious way out of the rank, moved sedately up a somnolent street, turned a corner and pricked up its heels to the tune of a long, silken snore, flinging over its shoulder two miles of white, well-metalled roadway with no appreciable effort whatever.

For a moment or two dwellings swept by like so many telegraph-poles past a car-window. Then they became more widely spaced, and were succeeded by a blurred and incoherent expanse of woods, fields, parks, hedges, glimpses of lawns surfaced like a billiard-table, flashes of white facades maculated with cool blue shadows.

Then, without warning if without a jar, the car slowed down to a safe and sane pace and swung off between two cobblestone pillars into a well-kept wilderness of trees that stood as a wall of privacy between the highroad and an exquisitely parked estate bordering the cliffs.

Debouching into the open, the drive swept a gracious curve round a wonderful wide lawn of living velvet and through the pillared porte-cochere of a long, white-walled building with many gaily awninged windows in its two wide-spread wings.

Sentinelled by sombre cypresses, relieved against a sapphire sky bending to a sea of scarcely deeper shade, basking in soft, clear sunlight, the house seemed to hug the earth very intimately, to belong most indispensably, with an effect of permanence, of orderliness and dignity that brought to mind instinctively the term estate, and caused Sally to recall (with misspent charity) the fulsome frenzy of a sycophantic scribbler ranting of feudal aristocracies, representative houses, and encroaching tenantry.

The solitary symptom of a tenantry in evidence here was a perfectly good American citizen in shirt-sleeves and overalls, pipe in mouth, toleration in his mien, calmly steering a wheelbarrow down the drive. Sally caught the glint of his cool eyes and experienced a flash of intuition into a soul steeped in contemplative indulgence of the city crowd and its silly antics. And forthwith, for some reason she found no time to analyse, she felt more at home, less apprehensive.

As the car pulled up beneath the porte-cochere a mild-eyed footman ran out to help the valet with the luggage; Savage skipped blithely down and gave a hand to his sister, offering like assistance to Sally in turn; and on the topmost of three broad, white, stone steps the chatelaine of Gosnold House appeared to welcome her guests—a vastly different personality, of course, from any in Sally's somewhat incoherent anticipations.

Going upon the rather sketchy suggestions of Mrs. Standish, the girl had prefigured Aunt Abby as a skittish female of three-score years and odd; a gabbling creature with a wealth of empty gesticulation and a parrot's vacant eye; semi-irresponsible, prone to bright colours and an overyouthful style of dress.

She found, to the contrary, a lady of quiet reserve, composed of manner, authoritative of speech, not lacking in humour, of impeccable taste in dress, and to all appearances not a day older than forty-five, despite hair like snow that framed a face of rich but indisputably native complexion.

In her regard, when it was accorded exclusively to Sally, the girl divined a mildly diverted question, quite reasonable, as to her choice of travelling costume. Otherwise her reception was cordial, with reservations; nothing warranted the assumption that Mrs. Gosnold (Aunt Abby by her legitimate title) was not disposed to make up her mind about Miss Manwaring at her complete leisure. Interim she was very glad to see her; any friend of Adele's was always welcome to Gosnold House; and would Miss Manwaring be pleased to feel very much at home.

At this point Mrs. Standish affectionately linked arms with her relation and, with the nonchalant rudeness that was in those days almost a badge of caste, dragged her off to a cool and dusky corner of the panelled reception-hall to acquaint her with the adulterated facts responsible for the phenomenon of Miss Manwaring.

"Be easy," Mr. Savage comforted the girl airily; "trust Adele to get away with it. That young woman is sure of a crown and harp in the hereafter if only because she'll make St. Peter himself believe black is white. You've got nothing to worry about. Now I'm off for a bath and nap; just time before luncheon. See you then. So-long."

He blew a most débonnaire kiss to his maternal aunt and trotted lightly up the broad staircase; and as Sally cast about for some place to wait inconspicuously on the pleasure of her betters, Mrs. Gosnold calledher.

"Oh, Miss Manwaring!"

The girl responded with an unaffected diffidence apparently pleasing in the eyes of her prospective employer.

"My niece has been telling me about you," she said with an engaging smile; "and I am already inclined to be grateful to her. It isn't often—truth to tell—she makes such prompt acknowledgment of my demands. And I'm a most disorderly person, so I miss very much the services of my former secretary. Do come nearer."

Sally drew within arm's-length, and the elder woman put out a hand and caught the girl's in a firm, cool, friendly grasp.

"Your first name?" she inquired with a look of keen yet not unpleasant scrutiny.

"Sarah," said Sarah bluntly. "Man'aring" stuck in her guilty throat.

"S-a-r-a," Mrs. Standish punctiliously spelled it out.

"Thank you; I recognise it now." A shrewd, sidelong glance flickered amusement at Mrs. Gosnold's niece. "You come from the middle West, I understand, and you've had rather a hard time of it in New York. What do you do best?" "Why—I've tried to write," Sally confessed shyly.

"Oh? Novels?"

"Not quite so ambitious; short stories to begin with and then special articles for the newspapers—anything that promised to bring in a little money, but nothing ever did."

"Then, I presume, you're familiar with typewriters?"

"Oh, yes."

"And can punctuate after a fashion?"

"I think so."

"You don't look it; far too womanly, unless your appearance is deceptive, to know the true difference between a semicolon and a hyphen. No matter; you have every qualification, it seems, including a good manner and a pleasant smile. You're engaged—on probation; I mean to say, for this one week we'll consider you simply my guest, but willing to help me out with my correspondence. Then, if you like the place and I like you as much as I hope I shall, you'll become my personal secretary at a salary of twenty-five dollars a week and all expenses. No—don't thank me; thank your sensible eyes."

Mrs. Gosnold laughed lightly, gave Sally's hand a final but barely perceptible pressure, and released it.

"Now Thomas will show you your room. Mrs. Standish tells me she has promised to outfit you; her maid will bring you more suitable things by the time you've had your tub and some rest. Plenty of time; we lunch at one-thirty."

The girl stammered some sort of an acknowledgment; she was never able to recall precisely what she said, in truth, but it served. And then she was amazedly ascending the broad staircase and following the flunky's back down a long, wide, drafty corridor to a room at one extreme of the building—a small room, daintily furnished and bright with summery cretonne, its individual bath adjoining.

"I'll be sending the maid to you at once, ma'am," said Thomas, and shut the door.

Sally wandered to a window, lifted the shade, and looked out with bewildered eyes.

From the front of the house to the edge of the cliff the grounds were as severely composed as an Italian formal garden; but to one side, screened by high box hedges, a tennis-court was in the active possession of four young people, none of them, apparently over twenty years of age. Their calls and clear laughter rang in the quietness, vibrant with careless joy of living.

They did not in the least suggest the crew of adventurers which Mrs. Standish had led Sally to expect.

Thus far, indeed, Sally had failed to detect anything in the atmosphere of the establishment or in the bearing of its mistress to bear out the innuendo that Gosnold House was infested by a parasitic swarm and "Aunt Abby" the dupe of her own unholy passions. Doubts hummed in Sally's head, and she was abruptly surprised to find the view obscured by a mist of her own making—by, in short, nothing less than tears.

The simple kindliness of Mrs. Gosnold's welcome had touched the impostor more deeply than she had guessed. All this was offered her, this life of semi-idleness and luxury in this spot of poetic beauty, in return for nothing but trifling services. But she was not worthy!

A little gust of anger shook her—anger with her benefactors, that they could not have introduced her to this mundane paradise as her simple self, Miss Manvers—Sarah with the vulgar *h*—by her own merits and defects to stand or fall... .

But, as though the fates were weaving the fabric of her destiny less blindly than is their commonly reputed custom, the young woman's conscience during those few first hours had little time in which to work upon her better nature. Its first squeamish qualms, when it at length got Sally alone, were quickly counteracted by a knock at her door and what followed—the entrance of a quiet-mannered maid whose fresh-coloured countenance loomed like some amiable, mature moon above a double armful of summery apparel.

"Mrs. Standish's compliments, ma'am, and I'm bringing your things. There's more to come—as much again I'm to fetch immediate—and the rest, Mrs. Standish says, there'll be time enough for after luncheon, when all her trunks is unpacked."

Carefully depositing her burden upon the bed, she beamed acknowledgment of Sally's breathless thanks and made off briskly, to return much too soon to suit one who would have been glad of longer grace in which to become more intimately acquainted with this new donation of her ravishing good fortune.

None the less, it didn't need another double armful of beautiful things to satisfy Sally that, whatever and how many might be the faults of her benefactress, niggardliness was not of their number.

"That's all for now, and Mrs. Standish's compliments, and will you be so kind as to stop and see her, when you're dressed, before going down to lunch. It's the last door on the left, just this side the stairs. Will I turn on your bath now?"

"Please don't trouble. I—"

"No trouble at all, ma'am. Indeed, and I'm sure you'll find us all very happy to do anything we can for you. It'll be a nice change to be waiting on a pleasant-spoken person like yourself after that"— with a sniff—"Miss Matring."

"Oh!" Genuine disappointment was responsible for the exclamation. But a moment's thought persuaded Sally she had been unreasonable to hope her secret might be kept from the servants. Even if Mrs. Standish had not betrayed it to this maid, there had been that flunky, Thomas, in the reception-hall close at hand during the establishment of Sally's status, with his pose of inhuman detachment of interest—quite too perfect to be true.

"Beg pardon, ma'am?"

"Oh, nothing!" Sally swallowed her chagrin bravely. "I mean, thank you very much, but I'm accustomed to waiting on myself—except when it comes to hooks up the back—and you must have enough to keep you busy with so many people in the house."

"Not a great many just now, ma'am—not more'n a dozen, counting in Mrs. Standish and her brother and you. This has been an off week, so to speak, but they'll be arriving in plenty to-morrow and Saturday, I'm told."

That gossip was the woman's failing was a fact as obvious as that her desire was only to be friendly; brief reflection persuaded Sally that it was to her own interest neither to snub nor to neglect this gratuitous source of information. With some guilty conceit, befitting one indulging in all most Machiavellian subtlety, she let fall an extravagantly absent-minded "Yes?" and was rewarded, quite properly, with a garrulous history of her predecessor's career, from which she disengaged only two profitable impressions: that the staff of servants was devoted to their mistress, and that it would little advantage a secretary to quarrel with the one in the hope of ingratiating herself with the other.

So she contrived, as soon as might be without giving offence, to interrupt and dismiss the maid; then steeled her heart against the temptation to try on everything at once, and profited by long practice in the nice art of bathing, dressing, breakfasting, and trudging two miles in minimum time—between, that is, the explosion of a matutinal alarm and the last moment when one might, without incurring a fine, register arrival on the clock at Huckster's entrance for employees. She hadn't the slightest notion what Mrs. Standish might want of her, but she was very sure that she didn't mean to invite displeasure by seeming careless of the lady's whims.

Consequently it was surprisingly soon that she stood, refreshed and comfortable in white linen, tapping at the door that Emmy, the maid, had designated.

Another maid, less prepossessing, admitted her to the dressing-room of the woman of fashion; and this last greeted Sally with a fretful, preoccupied frown, visible in the mirror, which reflected as well the excellent results obtainable from discreet employment of a high-keyed palette.

"Oh, it's you!" said Mrs. Standish shortly. "I was hoping you wouldn't be forever. Though you do look well in those duds. I've something quite important to say. You may go now, Ellen; I sha'n't want you again until evening."

With a scowl Ellen made off, an effort of masterly self-restraint alone enabling her to refrain from slamming the door.

"A most ridiculous thing has happened," Mrs. Standish pursued, delicately lining in her devastating eyebrows—"most annoying!" She jerked an impatient thumb at a telegram that lay open on the dressing-table. "Read that. It was waiting our arrival."

Sally obeyed with an opening wonder that swiftly gave place to panic consternation.

House entered by burglars last night discovered this morning forced entrance by scuttle extent of loss unknown but desk broken open safe cleaned out dining-room silver gone some clothing dresses missing one of gang evidently woman garments left in bath-room name indelible ink faded but apparently manners or manvers police notified detectives on case advise return please wire instructions-Riggs.

"Now don't have hysterics!" Mrs. Standish snapped as Sally, with a low cry of dismay, sank stunned into a chair. "There's nothing for you to fret about— you're all right, here, with me, under my protection. Nobody's going to look for you here; but think how fortunate it was I had the wit to change your name. No, it's I who have to worry!"

"But I don't understand," the girl stammered. "Of course there must be some mistake; you haven't really lost anything—"

"Oh, haven't I? I wish I could believe that. Don't you see what the telegram says—'safe cleaned out, dining-room silver gone'? That sounds suspiciously like a loss to me. Walter didn't 'clean out' the safe, and of course he didn't touch the silver. On the contrary, he's positive he shut the safe and fixed the combination before leaving. As for the dining-room, he didn't once set foot in it."

"Then—that burglar must have come back."

"That's our theory, naturally. Walter was so sure he'd scared the man off, he simply left the scuttle closed—"

"But he told me he found hammer and nails and fastened it up securely!"

"That was just his blague; he was having a good time, pretending to be what

64

you took him for—an amateur cracksman; he made up that story to fool you. The truth is, he made an uncommonly asinine exhibition, even for Walter—so excited and upset by that fight with the real burglar, to say nothing of the mystery of your interference, that he didn't stop to make sure he had got hold of the right jewel-case. As a matter of fact, he hadn't; everything I own of any real value was left behind; what Walter brought me was an old case containing a lot of trinkets worth little or nothing aside from sentimental associations."

"Oh, I am so sorry!"

"I'm sure you are, but that doesn't mend matters. The only thing that will is for you to make good here and keep away from New York until the whole affair has blown over and, above all, never, under any consideration, breathe a word of the truth to a living soul."

"I'm hardly likely to do that, Mrs. Standish; it wouldn't—"

"But you might. I've got to warn you. Everything depends on secrecy. Suppose some one were to question you, and you thought you had to tell the truth—a detective, for instance. It's not unlikely that one may come down here to interview me. Walter is leaving for New York by the first boat—in hopes of preventing anything of the sort—but still it isn't impossible. And if it ever comes out that Walter was in the house last night after dark—well, you can see for yourself what chance we'll have of making the burglar-insurance people pay us for what we've lost!"

CHAPTER VII

FRAUD

At Gosnold House that day, in an airy dining-room from which sunlight was jealously excluded by Venetian blinds at every long, wide window, creating an oasis of cool twilight in the arid heart of day, ten persons sat at luncheon— a meal of few and simple courses, but admirably ordered and served upon a clothless expanse of dark mahogany, relieved at each place by little squares of lace and fine linen, and in the center by a great, brazen bowl of vivid roses.

In this strange atmosphere the outsider maintained a covertly watchful silence (which, if rarely interrupted, was altogether of her own election) and was happily guiltless of any positive fault; long proscription to the social hinterland of dingy boarding-houses, smug quick-lunch rooms, and casual studio feeding had not affected her nice feeling for the sensible thing at table. She possessed, furthermore, in full measure that amazing adaptability which seems to be innate with most American women of any walk in life; whatever she might lack to her detriment or embarrassment she was quick to mark, learn, assimilate, and make as much her own as if she had never been without it.

And then—for in spite of reassurances persistently iterated by Mrs. Standish, the news from New York troubled her profoundly—preoccupation largely counteracted self-consciousness through those first few dreaded moments of Sally's modest social debut.

The men on either side of her she found severally, if quite amiably, agreeable to indulge her reticence. Savage, for one, was secretly, she guessed, quite as much disconcerted by the reported contretemps in town; but he dissembled well, with a show of whimsical exasperation because of this emergency that tore him so soon away from both Gosnold House and his other neighbour at table, a Mrs. Artemas—a spirited, mercurial creature, not over-handsome of face, but wonderfully smart in dress and gesture, superbly stayed and well aware of it; a dark, fine woman who recognised the rivalry latent in Sally's dark looks without dismay—as Sally conceded she might well.

On her other hand sat a handsome, well-bred boy of eighteen or so, one of the tennis four, answering to the name of Bob—evidently a cheerful soul, but at ease in the persuasion that comparative children should be seen and so forth. His partner of the courts sat next him—name, Babs—a frank-eyed, wholesome girl, perhaps a year his senior. Their surnames did not transpire, but they impressed Sally, and correctly, as unrelated save in community of unsentimental interests. The other players were not present.

Aside from these, the faces strange to her were those of a Miss Pride and Messrs. Lyttleton and Trego.

The last-named impressed her as a trifle ill at ease, possibly because of the blandishments of Mrs. Artemas, who had openly singled him out to be her special prey, and discovered an attitude of proprietorship to which he could not be said to respond with the ardour of a passionate, impulsive nature. A youngish man, with a heavy body, a bit ungainly in carriage, Mr. Trego had a square-jawed face with heavy-lidded, tranquil eyes. When circumstances demanded, he seemed capable of expressing himself simply and to the point, with a sure-footed if crushing wit. In white flannels his broad-shouldered bulk dwarfed the other men to insignificance.

Mr. Lyttleton—assigned to entertain his hostess, and (or Mrs. Gosnold flattered him) scoring heavily in that office—was as slenderly elegant and extreme a gallant as one may hope to encounter between magazine covers. He had an indisputable air, a way with him, the eye of a killer; if he perhaps fancied himself a trace too fervently, something subtle in his bearing toward Mrs. Standish fostered the suspicion that he was almost fearfully sensible of the charms of that lady.

Miss Pride, on Mrs. Gosnold's other hand, was a wiry roan virgin who talked too much but seldom stupidly, exhibited a powerful virtuosity in strange gestures, and pointedly designated herself as a "spin" (diminutive for spinster) apparently deriving from this conceit an amusement esoteric to her audience. Similarly, she indulged a mettlesome fancy for referring to her hostess as "dear Abigail." Her own maiden name was eventually disclosed as Mercedes —pronounced, by request, Mar-say-daze.

From her alone Sally was conscious at the very outset of their acquaintance of a certain frigidity—as one may who approaches an open window in the winter unawares. And it was some time before she discovered that Miss Pride accounted her a rival, thanks to a cherished delusion, wholly of independent inspiration, that dear Abigail was a forlorn widow-woman in sore want of some thoroughly unselfish friend—somebody whose devotion could not possibly be thought mercenary—somebody very much like Mercedes Pride, Spin.

The table talk was so much concerned with the sensation of the hour, the burglary, that Sally grew quickly indifferent to the topic, and thus was able to appreciate Savage's mental dexterity in discussing it with apparent candour, but without once verging upon any statement or admission that might count against the interests of his sister. He seemed wholly unconstrained, but the truth was not in him. Or, if it were, it was in on a life sentence.

The consensus pronounced Mrs. Standish a very fortunate woman to be so thoroughly protected by insurance, and this the lucky victim indorsed with outspoken complacence, even to the extent of a semiserious admission that she almost hoped the police would fail to recover the plunder. For while many items of the stolen property, of course, were priceless, things not to be duplicated, things (with a pensive sigh) inexpressibly endeared to one through associations, she couldn't deny (more brightly again) it would be rather a lark to get all that money and go shopping to replenish her treasure-chests from the most famous jewellers of the three capitals.

This aspect of the case made Mrs. Artemas frankly envious. "How perfectly ripping!" she declared. "I'm almost tempted to hire a burglar of my own!"

"And then," Lyttleton observed profoundly, "if one isn't in too great a hurry—

there's no telling—one may run across the lost things in odd corners and buy them back for a song or so. Anne Warridge did, when they looted her Southampton place, some time ago. Remember the year 'motor-car pirates' terrorized Long Island? Well, long after everything was settled and the insurance people had paid up, Anne unearthed several of her best pieces in the shops of bogus Parisian antiquaries, and bought them back at bargain rates."

"It sounds like a sin to me," Savage commented.

"But I call you all to witness that, if anything like that happens in this family, I hereby declare in on the profits. It's worth something, this trip to town—and nobody sorry to see me go!"

After luncheon the party dispersed without formality. Mrs. Artemas vanished bodily, Mrs. Standish in the car with her brother to see him off; Bob and Babs murmured incoherently about a boat, and disappeared forthwith; and Lyttleton, pleading overdue correspondence, Trego was snapped up for auction bridge by Mrs. Gosnold and Miss Pride, Sally being elected to fourth place as one whose defective education must be promptly remedied, lest the roof fall in.

She found it very pleasant, playing on a breeze-fanned veranda that overlooked the terrace and harbour, and proved a tolerably apt pupil. A very little practice evoked helpful memories of whist-lore that she had thought completely atrophied by long disuse, and she was aided besides by a strong infusion in her mentality of that mysterious faculty we call card-sense. Before the end of the second rubber she was playing a game that won the outspoken approval of Trego and Mrs. Gosnold, and certainly compared well with Miss Pride's, in spite of the undying infatuation for auction professed by dear Abigail's one true friend.

It was noteworthy that dear Abigail seemed to have no interests of any character that were not passionately indorsed by her faithful Mercedes.

Pondering this matter, Sally found time to wonder that Mercedes had not been deemed a sufficiently vigilant protector for the poor rich widow; it was her notion that Mercedes missed few bets.

A circumstance which Sally herself had overlooked turned out to be the tacit understanding on which the game had been made up; and when, at the conclusion of the third rubber, Mr. Trego summed up the score, then calmly presented her with a twenty-dollar bill and some loose silver—Mercedes with stoic countenance performing the same painful operation on her own purse in favour of dear Abigail—the girl was overcome with consternation.

"But—no!" she protested, and blushed. "We weren't playing for money, surely!"

"Of course we were!" Miss Pride snapped, with the more spirit since Sally's stupidity supplied an unexpected outlet. "I never could see the amusement in playing cards without a trifling stake—though I always do say five cents a point is too much for a friendly game."

"It's our custom," Mrs. Gosnold smiled serenely. "You haven't conscientious scruples about playing for money, I hope?"

"Oh, no; but"—Sally couldn't, simply couldn't confess her penniless condition before Miss Pride and Mr. Trego—"but I didn't understand."

"That's all right," Trego insisted. "You won it fairly, and it wasn't all beginners' luck, either. It was good playing; some of your inferences were as sound as any I ever noticed."

"It really doesn't seem right," Sally demurred.

None the less she could not well refuse the money.

"I must have my revenge!" Miss Pride announced briskly, that expression being sanctioned by convention. "To-night, dear Abigail? Or would you like another rubber now?"

Mrs. Gosnold shook her head and laughed. "No, thank you; I've had enough for one afternoon, and I'm sleepy besides." She thrust back her chair and rose. "If you haven't tried the view from the terrace, Miss Manwaring, I'm sure you'll find it worth while. And let your ill-gotten gains rest lightly on your conscience; put them in the war-chest against the rainy day that's sure to dawn for even the best players. I myself play a rather conservative game, you'll find, but there are times when for days on end I can't seem to get a hand much better than a yarborough."

"Do you," Sally faltered, timidly appreciating the impertinence, "do you lose very much?"

"I? No fear!" Mrs. Gosnold laughed again. "It amuses me to keep a bridge account, and there's seldom a year when it fails to show a credit balance of at least a thousand."

If Sally's bewilderment was only the deeper for this information, she was sensible enough to hold her tongue.

Why need Mrs. Standish deliberately have uttered so monumental a falsehood about the losses of her aunt at cards? She might, of course, be simply and sincerely mistaken, misled by over-solicitude for a well-beloved kinswoman.

On the other hand, the gesture of Adele Standish was not that of a woman easily deceived.

Thus the puzzle swung full circle.

"Mind if I show you the way, Miss Manwaring?"

"Oh, no!" Sally started from her abstraction to find Trego had lingered, and, smiling, turned to the steps that led down to the terrace. "I'll be very glad ..."

But the truth was that she was not glad of this unsolicited company; she wanted uninterrupted opportunity to think things over; furthermore, she thought the sheer weight and masculine force of Trego's personality less ingratiating than another's—Savage's, for instance, however shallow, was always amusing—or Lyttleton's, with his flashing insouciant smile, his easy grace and utter repose of manner.

But this Mr. Trego, swinging ponderously by her side down the terrace walks, maintaining what was doubtless intended as a civil silence but what achieved only oppressiveness, of a sudden inspired a sharp impression that he would prove a man easy to dislike intensely—the sort of man who is capable of inspiring fear and makes enemies without any perceptible difficulty.

And if that were so—if, as it seemed, she had already, intuitively, acquired a distaste for Mr. Trego—how could she at once retain her self-respect and his money—money which she had won in defiance of the rules of fair play?

It stuck in her fist, a hard little wad of silver wrapped in the bill; nearly twenty-one dollars, the equivalent of three weeks' pay for drudgery, the winnings of an idle hour, the increment of false pretences.

"There's your view," Trego's voice broke upon the reverie. "Pretty fine, isn't it?"

They paused in a corner of the terrace, where a low stone wall, grey, weathered and lichened, fenced the brow of the cliff; and Sally's glance compassed a panorama of sea and sky and rocky headlands, with little appreciation of its wild, exquisite beauty.

She uttered an absent-minded "Yes," hesitated, plunged boldly: "Mr. Trego, I do wish you'd let me give back this money!"

His slowness in replying moved her to seek an answer in his face. He was unquestionably sifting his surprise for some excuse for her extraordinary request; a deep gravity informed his heavy-lidded eyes that were keen with an intelligence far more alert than she had previously credited.

He said deliberately: "Why?"

"I'd rather not say." She offered the money in her open hand. "But I'd feel—

well, easier, if you'd take it back."

He clasped his hands behind him and shook his head. "Not without good reason. I don't understand, and what I don't understand I can't be party to."

She tried the effect of a wistful smile. "Please! I wish you wouldn't make me tell you."

"I wish you wouldn't put me in such an uncomfortable position. I don't like to refuse you anything you've set your heart on, but my notion of playing the game is to lose like a loser and—win like a winner."

"That's just it. I can't win like a winner because—because I didn't win fairly."

"You never cheated."

It was less a question than an assertion.

"How do you know?"

"I'd have known quick enough if you'd tried. Anyway, you're not that kind."

"How do you know I'm not?"

There was a pause. Then Trego smiled oddly. "Better not ask me. You don't know me very well yet."

She coloured faintly. "Then I must tell you you are wrong. I did cheat. I did, I tell you! I played for money without a cent to pay my losses if I lost. You don't call that fair play, do you?"

"Depends. Of course, it's hard to believe."

"I'm penniless. You don't understand my position here. I'm—nobody. Mrs. Standish took pity on me because I was out of work and brought me here to act as secretary to Mrs. Gosnold."

Trego nodded heavily. "I guessed it. I mean I felt pretty sure you were—well, of another world." He jerked a disrespectful head toward the smiling face of Gosnold House. "The same as me," he added. "That's why I thought … But it doesn't matter what I thought."

An unreasonable resentment held her true to the course of her purpose.

"Well, now you know, you must see it's impossible—"

"I don't," he contended stubbornly. "Maybe I'm the devil's advocate, but the way I see it—to begin with, I was playing for money; if I had won I'd have expected you to pay up."

"But I couldn't—"

"You would have; that is, Mrs. Gosnold would have paid for you. It was up to her. She meant it that way. She was staking you against the Pride person and myself; that's why you played together; if you and she had lost, she'd have paid for both. So, you see, you may as well quit trying to make me touch that money."

His sophistry baffled her. She shook her head, confused and a little angry in defeat, liking him less than ever.

"Very well. But I don't feel right about it—and I think it most unkind of you."

"Sorry. I only want to play the game as it lies, and this is my idea of doing it."

There was a brief pause while Sally, at a loss, stared out over the shining harbour, now more than ever sensible of the profound, peaceful beauty of its azure floor over which bright sails swung and swayed like slim, tall ladies treading a measure of some stately dance.

"If you ask my definition of unfair play," Trego volunteered, "it's this present attitude of yours—forcing a quarrel on me and getting mad because I stick up for my notion of a square deal!"

"Oh, you misunderstand!" she protested. "I'm only distressed by my conception of what's wrong."

"It's the worst of gambling," he complained: "always winds up in some sort of a row."

"Why gamble, then?"

"Why not? We've got to do something here to keep from yawning in one another's faces."

"Is there so much of it going on all the time—gambling—here?"

"Oh, not a great deal. Not bad gambling, at least." He smiled faintly. "Not what I call gambling. But I was bred on strong meat—in mining camps—where my father made his money. There men gambled with their lives. Here —*hmp!*" He grunted amusedly. "It's just enough like the real thing to make a fellow restless. Sometimes I wish the old man hadn't struck it quite so rich. If he hadn't, we'd both be happier. As it is, he fluffs around, making a pest of himself in Wall Street because he thinks it's the proper thing. And here am I, instead of earning dividends on what little knowledge I do happen to possess, sticking round with a set of idle egoists, simply because the old man's got his heart set on his son being in society! He won't be happy till he sees me married to one of these—er—women. Sometimes…"

Morosely he ruminated on the suppressed adjective for a moment.
"Sometimes I feel it coming over me that the governor's liable to be happy,

according to his lights, considerably quicker than I am."

CHAPTER VIII

A THIEF IN THE NIGHT

She sat beside the wide window of her bed-chamber, on that third midnight at Gosnold House, in a state of lawless exaltation not less physical than spiritual and mental, a temper that proscribed sleep hopelessly.

The window was open, the night air still and suave and warm, her sole protection a filmy negligee over a night-dress of sheerest silk and lace. And in that hour Sarah Manvers was as nearly a beautiful woman as ever she was to be—her face faintly flushed in the rich moonlight, faintly shadowed from within by the rich darkness of her blood, her dreaming eyes twin pools of limpid shadow, her dark lips shadowed by a slight elusive smile.

She was relishing the sensation of life intensely, almost painfully; she was intensely alive for the first time in all her life, it seemed; in throat and wrists and temples pulses sang, now soft, now loud; and all her body glowed, from crown of head to tips of toes nestling in silken mules, with the warmth and the languor of life.

She was deeply and desperately in love.

The genius of her curious destiny, not content with making her free of all the good material things of life, had granted her as well this last and dearest boon. For though her years were twenty-seven she had not loved before. She had dreamed of love, had been in love with love and with being loved, had believed she loved; but nothing in her experience compared with such rapture as to-night obsessed her being, wholly and without respite.

Life, indeed, grants no compensation for the ignominious necessity of love but this, that no other love was ever real but to-day's alone.

And so the beauty of that moonlight midnight seemed supernal. Becalmed, the island lay steeped in floods of ethereal silver, its sky an iridescent dome, its sea a shimmering shield of opalescence, its lawns and terraces argentine shadowed with deepest violet. There was never a definite sound, only the sibilance of a stillness made of many interwoven sounds, soft lisp of wavelets on the sands a hundred feet below, hum of nocturnal insect life in thickets and plantations, sobbing of a tiny, vagrant breeze lost and homeless in that vast serenity, wailing of a far violin, rumour of distant motor-cars. A night of potent witchery, a woman willingly bewitched... .

In fancy she still could feel the pulsing of his heart against her bosom, the caressing touch of his hands, the warm flutter of his breath in her hair and upon her cheek, as in that last dance; and with an inexpressible hunger at once of flesh and soul she yearned to feel them all again, to be once more within the magic circle of his arms, to live once more in the light of his countenance.

It mattered nothing that she loved hopelessly a graceless runagate—and knew it well. She had not needed the indirect warnings of Adele Standish and Mercedes Pride that the man was nothing better than an engaging scamp. Who was she to demand worthier object for her love? She was precisely Nobody, and might waste her passion as she would, and none but herself the worse for it.

Nor did it matter that her love was desperate of return. She knew that he recognised and was a little amused and a little flattered by her unspoken admiration, but more deeply than that affected not at all. But that was his imperial prerogative; she did not mind; temporarily she believed herself quite content, and that she would continue so as long as permitted to hug to her secret heart the unutterable sweetness of being in love with him. Again, she was Nobody and didn't count, while he was precisely all that she had longed for ever since she was of an age to dream of love. He was not only of an admirable person, he wore the habit of distinction like a garment made for him alone. In short, the man was irresistible, and the woman didn't even want to resist but only despaired of opportunity ever to capitulate.

She was as love-sick as a schoolgirl of sixteen; a hundred times, if once, her barely parted lips breathed his name to the sympathetic night that never would betray her: "*Donald—Donald—Donald Lyttleton... .*"

Now all the while she wasted sighing for him by the window Mr. Lyttleton spent idly speculating about her—lounging in a corner of the smoking-room, on the edge of a circle of other masculine guests making common excuse of alcohol to defer the tiresome formalities of going to bed and getting up again in the morning.

If this gentleman was Sally's junior in the matter of a year or two, he was overwhelmingly her senior in knowledge of his world—a world into which he had been brought neither to toil nor yet to spin, but simply to be the life and soul of the party. And at twenty-five he was beyond permitting sentiment to run away with judgment; he could resist temptation with as much fortitude as any man, always providing he could see any sound reason for resisting it—

any reason, that is, promising a profit from the deed of abstinence.

Mr. Lyttleton had ten thousand a year of his own, income from a principal fortunately beyond his power to hypothecate; he spent twenty thousand with an easy conscience; he earnestly desired to be able to spend fifty without fear of consequences. Talents such as his merited maintenance—failing independent means, such maintenance as comes from marrying money and a wife above suspicion of parsimony. If only he had been able, or even had cared to behave himself, Mr. Lyttleton's fortunes might long since have been established on some such satisfactory basis. But he was sorely handicapped by the weakness of a sentimental nature; women would persist in falling in love with him—always, unhappily, women of moderate means. He couldn't help being sorry for them and seeking to assuage their sufferings; he couldn't forever be running away from some infatuate female; and so he was forever being found out and forgiven—by women. Most men, meanly envious, disliked him; all men held him in pardonable distrust. Devilish hard luck.

Take this Manwaring girl—pretty, intelligent, artless little woman, perhaps a bit mature, but fascinating all the same, affectingly naive about her trouble, which was simply spontaneous combustion, one more of those first-sight affairs. He had noticed the symptoms immediately, that night of her introduction to Gosnold House. He hadn't paid much attention to her during luncheon, and only sought her out—when they got up, on the spur of the moment, that informal after-dinner dance by moonlight on the veranda— partly because he happened to notice her sitting to one side, so obviously longing for him to ask her, partly because it was his business to dance, and partly because—well, because it was less dangerous, everything considered, than dancing with Mrs. Standish.

And then the eloquent treachery of Sally's eyes and that little gesture of surrender with which she yielded herself to his guidance. It was really too bad, he thought, especially since she had made occasion to tell him frankly she hadn't a dollar to bless herself with. Still, he must give himself credit for behaving admirably; he hadn't encouraged the girl. Not much, at all events. Of course, it wasn't in human nature to ignore her entirely after that; moreover, to slight her would have been conspicuous, not to say uncivil. But one must draw the line somewhere.

To-night, for example, he had danced with her perhaps too often for her own good, to say nothing of his own. And they had sat out a dance or two— awfully old-fashioned custom; went out years ago—still, one did it, regardless, now and then.

Curious girl, the Manwaring; one moment almost melting into his arms, the next practically warning him against herself. And curiously reticent—said she was "Nobody"—let it go at that. Very probably told the truth; she seemed to know nobody who was anybody; and though she was apparently very much at her ease most of the time, and not readily impressed, he noticed now and then a little tensity in her manner, a covert watchfulness of other women, as though she were waiting for her cue.

At this juncture in his reverie Mr. Lyttleton peremptorily dismissed luckless Miss Manwaring from his mind, compounded his nightcap at the buffet, and joined in the general conversation.

Coincidentally the reverie of Miss Manwaring at her bedchamber window digressed to review fragmentarily the traffic and discoveries of three wonderful days.

Days in whose glamorous radiance the romance of Cinderella paled to the complexion of a sordidly realistic narrative of commonplaces; contemplating them, Sally, for the sake of her self-conceit, felt constrained to adopt an aloof, superior, sceptical pose. Conceding freely the incredible reality of this phase of her history, she none the less contended that in it no more true permanence inhered than in a dream.

She recapitulated many indisputable signs of the instability of her affairs. And of all those the foremost, the most glaring, was her personal success, at once actual and impossible. She saw herself (from that remote and weather-beaten coign of scepticism) moving freely to and fro in the great world of the socially elect, unhindered, unquestioned, tacitly accepted, meeting, chatting, treating and parting with its denizens with a gesture of confidence that was never the gesture of S. Manvers of the Hardware Notions; a Nobody on terms of equality with indisputable Somebodies—vastly important Somebodies indeed, for the most part; so much so that by common consent mankind had created for them a special world within the world and set it apart for their exclusive shelter and delectation, for them to live in and have their being untroubled and uncontaminated by contact with the commonalty.

For all that, Sally couldn't see why they must be so cared for and catered to. The only thing that apparently distinguished them from those who lacked their advantages, who looked up reverently to them and read enviously of their doings in the papers, was their assurance, a quality ostensibly inimitable; yet she imitated it with seemingly flawless art. A contradiction that defied her wits to reconcile.

She wasted time in the endeavour; her own personality was prepossessing; she had sufficient tact never to seek to ingratiate herself; her solecisms were few and insignificant, and the introduction of Abigail Gosnold was an unimpeachable credential.

As for her antecedents, the lie which credited her to the city of Massillon passed unchallenged, while a conspiracy of silence kept private to the few acquainted with it that hideous secret of her department-store servitude. Mrs. Gosnold would have said nothing out of sheer kindness of heart even if it had not been her settled habit to practise the difficult arts of minding her own business and keeping her own counsel. Savage was still in New York, but had he been at Gosnold House would have imitated the example set by his amiable sister and held his tongue even when most exasperated with Sally. Mr. Trego, of course, knew no more than what he had been free to surmise from the girl's impulsive confession that she had been out of both work and money when befriended by Mrs. Standish; but, whatever his inferences, he kept them to himself.

A simple, sincere, stubborn soul, this Mr. Trego; so, at least, he made himself appear to Sally, persistently seeking her and dumbly offering a friendship which she, in the preoccupation of her grand passion, had neither time nor wish to cultivate, and which he himself ingenuously apologised for on the plea of self-defence. He frankly professed a mortal dread of "these women," one of whom, he averred mysteriously, was bent on marrying him by main strength and good-will first time she caught him with lowered guard.

His misgivings were measurably corroborated by the attitude toward Sally adopted by Mrs. Standish in her capacity as close friend, foil, and confidant of Mrs. Artemas. In the course of those three days the girl had not been insensible to intimations of a strong, if as yet restrained, animus in the mind of the older woman. In alarm and regret she did her futile best to discourage this gentleman without being overtly discourteous. She could hardly do more; impossible to explain to her benefactress that he was not the man of her heart's choice.

Unfortunately, Trego was indifferent to tempered rebuffs.

"If you don't mind," he interrupted one of Sally's protracted snubs, "I'll just stick around and keep on enjoying the society of a human being. Of course, I know these others are all human in their way, but it isn't your way or mine. Perhaps it only seems so to me because I don't understand 'em. It's quite possible. One thing's sure, they don't understand me. At least, the women don't; I can get along with the men—most of 'em. They're not a bad lot, if immature. You can stand a lot of foolishness from children once you realise their grown-uppishness is only make-believe."

"They don't know how to enjoy themselves," he expatiated; "they've got too much of everything, including spare time. What's a holiday to anybody who has never done a stroke of work? You and I know the difference; we can appreciate the fun of loafing between spells of work; but these people have

77

got no standards to measure their fun by, so it's all the same to them—flat, vapid, monotonous, unless they season it up with cocktails and carrying on; and even that gets to have all the same flavour of tastelessness after a while. That's why so many of these women are going in for the suffragette business; it isn't that they care a whoop for the vote; it's because they want the excitement of wanting something they haven't got and can't get by signing a check for it."

"You're prejudiced," the girl objected. "You're at loose-ends yourself, idle and restless, and it distorts your mental vision. For my part, I've never met more charming people—"

"That's your astigmatism," he contended. "You've been wanting this society thing all your life, and now you've got it you're as pleased as a child with a new toy. Wait till the paint wears off and it won't shut its eyes when you put it down on its back and sawdust begins to leak out at the joints."

"Wouldn't it be more kind of you to leave me to discover the sawdust for myself?"

"It unquestionably would, and I ought to be kicked," Trego agreed heartily. "I only started this in fun, anyway, to make you see why it is you look so good to me—different—so sound and sane and wholesome that I just naturally can't help pestering you."

She did not know what to say to that. She suffered him... .

Her duties as secretary to Mrs. Gosnold proved, when inaugurated the second morning after her arrival, to be at once light and interesting. Her employer was conservative enough in an unmannerly age to insist on answering all personal correspondence with her own hand; what passed between her and her few intimates was known to herself alone. But she carried on, in addition, an animated correspondence with numberless frauds—antique dealers, charities, professional poor relations, social workers, and others of that ilk—which proved tremendously diverting to her amanuensis, especially when it transpired that Mrs. Gosnold had a mind and temper of her own, together with a vocabulary amply adequate to her powers of ironic observation. This last gift came out strongly in her diary, a daily record of her various interests and activities which she dictated, interspersing dry details with many an acid annotation.

When all was finished Sally found she had been busied for little more than two hours, and was given to understand that her duties would be made more burdensome only by the addition of a little light bookkeeping when she settled down to the routine of regular employment.

Of the alleged high play, at cards or otherwise, she had yet, at this third midnight, to see any real evidence. Mrs. Gosnold most undoubtedly played a stiff game of bridge, but she played it with a masterly facility, the outcome of long practice and profound study; her losses, when she lost, were minimised. Nor was there ever a sign of cheating that came under Sally's observation. Everybody played who didn't dance, and vice versa, but nobody seemed to play for the mere sake of winning money. And while the influx of week-end guests by the Friday evening boat brought the number at Gosnold House up to twenty-two, they were all apparently amiable, self-centred folk of long and intimate acquaintance with one another as well as with their hostess and all her neighbours on the Island. Of that dubious crew of adventurers she had been led to expect there was never a hint.

Such provision as their hostess made for her guests' entertainment and amusement they patronised or ignored with equal nonchalance, according to individual whim; they commanded breakfasts for all hours of the morning, and they lunched at home and dined abroad, or reversed the order, or sought all their meals in the homes of neighbouring friends, quite without notice or apology. Such was the modish manner of that summer of 1915—a sedulous avoidance of anything resembling acknowledgment of obligation to those who entertained. Indeed, if one interpreted their attitude at its face value, the shoe was on the other foot.

And they brimmed the alleged hollowness of their days with an extraordinary amount of running about. There was incessant shifting of interest from one focal point to another of the colony, a perpetually restless swarming hither and yon to some new centre of distraction, a continual kaleidoscopic parade of the most wonderful and extravagant clothing the world has ever seen.

To the outsider, of course, all this was not merely entertaining and novel, if much as she had imagined it would be, it was more—it was fascination, it was enchantment, it was the joy of living made manifest, it was life.

If only this bubble might not burst!

Of course, it must; even if not too good to be true, it was too wonderful to be enduring; the clock strikes twelve for every Cinderella, and few are blessed enough to be able to leave behind them a matchless slipper.

But whatever happened, nothing now could prevent her carrying to her grave the memory of this one glorious flight: "better to have loved and lost—" The wraith of an old refrain troubled Sally's reverie. How did it go? "Now die the dream—"

Saturate with exquisite melancholy, she leaned out over the window-sill into the warm, still moonlight, drinking deep of the wine-scent of roses, dwelling upon the image of him whom she loved so madly.

What were the words again?

"… The past is not in vain, For wholly as it was your life, Can never be again, my dear, Can never be again."

She shook a mournful head, sadly envisaging the loveliness of the world through a mist of facile tears; that was too exquisitely, too poignantly true of her own plight; for, wholly as it was, her life could never be again.

And not for worlds would she have had it otherwise.

Below, in the deserted drawing-room, a time-mellowed clock chimed sonorously the hour of two.

Two o'clock of a Sunday morning, and all well; long since Gosnold House had lapsed into decent silence; an hour ago she had heard the last laggard footsteps, the last murmured good nights in the corridor outside her door as the men-folk took themselves reluctantly off to their beds.

She leaned still farther out over the sill, peering along the gleaming white facade; no window showed a light that she could see. She listened acutely; not a sound but the muttering of fretful little waves and the drowsy complaint of some bird troubled in its sleep.

Of all that heedless human company, it seemed, she alone remained awake.

Something in that circumstance proved almost resistlessly provocative to her innate lust for adventure. For upward of two hours she had been passive there in her chair, a prey to uneasy thoughts; now she was weary with much thinking, but as far as ever from the wish to sleep; never, indeed, more wide awake—possessed by a demon of restlessness, consumed with desire to rise up and go out into the scented moonstruck night and lose herself in its loneliness and—see what she should see.

Why not? No one need ever know. A staircase at her end of the corridor— little used except by servants—led to a small door opening directly upon the terrace. Providing it were not locked and the key removed, there was no earthly reason why, if so minded, she should not go quietly forth that way and drink her fill of the night's loveliness.

To a humour supple to such temptation the tang of lawlessness in a project innocent enough was irresistible. Besides, what was the harm? What could be the objection, even were the escapade to be discovered by misadventure?

Among other items in her collection of borrowed plumage she possessed an evening wrap, somewhat out of fashion, but eminently adapted to her purpose —long enough to cloak her figure to the ground, thus eliminating all necessity for dressing against chance encounter with some other uneasy soul. Worn with black stockings and slippers, it would render her almost invisible in shadow.

In another minute, without turning on a light, she had found and donned those several articles, and from her door was narrowly inspecting the hallway before venturing a step across the threshold.

It was quite empty and silent, its darkness moderated only by the single nightlight burning at the head of the main staircase.

Satisfied, she closed the door and crept noiselessly down the steps, to find the side door not even locked.

Leaving it barely ajar, she stepped out beneath the stars, hesitated for a moment of cautious reconnaissance, then darted across an open space of moonlight as swiftly as the shadow of a cloud wind-sped athwart the moon, and so gained the sheltering shadow of the high hedge between the formal garden and tennis-court.

The dew-drenched turf that bordered the paths muffled her footsteps as effectually as could be wished, and keeping circumspectly in shadow, the better to escape observation from any of the windows, she gained at length that corner of the terrace overlooking the water where she and Trego had paused for their first talk.

Nothing now prevented her from appreciating the view to the full. Enchanted, she withdrew a little way from the brow of the cliff to a seat on the stone wall, overshadowed by the hedge, and for a long time sat there motionless, content.

Below her the harbour lay steel-grey and still within its guardian headlands, a hundred slim, white pleasure craft riding its silent tide. Far out a Sound steamer crawled like some amphibious glowworm, its triple tier of deck-lights almost blended into one. Farther still the lights of the mainland glimmered low upon the horizon. .

At a little distance, from a point invisible, an incautious footstep grated upon a gravel path of the terrace and was instantly hushed.

But the girl, stiffened to rigidity in her place, fancied she could hear the whisper of grass beneath stealthy feet.

Abruptly a man came out into broad moonlight and, pausing on a stone platform at the edge of the cliff by the head of the long, steep, wooden zigzag of stairs to the sands, looked back toward the house.

Sally held her breath. But her heart was like a mad thing—the man was Donald Lyttleton. He still wore evening dress, but had exchanged the formal coat for that hybrid garment which Sally had lately learned should *not* be termed a Tuxedo. The brim of a soft, dark hat masked his eyes. He carried one shoulder stiffly, as if holding something in the hollow of his arm. She could not make out or imagine what this might be.

His hesitation was brief. Satisfied, he swung round to the stairway, in another instant had vanished. Only light footfalls on the wooden steps told of a steady descent, and at the same time furnished assurance that Sally had not victimised herself with a waking vision bred of her infatuation.

The footfalls, not loud at best, had become inaudible before she found courage to approach the platform. With infinite pains to avoid a sound, she peered over the edge of its stone parapet.

For a little the gulf swam giddily beneath her who was never quite easy at any unusual height. But she set herself with determination to master this weakness and presently was able to examine the beach with a clear vision.

It was only partially shadowed by the cliffs, but that shadow was dense, and outside it nothing stirred. None the less, after a time she was able to discern Lyttleton's figure kneeling on the sands at the immediate foot of the cliff, a hundred feet or so to one side of the steps. And while she watched he rose, stood for a little staring out to sea, wasted a number of matches lighting a cigarette (which seemed curious, in view of the unbroken calm) and moved on out of sight beyond a shoulder of stone.

She waited fully ten minutes; but he did not reappear.

Then, retreating to her seat on the stone wall, she waited as long again—still no sign of Lyttleton.

But something else marked that second period of waiting that intrigued her no less than the mysterious actions of her beloved—this although she could imagine no link between the two.

Some freak of chance drew her attention to a small, dark shape, with one staring red eye, that was stealing quietly across the Sound in the middle distance—of indefinite contour against the darkening waters, but undoubtedly a motor-boat, since there was no wind to drive any sailing vessel at its pace, or indeed at any pace at all.

While she watched it incuriously it came to a dead pause, and so remained for several minutes. Then, deliberately, with infinitely sardonic effect, it winked its single eye of red at her—winked portentously three times.

She made nothing of that, and in her profound ignorance of all things nautical might have considered it some curious bit of sea etiquette had she not, the next instant, caught out of the corner of her eye the sudden glow of a window lighted in the second story of Gosnold House.

As she turned in surprise the light went out. A pause of perhaps twenty seconds ensued. Then the window shone out again—one in the left wing, the wing at the end of which her bedchamber was located. But when she essayed to reckon the rooms between it and her own it turned black again, and after another twenty seconds once more shone out and once more was lightless.

After this it continued stubbornly dark, and by the time Sally gave up trying to determine precisely which window it had been, and turned her gaze seaward again, the boat had vanished. Its lights, at least, were no longer visible, and it was many minutes before the girl succeeded in locating the blur it made on the face of the waters. It seemed to be moving, but the distance was so great that she could not be sure which way.

A signal—yes, obviously; but between whom and for what purpose?

Who was on that boat? And who the tenant of that room of the flashing window? She was satisfied that the latter was one of a row of six windows to three rooms occupied by Mrs. Standish, Mrs. Artemas, and a pretty young widow who had arrived late Saturday afternoon and whose name Sally had yet to learn.

She pondered it all with ever-deepening perplexity until a change came over the night—a wind stirred, leaves rattled, boughs soughed plaintively, the waters wakened and filled the void of silence with soft clashing. Then, shivering, Sally rose and crept back toward the house.

But when she paused on the edge of the last shadow, preparatory to the dash across the moonlit space to the door, a step sounded beside her, a hand caught at her cloak.

She started back with a stifled cry.

"Steady!" Lyttleton's voice counselled her guardedly. "Don't make a row! Blessed if it ain't Miss Manwaring!"

CHAPTER IX

PICAROON

Plucking peremptorily at her cloak, Lyttleton drew the girl to him and, seizing her hand, without further ceremony dragged her round the clump of shrubbery to a spot secure from observation.

She submitted without a hint of resistance. But she was trembling violently, and the contact with his hand was as fire to her blood.

Pausing, he stared and laughed uncertainly.

"Of all people!" he said in an undertone. "I never for an instant thought of you!"

Controlling her voice tolerably, she asked directly: "How did you get up again without my seeing you?"

"Simply enough—by the steps of the place next door. I saw you watching me —saw your head over the edge of the landing, black against the sky—and knew I'd never know who it was, unless by strategy. So I came up the other way and cut across to head you off."

He added, after a pause, with a semi-apologetic air: "What do you mean by it, anyway'?"

"What—?"

"Watching me this way—spying on me—?"

"But I didn't mean to. I was as surprised to see you as you were, just now, to see me."

"Honestly?"

His eyes searched hers suspiciously. Flushing, she endeavoured to assume some little dignity—drew up, lifted her chin, resumed possession of her hand.

"Of course," she said in an injured voice.

"Sure Mrs.—sure nobody sent you to spy on me?"

"Mr. Lyttleton!"

"I want to believe you."

"You've no right not to!"

"But what, will you tell me, are you doing out here this time of night?"

"I came out because I wanted to—I was restless, couldn't sleep."

He reflected upon this doubtfully. "Funny freak," he remarked.

"You're impertinent!"

"I don't mean to be. Forgive me. I'm only puzzled—"

"So am I puzzled," she retorted with spirit. "Suppose you tell me what you're doing out here at this time of night—down on the beach—anxious to escape notice. If you ask me, I call that a funnier freak than mine!"

"Quite so," he agreed soberly; "and a very reasonable retort. Only I can't tell you. It's—er—a private matter."

"So I presumed—"

"Look here, Miss Manwaring; this is a serious business with me. Give me your word—"

"What makes that essential? Why do you think I'd lie—to you '?"

It was just that little quaver prefacing her last two words which precipitated the affair. Otherwise a question natural enough under the circumstances would have proved innocuous. But for the life of her she could not control her voice; on those simple words it broke; and so the question became confession —confession, accusation and challenge all in, one.

It created first a pause, an instant of breathless suspense, while Lyttleton stared in doubt and Sally steeled herself, with an effect of trembling, reluctant, upon the brink of some vast mystery.

Then: "To me?" he said slowly. "You mean me to understand you might lie to another-but not to me?"

Her response was little better than a gasp: "You know it!"

He acknowledged this with half a nod; he knew it well, too well.

Now she must have seemed very lovely to the man in that moment of defiance. She saw his eyes lighten with a singular flash, saw his face darken suddenly in the paling moonlight, and heard the sharp sibilance of his indrawn breath.

And whether or not it was so, she fancied the wind had fallen, that the night was hushed once more, and now more profoundly than it had ever been, as though the very world were standing still in anticipation.

She heard him cry, almost angrily: "Oh, damn it, I must not!"

And with that she was in his arms, sobbing, panting, going to heaven against his lips... .

Then fell a lull. She was conscious that his embrace relaxed a trifle, heard the murmur of his consternation: "Oh, this is madness, madness!"

But when she tried to release herself his arms tightened.

"No!" he said thickly, "not now—not after this. Don't. I love you!"

She braced her hands against his breast, struggled, thrust him away from her, found herself free at last.

"You don't!" she sobbed miserably; "You don't love me. Don't lie to me! Let me go!"

"Why do you say that? You love me, and I—"

"Don't say it! It isn't true! I know. I threw myself at your head. What else could you do? You care nothing about me; to you I'm just one more silly woman. No; let me be, please! You do not love me—you don't, you don't, you don't!"

He shrugged, relinquished his effort to recapture her, muttered uncertainly: "Blessed if I know!"

Recovering a little, she drew her hands swiftly across face and eyes that still burned with his kisses.

"Oh!" she cried brokenly, "why did you—why did I—?"

"What's the good of asking that? It's done now," he argued with a touch of aggrieved resentment. "I didn't mean—I meant to—I don't know what I meant. Only—never this."

He took an impatient stride or two in the shelter of the shadow, turned back to her, expostulant: "It's too bad! I'd have given worlds—"

"But now I've gone and done it!" she retorted bitterly. In chagrin, her own indignation mounted. "It is too bad, poor Mr. Lyttleton!"

That was too much; he came closer and grasped her wrist. "Why do you talk that way to me?" he demanded wrathfully. "What have I done—?"

"You? Nothing!" she broke in, roughly wrenching her hand free in a fury of humiliation. "Do you ever do anything? Isn't the woman always the aggressor? Never your fault—of course not! But don't, please, worry; I shan't ever remind you. You're quite free to go and forget what's happened as quickly as you like!"

She scrubbed the knuckles of one hand roughly across her quivering lips. "Forget!" she cried. "Oh, if only I might ever … But that's my penance, the mortification of remembering how I took advantage of the chivalry of a man who didn't care for me—and couldn't!"

"You don't know that," Lyttleton retorted.

Provoked to imprudence by this sudden contrariety, this strange inconsistence, he made a futile attempt to regain her hand. "Don't be foolish. Can't you see I'm crazy about you?"

"Oh, yes!" she laughed, contemptuous.

"You're no fool," he declared hotly. "You know well you can't—a woman like you—play with a man like me as if he were a child. I tell you I—"

He checked himself with a firm hand; since, it seemed, she was one who took such matters seriously. "I'm mad about you," he repeated in a more subdued tone, "and I'd give anything if ... Only ... the deuce of it is, I can't ..."

"You can't afford to!" she snapped him up. "Oh, I understand you perfectly. Didn't I warn you I was penniless? You can't afford to love a penniless Nobody, can you—a shop-girl masquerading in borrowed finery! No—please don't look so incredulous; you must have guessed. Anyway, that's all I am, or was—a shop-girl out of work—before I was brought here to be Mrs. Gosnold's secretary. And that's all I'll be to-morrow, or as soon as ever she learns that I way lay her men guests at all hours and—steal their kisses!"

"She won't learn that from me," said Lyttleton, "not if you hold your tongue."

She drew back a pace, as though he had made to strike her, and for a moment was speechless, staring into the new countenance he showed her—the set, cold mask of the insolent, conquering male. And chagrin ate at her heart like an acid, so that inwardly she writhed with the pain of it.

"I—!" she breathed, incredulous. "I hold my tongue! Oh! Do you think for an instant I'm anxious to advertise my ignominy?"

"It's a bargain, then?" he suggested coolly. "For my part, I don't mind admitting I'd much rather it didn't ever become known that I, too, was—let's say—troubled with insomnia to-night. But if you say nothing, and I say nothing—why, of course—there's not much I wouldn't do for you, my dear!"

After a little she said quietly: "Of course I deserved this. But I'm glad now it turned out the way it has. Two minutes ago I was wild with the shame of making myself so cheap as to let you—of being such a fool as to dream you would lower yourself to the level of a woman not what you'd call your social equal, who could so far forget her dignity as to let you see she cared for you. But, of course, since I am not that—your peer—but only a shop-girl, I'm glad it's happened. Because now I understand some things better—you, for example. I understand you very well now—too well!"

She laughed quietly to his dashed countenance: "Oh, I'm cured, no fear!" and turned as if to leave him.

He proved, however, unexpectedly loath to let her go.

Such spirit was not altogether new in his experience, but it wasn't every day one met a girl who had it; whatever her social status, here was rare fire—or the promise of it. Nor had he undervalued her; he had suspected as much from the very first; connoisseur that he was, his flair had not deceived him.

His lips tightened, his eyes glimmered ominously.

And she was, in a way, at his mercy. If what she said of herself were true, he need only speak a word and she would be as good as thrown out. Even Abigail Gosnold couldn't protect her, insist on people inviting a shop-girl to their houses. And if such drudgery were really what she had come up from, you might be sure she'd break her heart rather than forfeit all this that she had gained.

And then again she had been all for him from the very first. She had admitted as much out of her own mouth. Her own mouth, for that matter, had taken his kisses—and hungrily, or he was no judge of kissing. Only the surprise of it, his own dumb unreadiness, his unwonted lack of ingenuity and diplomatics had almost lost her to him. Not quite, however; it was not yet too late; and though the risk was great, the penalty heavy if he were discovered pursuing an affair under this roof, the game was well worth the candle.

Thus Mr. Lyttleton to his conscience; and thus it happened that, when she turned to go, he stepped quickly to her side and said quietly: "Oh, please, my dear—one minute."

The unexpected humility of his tone, mixed with the impudence of that term of endearment, so struck her that she hesitated despite the counsel of a sound intuition.

"We mustn't part this way—misunderstanding one another," he insisted, ignoring the hostility in her attitude and modulating his voice to a tone whose potency often had been proved. "Three words can set me right with you, if you'll only listen—"

She said frostily: "Well?"

"Three words." He drew still nearer. "I've said them once to-night. Will you hear them again? No—please listen! I meant what I said, but I was carried out of myself—clumsy—bungled my meaning. You misunderstood, misconstrued, and before I could correct you I'd lost my temper. You said cruel things—just enough, no doubt, from your point of view—and you put words into my mouth, read thoughts into my mind that never were there. And I let you do me that injustice because I'm hot-tempered. And then, I'm not altogether a free agent; I'm not my own master, quite; and that's difficult to explain. If I could make you understand—"

Grown a little calmer, she couldn't deny there was something reasonable in his argument. She really had given him little chance; impulse and instinct had worked upon her, causing her to jump at conclusions which, however well founded in fact, were without excuse in act. If he had kissed her, it wasn't without provocation, nor against her will; she had got no more than she asked for. The trouble was, she no longer wanted it. She had been the dupe of her own folly, by her own romantic bent and the magnetism of the man blinded to the essentially meretricious spirit clothed in the flesh of his engaging person.

It had been a simple and perhaps inevitable infatuation of a mind all too ready to be infatuated, needing heroic treatment—such as she'd had and blushed to remember—to cure. And the shock of waking from that mad dream, no less than the shock of physical contact, had made her frantic and unreasonable. She could but admit that and, admitting it, be generous enough to let him clear himself.

If only he would not insist on his declaration of love, that she knew to be untrue, as if the compliment of it must be a balm to a spirit as bruised as her own!

He went on: "And all this because I seemed to hesitate—because I did hesitate, knowing I couldn't say all I wanted to. And before I could explain —"

"You're not married?" she inquired with an absence of emotion that should have warned him.

"Of course not. But I'm dependent, and good for nothing in a business way. My income is from my family, and depends on their favour. What can I say? I love you—I do—on my soul, I do!"

He put his arms once more round her shoulders, and she did not resist him, but none the less held her head up and back, eying him steadily.

"I love you desperately, but I can't ask you to marry me until I get the permission of my family. Till then … is there any reason …? Be kind to me, be sweet to me, O sweetest of women! I'm mad, mad about you!"

With no more warning he lowered his head, fastening his lips to the curve of her throat; and discovered suddenly and definitely his error. In a twinkling it was a savage animal he held in his arms, and before he knew what was happening she had broken his grasp and he was reeling back with a head that rang from the impact of an open hand upon his ear.

"You shrew!" he chattered. "You infernal little vixen! And I thought—!"

He sprang toward her, beside himself, with a purpose that failed only through the intervention of a third party.

A man swinging suddenly round the end of the hedge shouldered between Lyttleton and the object of his rage—a man whose bulk, in the loose flannels of a lounge suit, seemed double that of Lyttleton.

"Oh, here!" said Trego impatiently, but without raising his voice. "Come, come!" He caught Lyttleton's wrists and forced them down. "Don't be an idiot—as well as a cad. Do you want to rouse the household? If you do, and get kicked out, you'll never get another chance on this island, my friend."

"Damn your impudence!" Lyttleton stuttered, sufficiently recalled to his senses to guard his tone, and wrenched at his wrists. "Let me go! I'll—"

"Sure I'll let you go," Trego agreed cheerfully. "But unless you want a thrashing in the presence of a lady, you'll do nothing foolish."

With this he released Mr. Lyttleton in such wise that he was an instant later picking himself up from the gravel path.

And while he was picking himself up he was also reflecting swiftly, this notwithstanding that Sally was no longer present to be a stay upon their brawling.

If his look was vicious, his tone was subdued as he stood brushing off the dust of his downfall.

"Lucky you came when you did," he said, with an effort to seem composed. "I presume I ought to thank you for knocking me about. This confounded temper of mine will get me into serious trouble yet if I'm not careful. I was driven pretty nearly wild by that little devil—"

"Cut it right there!" Trego interrupted sharply. "I don't know anything about your row—didn't hear a word that passed between you two—and it's none of my business. But if there's any blame to be borne, you'd better shoulder it yourself, for I warn you, I'm not going to hear any woman called names by a pup like you!"

CHAPTER X

LEGERDEMAIN

With a mind half distracted, the battlefield of a dozen unhappy emotions of which the most coherent were seething self-reproach and frantic irritation with Trego (why must it have been he, of all men?) Sally inconsiderately left the two to conclude their quarrel without an audience—took to her heels incontinently and sped like a hunted shadow across the open lawn. She flung through the side door and left it wide, stumbled blindly up-stairs to her bedchamber door, and shut this last behind her with no anticipation so fond as that of solitude and freedom to cry her eyes out.

But she had no more than turned from the door toward her bed, in the same movement shrugging off her black cloak and letting it fall regardless to the floor, when she became aware that solitude was no more in that room, that she shared it with an alien Presence—a shape of misty pallor, filling the armchair, silhouetted vaguely against the moonlight rectangle of the window.

And she faltered and stopped stock-still, with a strangled whimper, due in part to sheer surprise, but mostly to semi-superstitious dread.

The Presence did not move; but she was frightfully aware of the fixed regard of its coldly hostile eyes.

"Who are you?" she demanded in a choking whisper. "What are you doing here? What do you want?"

"Where have you been?" the Presence retorted in a level voice instantly identified as that of Mrs. Standish. "What have you been doing"—a spectral arm gestured vaguely toward the terrace—"out there?"

Sally took firm hold of herself and mustered all her wit against this emergency.

"I went out," she said slowly, "because I couldn't sleep, and—everything seemed so lovely... ."

"Dressed like that!"

Profound scorn informed this comment. The girl writhed, but held herself well in hand.

"It was so late," she explained, "I didn't think it possible there'd be anybody else about."

"Of course you didn't." The woman's tone was saturated with hateful innuendo. "On the other hand, you soon discovered your mistake, didn't you?"

Sally muttered a sullen "Yes ..."

"You're wise not to lie I to me," her patroness remarked with just a suspicion of satisfaction. "I knew, you see. I've been sitting here, waiting, the better part of an hour, listening to you two bickering behind the hedge. You little fool!"

Sally said nothing. Her mood was all obsessed now with the conviction that this was the end to her life of a moth. An end to everything; come morning and she must be cast forth in disgrace, to go back to ...

She choked upon an importunate sob and dug nails into the palms of her hands.

"Who was the man?" Mrs. Standish pursued inexorably.

Then she didn't know!

"Does it matter?" Sally fenced.

"Certainly. I insist upon knowing. Remember your position here—and mine. I have assumed responsibility for you; but I cannot permit you to make me answerable for the antics of a man-crazy woman. If you can't behave yourself and refrain from annoying my aunt's guests, you must go. I thought you understood that."

"Of course," the girl muttered. "You didn't think I expected anything else, did you?"

"Who was the man you followed out there?"

The calculated offensiveness of this was balanced by its sudden revelation to Sally's mind of the fact that Mrs. Standish didn't know there had been two men. It was, however, true that the window did not command a view of the approach to the side door.

"Are you going to tell me?"

"Please, Mrs. Standish, I'd rather not."

"Think again, my girl, and don't forget the circumstances under which I was persuaded, against my better judgment, to introduce you here."

"What do you mean?"

"Have you forgotten you were caught in the act of burglarising my house— that I first saw you wearing clothes stolen from me? You told a story, but how do I know it was true? You may well have been an accomplice of the ruffian who nearly killed my brother."

"That's hardly likely, is it?"

"How am I to judge? You may have quarrelled and turned on him in revenge. Judged by your conduct here, I'm sure you're capable of anything. Or you may have thought you saw a way to win greater profit by aiding my brother."

"That's all nonsense," Sally retorted hotly, "and you know it."

If dismissal from Gosnold House were inevitable, then there was no reason why she should not call her soul her own.

A pause was filled by the dramatic effect of Mrs. Standish nobly holding her temper in leash.

"When are you going to answer my question?"

Sally was dumb.

"Was it—that man you went out there to meet—"

"I didn't go to meet anybody. It was an accident."

"So *you* say. Was it some one of the guests here?"

Silence was all the answer.

"If you persist in your present attitude, remembering your dubious history, I

93

have every right to take it for granted you went to meet an accomplice in crime—"

"Oh, rot!" Sally interjected impatiently.

And then, encouraged by consciousness of her audacity, she let her temper run away with her for an instant.

"All that's no good," she declared forcibly, "and you know it. If you mean to speak to Mrs. Gosnold about me in the morning, and have me sent away merely because I've had an unpleasant experience and refuse to discuss it with you—when it's none of your affair—why, I can't stop you. But I'm not a child, to be bullied and browbeaten, and I'm certainly not going to humour your curiosity about my private business. And that's flat. Now run and tell, if you really must—but you won't."

"Oh-indeed?" Mrs. Standish rose with vast dignity. "And why won't I, if you please?"

"Because you won't dare risk that insurance money, for one thing—"

"So you think you can blackmail—"

"Call it anything you like," Sally flashed defiantly. "Only bear in mind, I'm not going to submit tamely and be sent away in disgrace, like a kitchen-maid. I'll go, right enough—you don't need to worry about that—but I'll go on my own excuse. If you tell on me, I'll tell on you, and I'll tell everything I know, too."

"And what, please," the woman purred dangerously, "do you think you know —?"

"What about your signalling that yacht just now?"

It was shot at a venture; she had no real knowledge that the lighted window had been that of Mrs. Standish's bedroom; but it was just possible, and she chanced it, and it told, though she was not yet to know that with any certainty.

"What are you talking about?" Mrs. Standish hesitated with a hand on the door-knob.

"You know well enough. I saw what I saw. People don't do things like that unless there's something secret about it, something they don't want known."

"I think you must be out of your head," the woman responded with crushing hauteur. "I haven't the slightest notion what you mean, and you needn't trouble to enlighten me. I don't in the least care. But you may sleep on this— that your insolence shall be properly rewarded as soon as I can see my aunt in the morning. Good night."

With a defiant sniff that covered a spirit cringing in consternation, Sally turned her back and threw herself angrily into a chair. But the sound that she had expected of the door closing did not come, and after a minute she looked round to find Mrs. Standish still at pause upon the threshold.

"Oh," said Sally, with an impertinent assumption of remedying an oversight, "good night, I'm sure!"

Instead of audible reply, the woman shut the door and turned back to the middle of the room.

"I don't wish to be unjust," she said quietly.

"I am quick-tempered, just as you are, but I always try to be fair in the end. Perhaps I was unpleasant and too exacting just now; but, you must admit, I really know little or nothing about you, and have every right to watch you closely."

She paused, as if expecting an answer; but before Sally could overcome her astonishment she resumed in the same level, reasonable tone:

"I was greatly distressed when I came here and found you had gone out at this hour of the night: certainly, you must allow, a queer proceeding on the part of a young woman in your position. And when you come back, after a long talk with a strange man in the shelter of a hedge, and refuse to give an account of yourself, I confess you exasperated me. At the same time, accidents do happen; and it's true you have rights of privacy that even I must respect—to whom you owe a great deal, you must admit. And now I think I've gone as far toward making amends as even you could ask."

Astonishment and incredulity yielded to penitence. Sally sat up with a little gesture of contrition and appeal—an outflung hand instantly withdrawn; this was not a woman whose susceptibilities were to be touched by such means; even now, beneath her ostensible generosity, one divined a nature cold and little placable.

Then, with a remorseful cry, "Oh, I'm sorry!" the girl yielded to the tension of overwrought nerves and broke down completely, crushed, confounded, shaken by spasms of silent sobbing.

In the course of this she was conscious of the touch of a hand on her shoulder; no more than that. And when she had spent herself in tears and grew more calm, it was to find Mrs. Standish seated opposite her and waiting patiently; at all events with a fair imitation of that virtue.

"Please," Sally begged between gulps, "please forgive me. I'm so excited and unstrung—"

"I quite understand. There—compose yourself."

"If you still wish me to—if you insist—of course I'll tell you—"

"No." It cost the other woman an effort of renunciation, but she was steadfast to her secret purpose. "Forget that. It doesn't matter. I had no right to ask, and really do not care to know. But if you're quite able to pay attention, I'd like to consult with you—about what got me out of bed and brought me here this morning."

"I don't understand."

"Of course you don't. But it has been on my nerves all evening, until I felt as if I must talk to somebody—and you are the only one I can trust."

Sally stared in a state of dumb bewilderment that eclipsed all she had experienced before. Truly the world was topsyturvy this madcap night! What under the moon now?

"You know how worried I've been about that affair in town. Men are so inconsiderate; simply because he knew how things were going—and I presumed they must have been going well—Walter left me without a word till this evening. Then he telegraphed he'd be here to-morrow afternoon and that everything was all right; but that he is bringing with him one of the adjusters for the burglar-insurance people—a detective, I presume, the man is, really— and I'll have to answer some questions before we can collect the money to cover my loss."

"A detective!"

"Adjuster is a much more pleasant name. And I know it's merely a matter of formality, and I oughtn't to be silly about it, but I can't help it. I've been on edge ever since, fretting for fear something would come out about that case that Walter did bring me from the safe, you remember. If that were found—as it might be, if they ask me to produce what jewelry I have with me—well, I simply can't think what to do."

"Why not hide the case?"

"That's just it. But where? I can't imagine. Of course I can't very well smuggle it out of the house myself. So I thought perhaps you … At any rate, I've brought it to you."

"To me?"

"Don't be alarmed. Nobody will ever suspect you of any connection whatever with the affair. It'll be perfectly safe here, in your keeping, until you find a way to dispose of it. To-morrow night, for instance, as soon as it's dark, you might take it down to the shore, put a stone in it, and throw it out into the water. Or bury it in the sand. Anything. Nobody will pay any attention if you excuse yourself to go to your room or out to the terrace for half an hour. But I —well, you must see. I've hidden the case under your pillow. You may find some better place for it—but then you haven't a maid to hoodwink. I declare it has nearly driven me mad, these last few days, trying to keep the thing out of Ellen's sight. She's such a nosy, prying creature."

Mrs. Standish rose. "You will do this for me, won't you? I was sure I could depend on you. And—let us forget our little misunderstanding. I've forgotten it already."

She had left the room before Sally could formulate reasonable protest— reasonable, that is, remembering her burden of obligation to this woman.

It was an hour later before she at length settled upon satisfactory concealment for the incriminating jewel-case—in the recess behind a bureau-drawer, where it fitted precisely in the wrappings she did not trouble to remove.

In the grey twilight of the dawn at last, she flung herself upon the bed—and fell instantly asleep.

CHAPTER XI

THE THIRD DEGREE

In the sequel to that night of mischief and misadventure Sarah Manvers had sound reason to be thankful for the resilient youth which still animated her body. But of course she wasn't; youth will ever misprize till it must mourn its blessings.

Yet by virtue of that inestimable attribute alone was she able to do with only four hours' sleep (when Adele Standish, for example, needed eight, and then was seedy) and be the first of the household to appear for breakfast—clear of eye and fresh of colour, with a countenance as serene as her temper and a temper as normal as her appetite.

As for this last, she made an excellent breakfast, alone in the sun-bright dining-room. And if at times, as she sat and munched, her look was pensive and remote, this was due less to misgivings than to mystification.

The quarrel and reconciliation with Mrs. Standish had cleared the atmosphere of their relations; henceforward there could be no more misunderstanding;

they hated each other heartily; neither entertained any illusion as to that; but their interests were too far interdependent to license any play of private feeling. Sally wanted to stay on at Gosnold House, and Mrs. Standish was resigned; Mrs. Standish wanted her insurance money, and Sally would help her get it—by keeping quiet. Sally might be dealt with severely by the law if Mrs. Standish said the word, and Mrs. Standish, if Sally spoke, would suffer not only in her pocketbook, but in the graces of her aunt.

But Sally was not without compunction in respect to the deception practised on her still prospective employer. It wasn't possible to know Mrs. Gosnold and not like her; if that personality enforced respect, it was a lodestone for affection, and Sally meant with all her heart to serve faithfully and well; if she was to have her way, neither would know a single regret because of their association until time and chance conspired to sunder it.

Then, too, sleep had appreciably changed the complexion of her mind toward the Lyttleton episode. She was not yet able to recall that chapter of infatuation without a cringe of shame; but that would pass with time, and the experience had not been without a value already apparent. For even as she had said to him, she was cured—and more than cured, she was instructed; she was not only better acquainted with herself, but had learned to read the Lyttleton temperament too well ever to require repetition of the lesson. If she had played the fatuous moth, she had come through cheaply, with wings not even singed; for what she had taken for flame had proved to be no more than cheapest incandescence. She felt so sure of all this that she could even contemplate the affair with some inklings of the amusement that it would yet afford her. And she was fixed to make this the key of her attitude toward the man in all such future intercourse as was unavoidable.

But Trego …

Trego was a horse of another colour altogether. The very name of Trego was hateful in her hearing. There was little she would not willingly have done, however unjust and unfair, to avoid further communications with this animal of a Trego.

And yet, as she had learned, the term of his stay at Gosnold House had still another week to run, and he was in some way a favourite and intimate of Mrs. Gosnold, apt frequently to figure as her guest; and since this was so, and Sally herself bade fair (barring accidents) to prove a fixture in the household, it seemed inevitable that they must be often thrown together. So she must at all costs school herself to treat him civilly—at least without overt animosity.

She could imagine no task more difficult or distasteful; short of forfeiting her place in this new sphere, she would have paid almost any price for remission of that duty.

The irony of life seemed a bitter draft. Granting it had been requisite to some strange design of fate, in its inscrutable vagary, that several persons should suffer a night of broken rest at Gosnold House, why must they have been those four and none other—Sally, Adele Standish, Lyttleton, Trego? Especially Trego! Why that one? Palpable bonds of mutual interest linked the three first named; their common affliction might conceivably have been ascribable to subtle psychological affinity. But Trego was well outside the triangle, even as perceptibly out of sympathy with a majority of Mrs. Gosnold's guests.

Mrs. Standish was studious in her avoidance of him without appearance of open slight. His nature and Lyttleton's were essentially antagonistic. Sally's animus had been well defined from the very beginning, when she had resented his being both physically and temperamentally so completely out of the picture of that existence to which she aspired.

But reconnaissance up that dark alley demonstrated it an indisputable impasse and Sally gave it up, reserving the grievance for tender nursing (she had a very human weakness for selected wrongs) and turned her attention to the puzzle involving Lyttleton's business on the beach at 2 A. M. and the signals exchanged between yacht and window.

Nor did she make much headway in this quarter. Instinct indicated a delicate harmony between those events and the formless shadow to which Sally had all along been sensitive, of something equivocal in the pretensions of Mrs. Standish. But that clue played will-o'-the-wisp with her fancy, leading it ever farther astray in a bottomless bog of black bewilderment.

None the less, she had just succeeded in establishing to her own satisfaction the probability that her sponsor had been, if not active in, at least acquainted with the business of the signals—reasoning shrewdly upon that lady's high-handed treatment of Sally's insinuation as inconsequential—when Mr. Trego elected to appear for breakfast.

That unhappy young man had been more wise if he had not taken it for granted that nine o'clock would be too early for Sally as well as for everybody else who didn't make breakfast in bed a habit; and a more diplomatic person would have been at pains to prepare himself against that inevitable rencontre with a young woman of exacerbated sensibilities. Nothing could have been more surely predestined to ghastly failure than his cheerful assumption of a complete understanding, with the hint implicit that, having done Sally a signal service, he was willing to let bygones be bygones and take as tacit a sense of obligation not easy for her to express.

"Hel-lo!" he saluted the charming vision of her with undisguised pleasure and surprise. "You down already? Why, I made sure I had at least two hours' lead of the field."

"Yes," Sally agreed quietly; "I am early, I presume."

"Want to be careful," Trego cautioned; "it's hardly the thing, this early rising, you know; it's not really clawss; it isn't done."

Sally said nothing. It was safer not to. And cheerfully unaware of her self-restraint, Trego armed himself with a plate and foraged at the side-table, with its array of silver-hooded hot-water dishes.

"Been for a swim," he volunteered with a thrill of coarse creature satisfaction in his tone. "Wonderful water along this coast—not too warm, like the Jersey beaches—to my taste, anyway, and not too all-fired cold, as it generally is north of the Cape, but just right. Like bathing in champagne properly chilled. No such pick-me-up in the world as a dip in the cool of the morning. You should have tried it."

"I dare say," said Sally briefly, and was very glad she hadn't. "But that dreadfully long climb up from the beach—" she amended, feeling it obligatory upon her not to seem too short of civility.

"You don't mind that when you come to it after a swim," Trego declared. "It's only in anticipation, when you're snug between sheets and debating the rival claims of the distant beach and your handy bathtub; then, I grant you, the climb up the cliff weighs heavily in the scale of disadvantages."

He drew out the chair adjoining Sally's and attacked the half of an iced canteloup, but after the first mouthful put down his spoon.

"Sugar, please," he said with a deprecatory grimace, indicating the bowl just beyond the girl's place. "I know I ought to go in for salt if I want to come through as a regular guy; but if you won't tell on me, I'm going to enjoy this melon in my own primitive Western way. Thanks."

He committed the unpardonable deed with a liberal hand. "Frightfully weird, you know," he mimicked with a chuckle, adding: "It takes the rude, untutored mind of a barbarian to be satisfied with sweetening a thing with sweetness instead of bitterness, doesn't it'?"

"But I prefer salt myself," said the girl; "it brings out the flavour."

She concluded her defence in some confusion due to Trego's practically synchronous utterance of her identical phrase: "it brings out the flavour." Then she realised that he had deliberately trapped her and was meanly laughing in the triumph of his low cunning. And she had to laugh, too, to save her face; but it was an empty laugh and accompanied by a flush that might have warned the man had he not too soon returned attention to his melon.

"Never fails," he remarked. "Though, of course, it isn't safe to work it on anybody in this outfit—not, at least, unless you're pretty sure there's a trace of human humour in the make-up of the specimen. I'm making a collection of those stereotypes; it helps a lot. O table-talk! where is thy sting—when a fellow knows all the answers?"

He rose, set aside the shell of the maltreated melon, and returned with his plunder from the hot-water dishes, to find Sally on the point of leaving.

"Not going?" he protested more soberly. "Don't tell me I offended you, catching you up like that!"

"How absurd!" the infuriated girl replied, smiling falsely. "But—"

"Then, if you've nothing pressing on, keep me company for a little. I want to ask your advice. I'm puzzled. Maybe you can suggest something."

She couldn't well go, then, without betraying umbrage, so she settled herself with a resigned temper, and for want of a better lead contented herself with a conversational stop-gap—"Puzzled?"—spoken in an encouraging tone.

"Yes. Something I noticed this morning. But it weaves into last night— maybe. Maybe not. I'm a slow thinker when it comes to puzzles."

He filled a cup with coffee from the shining urn and resumed his chair.

"You see …" Some intimation of his gaucherie made him stumble. "Of course," he went on, semi-apologetic, "you understand that I'm going on the assumption that you're as human as I am."

"Thank you," said Sally sweetly.

"Human enough," he explained, "not to think I'm a savage because I've reminded you of last night."

"I see no reason—" she began with dignity.

"And there isn't any," he argued heartily. "We're both old enough to behave like grown-ups. Only, a fellow never can tell where he stands with most of these festive dames. I've been lorgnetted until I'm scared to open my mouth. But with you—well, it's like meeting somebody from home to talk to you."

"But the puzzle?" she reminded him with more patience than he knew.

"Oh, yes. I was going to say when I side-tracked myself: what got me up was Lyttleton. He has the room next mine, you know. I'd just turned out my bedside light—been reading, you understand—when I heard his door open very gently and somebody go pussy-footing down the hall. And for some reason that kept me awake—because it was none of my business, I guess—waiting for him to come back and wondering what in thunder took him out on the prowl like that. And when I had wondered myself wide awake I got up and dressed—thought I'd take a walk, too, since the night was so fine. I honestly had no idea of following him—that was all an accident, my butting in the way I did."

Sudden perception of a footing upon ground properly taboo even to angels caused the man to flush brick-red. His eyes sought Sally's in honest consternation.

"Hope you don't mind," he mumbled.

"Please go on," she said, conscious of the heat in her own cheeks, and holding him in an esteem proportionately more poisonous.

"Well. About this morning: As I say, I went down to the beach for a dip. You know how that beach is—about a twelve-foot breadth of sand from the bottom of the cliff when the tide's high, with about twenty feet more when it's low. So foot-prints show until the weather rubs them out—takes a tolerable storm, as a rule. Below high-water mark it's different; the sand is covered up and smoothed out twice a day. Well, then, just below high-water mark—that is, about five feet below it, or at quarter-tide mark—I noticed the print of a rowboat's bows on the sand. It had landed there and waited a while—drawn up only part way out of the water—about three o'clock this morning. Two men had got out; one waited with the boat, the other went up toward the foot of the steps and mixed his footprints up with all the others. I don't know what for and can't imagine; but that's what happened, and presently he turned round and went back to the boat, and the two of them shoved her off again—trusting, I guess, to the tide to cover up the signs of their landing.

"Why they should want to be secret about it, God only knows; but if they didn't, why three o'clock? It's all private beach along here, and whereas I believe there are no property rights below high-water mark, and anybody has a right to land anywhere in an emergency—where was the emergency? There was no gale last night, and if there had been, you'd think distressed mariners would have sense enough to come ashore farther along, toward the village, where they could find shelter—and all that. The more I think about it, the funnier it looks to me."

He finished his breakfast and his statement at the same time, pushed back his chair, and produced a cigarette-case.

"You don't mind? Thanks. Now what do you think?"

Sally shook her head and looked blank. "Three o'clock? How can you be so sure about that?" she inquired obliquely.

"Because it's high tide twice a day—approximately every twelve hours. I looked up a tide-table in the hall out there and found it was high at one eleven this morning and low at seven thirty-five—just about an hour turned when I had my swim, the water-line then about twelve feet short of the marks of the boat. It'll be high again about one forty-eight this afternoon—at least noon before water begins to wash over those marks."

He puffed voluminously. "If there was any shenanigan afoot last night, a couple of thick-heads footed it—that is, if they cared whether they left any clues or not."

Constrained to fill in his expectant pause, she made shift with a "How very odd!" that was a triumph of naturalness.

"Isn't it?" he agreed. "Now what do you make of it?"

"Nothing," she replied truthfully, for she was entirely at a loss to fit this new development into the adventures of Lyttleton and the lighted window—and make sense of it. "I can't imagine—"

"What I want to know is this," Trego propounded cunningly: "had Lyttleton anything to do with it?" She had prepared for that question, had settled her answer beforehand; even with any real reason to suspect Lyttleton of complicity in something underhand, she would not have betrayed him to this man—if to anybody.

"I'm sure I can't say."

"Well—it's funny, anyhow. Guess we better not say anything about it. After all, it's no concern of ours."

She couldn't refrain from the question: "But why should you think he—?"

"Well, what *was* he doing all that time—?"

He checked and stammered with embarrassment. "I beg your pardon!"

"You needn't. He wasn't—with me—all that time."

The situation grown intolerable, Sally got up suddenly and without a word of excuse took her scarlet cheeks out of the dining-room and back to her bedchamber.

On the dot of their standing appointment she found Mrs. Gosnold unconsciously, perhaps, but none the less strikingly posed in the golden glow of her boudoir window for the portrait of a lady of quality on fatigue duty— very much at her ease in a lavender-silk morning gown and stretched out in a *chaise longue*, a tray with fruit, coffee and rolls on her left dividing attention with a sheaf of morning notes on the other side and the portable writing-case on her knees.

Acknowledging Sally's appearance with a pleasant if slightly abstracted smile, she murmured: "Oh, is it you, Miss Manwaring? Sit down, please. Half a minute ..."

On the *qui vive* for any indication that Mrs. Standish had been false to her word or Mrs. Gosnold informed through any other channel of the secret history of that night and consequently inclined to hold her secretary in distrust, Sally detected nothing in the other's manner to add to her uneasiness. To the contrary, in fact. She sat and watched in admiration, and thought that she had never known a woman better poised, more serenely mistress of herself and of the technique of life. If Mrs. Gosnold nursed a secret sorrow, anxiety, or grievance, the world would never learn of it through any flaw in the armour of her self-possession.

She wrought busily with a fountain pen for little longer than the stipulated period of delay, then addressed and sealed a note and looked up again with her amiable, shrewd smile.

"Good morning!" she laughed, quite as if she had not till then recognised Sally's presence. "You've slept well, I trust?"

Sally did not hesitate perceptibly; the honest impulse prevailed. Secretly she was determined to tell no more major lies, though the heavens fell—only such minor fibs as are necessary to lubricate the machinery of society. She would do her best, of course, to preserve the hateful truth that had been so cunningly covered up by the lies of Mrs. Standish's first invention; but she would do that best, if possible, more by keeping silence than by coining and uttering fresh falsehoods.

"Not so well last night," she confessed. "I don't know what was the matter with me, but somehow I didn't seem even to want to sleep."

"I know," Mrs. Gosnold nodded wisely. "I'm not yet old enough to have forgotten these midsummer moonlight nights of ours. When I was a girl and being courted, from this very house, I know I used to wait until everybody had gone to bed and creep out and wander for hours ..."

Her pause invited confidences. And momentarily Sally's heart thumped like a trip-hammer. Did she, then, either know or guess?

"I did that last night," she responded; "but I hadn't your excuse."

"You mean, you're not being courted? Don't be impatient. Once to every woman—once too often to most. And it's well to take one's time nowadays. Perhaps it's a sign of age, and I shouldn't own it, but it does seem to me that the young men of to-day are an uncommonly godless crew. I should be sorry to have you make a mistake ..."

She contented herself with that much warning and no more; but Sally knew their thoughts were one, focused upon a singular though by no means strange example of the young men of the present day.

"I think," her employer pursued, with a look excusing the transient keenness of her scrutiny, "our Island air agrees with you. If you have had one poor night, all the same you're quite another girl than the one who came here—was it only four days ago? I hope you're quite comfortable."

"Oh, yes, indeed."

"And would you care to stay on?"

"With all my heart!"

"I see no reason why you shouldn't. I like you very well; you're quick and willing—and you humour my weakness for the respect of my associates. I don't ask for their dependence. If you like, we'll say your engagement begins to-day, the first of the week."

"You are very kind."

"I'm very selfish. I like intelligence, prettiness, and youth—must have them at any cost! So that's understood. Of course, there are certain questions to be settled, arrangements to be made. For example, I assume responsibility for your losses at bridge, because playing when I wish you to is one of your duties. But these matters adjust themselves as they come up from time to time."

"Thank you," said Sally in a tone that, though little more than a whisper, was more eloquent of her gratitude than the mere phrase could possibly have been.

"So now I shall stop calling you Miss Manwaring."

"Please do."

"It's much too formal, considering I'm old enough to be your mother."

"Oh, no!" Sally protested involuntarily. "That isn't possible."

"I'll not see fifty-five again," Mrs. Gosnold announced. "But that's a boudoir secret."

"I'll never—"

"And a secret of Polichinelle besides," the other laughed; "everybody I know or care a snap for knows it. At the same time, no woman cares to have her age discussed, even if it is public property and she quite old enough to be beyond such vanity. No matter; I'm going to call you Sara, if you've no objection."

"Why not Sally?" the girl suggested tentatively. "That's my name—I mean, what I'm accustomed to."

"Thank you; I like it even better," Mrs. Gosnold affirmed. "I'm conservative enough to favour old-time names. My own, for instance, Abigail, pleases me immensely, though I seldom meet a young woman these days who can hear it without looking either incredulous or as though she doubted the sanity of my sponsors in baptism."

She stayed the obvious reply with an indulgent toss of a hand still fair.

"Now to work. I've mapped out a busy morning for you. To begin with, here are a dozen or so notes to deliver. You may take the dog-cart—no, to save time, one of the motors. We must give these good people as much time as possible, considering it's a spur-of-the-moment affair. That is why, you understand, there are so few invitations—because I'd no time to write and post a number. But each of these is a bid to some friend with a houseful of people to come and bring all her guests.

"Oh!" she laughed, catching the look of puzzlement on the girl's face, "I haven't told you what it is. Well, my dear, it's an old woman's whim. Every so often I break loose this way and keep my memory green as one who, in her day, never entertained but in some unique fashion. I was once famous for that sort of thing, but of late years I haven't exerted myself except when bored to extinction by the deadly commonplace amusements most people offer us.

"For some time I've had this in mind, and everything prepared; you may, if you like, call it a spontaneous masquerade by moonlight. Half the fun of such affairs comes of the last-moment, makeshift costumes; if you give people much time to think them up it is always a stiff and frigid function. Moreover, it demands a perfect night—and we can't count on our Island weather twenty-four hours in advance. But to-day is perfect, and to-night will be fair with the moon at its full. You may dance on the veranda or make love on the terrace, just as you please, from ten o'clock till three—or later. Supper will be served from midnight on. At one we shall unmask.

"As I say, all preparations had been made, weather permitting; I had merely to telephone the caterers, electricians, and musicians, and scribble these invitations. I'd advise you to arrange your day to include a good long nap before dinner, for you'll be up till all hours very likely. I fancy I can promise you some fun."

Mrs. Gosnold ceased upon a note of mischievous enjoyment in anticipation that would have suited a girl of sixteen, then analysed the trouble behind Sally's perturbed countenance.

"As for your costume, you're not to give it a thought! I have arranged for it to be brought to your room at half past nine, and I pledge you my word you'll find it becoming. I have only two requests to make of you: that you refrain from unmasking or admitting your identity until one o'clock, and that if you recognise me, you hold your tongue. Is it a bargain?"

"You're so good to me," said Sally simply, "I can't think how to thank you."

"Leave that, too, to me. It's quite possible I may suggest a way." Mrs. Gosnold smiled curiously as at a thought reserved. "Now run along—order the car and put on your prettiest hat. But a moment!"

She illustrated the process of taking thought by puckering her brows and clipping her chin between a thumb and forefinger.

"Let me see. Have I remembered everybody?" She conned, half aloud, a list of names. "But no! What an oversight! I should never have forgiven myself— or have been forgiven. And my fountain pen needs refilling. No"—as Sally offered to take the pen—"sit there at the desk and write at my dictation. I will sign it."

Obediently Sally took her place at the escritoire, arranged a sheet of the monogrammed note-paper used by Mrs. Gosnold for correspondence with personal friends (as distinguished from the formal letter-head of Gosnold House, with its bristling array of telephone numbers and telegraph, post-office, railroad and steamboat addresses), dipped a pen, and waited with a mind preoccupied by visions of the night to come. Her first ball! Her first real function in Society!

"My dear friend," Mrs. Gosnold enunciated deliberately in a colourless, placid voice. "(Colon, dash, paragraph) It was only late last night, and then by merest chance, I learned you had come to the island yesterday instead of sailing last week, in accordance with your announced intention (period). So I cannot decently begin by berating you (dash) as I should, had you been here twenty-four hours without personally letting me know (period)."

A pause. Sally dreamed a beautiful dream of a crinoline costume, beflowered and beflounced, such as Vogue had lately pictured as a forecast of autumn fashions, an iridescent bubble of a dream shattered by the query: "Where was I, please?"

"'Letting me know,'" she quoted absently.

"Oh, yes. (Paragraph.) I hope with all my heart your change of plans was not brought about by any untoward accident (semicolon); but Italy's loss is the island's gain (semicolon); and I am looking forward with the keenest pleasure to seeing you again (period, paragraph). May I hope that it will be not later than to-night (point of interrogation)? I have arranged an impromptu masquerade by moonlight on the terrace (period). It should be a pretty sight (period). From ten o'clock till any time you like (dash) masks until one (period). Do come and help make the evening a happy one for me (period)."

Another contemplative pause. But this time Sally did not dream. She sat quite still in speculative wonder, troubled with a vague alarm as disturbing as the sound of distant thunder in the evening, of an August day.

"Cue, please?"

The girl replied in a low tone: "'Evening a happy one'—"

"Yes. Add: affectionately yours—or wait! Have you written—?"

"'Affectionately yours'—yes."

"No matter; leave a space for my signature, and add this: P. S. You will be glad to see, no doubt, that your letter to Adele has borne fruit (period). Miss Manwaring does splendidly as an amanuensis (period). Your judgment was always trustworthy (period). And address the envelope, of course, to Mrs. Cornwallis English. She is stopping, I hear, with the Lorimers at Bleak House —the grey stone house on the hill at the end of West Harbor Drive."

After a time Mrs. Gosnold said almost sharply: "Well, Miss Manwaring! You have little time to waste. Bring me the note, please, and a pen."

With a gesture of despair the girl twisted in her chair and showed the woman a stricken face.

"Are you sure—?" she stammered.

"Yes?" Mrs. Gosnold prompted with an accent of surprise. "What is it, Sally?"

The girl gulped hard, and mechanically put a hand to her throat, rising as she spoke.

"Are you sure Mrs. English is on the Island?"

"What of it? Why, I presumed you would be glad of the opportunity to thank her for that letter of—"

"There was no letter!"

"I beg pardon?" Mrs. Gosnold opened wide her eyes.

"I say," Sally faltered, yet with determination, "there was no letter. Mrs. Standish—that is—we both lied to you. I don't know Mrs. English; I never spoke a word to her in all my life. I didn't take any letter to Mrs. Standish. That was a story manufactured out of whole cloth to account for me—get me this position here."

"Oh, yes," Mrs. Gosnold assented coolly. "I felt quite sure of that in the beginning. You never could believe a word Adele said from the time she was able to talk. Even if the truth would have served as well and with less trouble, she was sure to disfigure it beyond identification. And Walter's just as bad. But you, my dear, will never make a good liar; the first words we spoke together I saw your eyes wince, and knew you were tormented by something on your conscience. Moreover, the last person Edna English would send anyone with a letter of recommendation to is my niece, who has not yet been proved guilty of one unselfish act. So I thought I'd test the story. Now you may tear up that note—Mrs. English is in Italy this very day, to the best of my belief—and tell me what it's all about."

CHAPTER XII

MACHIAVELLIAN

Within the span of an exceedingly bad quarter of an hour for Sally the cat was completely out of the bag, the fat as irretrievably in the fire; Sally was out of breath and in tears of penitence and despair; Mrs. Gosnold was out of her chair, thoughtfully pacing to and fro, and in full possession of all facts materially bearing upon the translation of S. Manvers of the Hardware Notions into S. Manwaring of the Golden Destiny.

No vital detail had escaped her penetrating probe; she proved herself past mistress in the art of cross-examination, and found in Sally a willing witness.

For the latter, however, it had seemed less giving of testimony than a hysteric confessional. She had wrung her conscience dry, deriving from the act a sort of awful joy mitigated by the one regret: that she had not more to confess, that the mystery of her favouring must remain a mystery which, with all the good-will in the world, no word of hers could elucidate.

As for the secret history of last night's dark transactions, however, that was not altogether hers to disclose. The interests and affairs of others were involved, she dared not guess how disastrously; she was only sensitive to the feeling that something black and foul and hideous skulked behind that shut door. Heaven forfend that hers should be the hand to open it and let ruin loose upon this pleasant world of Gosnold House!

It seemed incumbent upon her to explain that Mrs. Standish had brought to her room a jewel-case for Sally to hide or otherwise dispose of. Beyond this she feared to go. She would not mention Lyttleton or Trego or the yacht, or the window of the signals.

In the end, stopping tears and sobs as best she might, she waited listlessly her sentence of expulsion. Now nothing mattered; if her heart was lighter, her future was darker; and presently the nobody that she was would return into that drab nowhere whence some ill wind of chance had wafted her.

"Don't be a fool!" Mrs. Gosnold counselled her abruptly with unwonted brusqueness. "Do you really think I'm capable of baiting a trap for you with fair words and flattery for the sheer, inhuman pleasure of seeing you suffer until I choose to set you adrift? See how you've upset me already; metaphor is never safe in a woman's hands, but I'm seldom as bad as all that!"

Sally sniffed abjectly. "I'm willing to do anything ..."

"You've done enough. Be content. If it were not for you and what you've been able to tell me, I'd ... Well, no matter; I don't know what I'd do. As it is ... Look here!"

She paused in front of Sally, dropped one hand kindly on the girl's shoulder, with the other lifted her chin, exploring her tear-wet eyes with a gaze at once charitable and discriminating.

"I've taken a fancy to you, if you are a bit of an idiot. And I believe implicitly every word you've uttered. Perhaps I oughtn't to, and I probably wouldn't, if your account of yourself didn't chime so exactly with what I know about my dutiful niece and nephew. But, you see, I do know them, and very well—and that they're quite capable of all you say, and more to boot. Adele Standish in especial I know far too well to believe for an instant she'd burden herself with benevolent intentions toward another woman without expecting to reap some wildly inadequate reward. That's all that bothers me. I can't understand what they wanted with you. But I'm not going to let my mystification lose me the services of a promising amanuensis—not in these days, when intelligence is scarce and far to seek."

"Do you mean I'm to stay?" Sally gasped incredulously.

"Most assuredly I mean you're to stay. Why not? You're modest and well-mannered, and you've got too much sense to try again to pull wool over my eyes, even if you're wicked enough to want to, which I don't believe. No; as far as you're concerned, your position here is far more firmly established now than an hour ago, when everything was against my liking you—in spite of the fact that I did—especially your loyalty to those hopeless ingrates!"

She fumed in silence for a moment. "I could have forgiven almost anything—but this! The insolence of it! To dare picture me to you—or anybody—as a silly old fool of a woman without the wit to protect herself from being fleeced by a gang of adventurers. My friends!" she broke off with a snort of superindignation. "My guests here a set of rogues and vagabonds—and worse!"

She flopped into her chair with a helpless "Oh dear!" and began to laugh.

"It's too ridiculous!" she exclaimed. "If it ever got out, I'd almost be ashamed to show my face in public again. Promise you'll never breathe a syllable—"

"Oh, I promise—I do promise!" Sally protested fervently. "But, Mrs. Gosnold …"

"Well, what now?"

"I suppose," said Sally, "the only way to show my gratitude is by serving you faithfully—"

"You might," the elder woman interposed in a quizzical turn, "spare me, if you can, a little affection, since it seems I've lost that of my sister's children, together with their respect."

"I don't think you'll ever complain for want of that," Sally told her very seriously. "But can you afford to run the risk of the police coming here to find Sarah Manvers, who disappeared last week after breaking into a house—burglarising it—leaving her discarded clothing behind her for one positive clue—"

"You must make your mind easy as to that; unless I'm vastly mistaken, no police will ever look for you in Gosnold House; if any did, they wouldn't be admitted; and if by any chance they did happen to get in, they wouldn't find Sarah Manvers. Please understand, you're to remain Sara Manwaring for some time to come—for good, if I think best. Don't imagine I'm going to permit you to resume your right name and spoil everything. I hope I make myself clear."

"Oh, yes, Mrs. Gosnold!"

"And—attend to me—you're not to give Adele—or Walter, either, when he gets here, any reason to suspect you've confided in me. I wish everything to go on precisely as it has been going—so far as they can see. Avoid them as much as possible; when it isn't possible, give them a dose of their own medicine if necessary—I mean, lie. There's an explosion coming, but I don't wish it to happen until I'm sure who and what are going to be blown sky-high, and I am quite prepared to stand by and enjoy the fireworks. Meantime, don't let anybody frighten you; no matter how serious matters may seem or be represented to you, rely implicitly on me. And whatever is said to you that seems of any consequence—or if you should see anything—find some way to report quickly to me. Now what did you say you did with that jewel-case Adele gave you?"

Sally repeated her account of its hiding-place.

"You didn't unwrap it, you say. Well and good!" Mrs. Gosnold nodded intently. "Then don't; leave it as it is, and some time to-day, if I can manage without being observed, I'll drop into your room and have a look at the box myself. But you are on no consideration whatever to touch it until I give you leave."

"I understand."

"If Adele and Walter want to know what you've done with it, tell them the truth—you've done nothing. Say you've not yet found a good chance to. Tell them where it is, but assure them it's perfectly safe there."

"Yes, Mrs. Gosnold."

Momentarily the older woman was lost in a reverie of semimalicious cast, to judge by the smile that faintly shadowed the firm lines of her handsome face.

"A surprise patty …" she observed obscurely.

Of a sudden, with a sort of snap, she roused herself back to more immediate issues. "Oh, come! the morning almost gone already and nothing accomplished! Off with you! But before you go, do, for goodness' sake, attend to your eyes; if some one were to see you going through the halls the way you are—it might be ruinous. Bathe them with cold water in the bath-room there—and you'll find plenty of powder and stuff on my dressing-table."

And while Sally hastened to profit by this advice, the other pursued: "You should school yourself never to cry, my girl. You're too sensitive and emotional by half. If you go on this way, at the least excuse—great Heavens! what a moist married life you'll lead! Now let me look at you. That's much better. You'll do very well—if only you've wit enough not to worry—to trust me, whatever the emergency. Now, please, get about my errands. And when you come back, tell Thomas to let me know. If I need you during the day I'll send for you."

As it happened, she didn't send for Sally before nightfall; but she kept her busy with commissions delivered by word of mouth—so busy, perhaps considerately, that the girl found little time to waste in futile fretting, but was ever conscious, when now and again her thoughts did inevitably revert to the status of her personal affairs, of contentment crooning in her heart like the soft refrain of some sweet old song.

Her social education had made a gigantic forward stride with her surprising discovery that confession is good for the soul, that honesty in all things is not only expedient but wholesome. If material advantage had accrued unto her through that act of desperate honesty, if she basked all this day long in the assurance of immunity from the consequences of her folly and imprudence, it was less with the arrogance of Fortune's favourite daughter than with the humility of one to whom life had measured out benefactions of which she was consciously undeserving. The assertion that the world owed her a living was forgotten, and if recalled, would have been revised to the sense that she owed the world the duty of honourable and conscientious living. If her temper was tolerably exalted, it was well chastened to boot.

Thanks to the tardy advertisement of the fete, the avidity of a people ever seeking some new thing, and the fame of Abigail Gosnold as an entertainer of eccentric genius, that day could hardly be said to wane; rather, it waxed to its close in an atmosphere of electric excitement steadily cumulative. The colony droned like some huge dynamo with the rumour of secret preparation against the night. Other than servants scurrying to and fro on pressing but mysterious errands, few folk were visible in the afternoon; the drives and beaches; the lawns, terraces, courts, gardens, verandas and casinos were one and all deserted.

At Gosnold House, below-stairs, in kitchens and servants' halls, and all about the grounds as well, a multitude of work-people swarmed like an invading army of ants. Astonishing feats of preparation were consummated as if by legerdemain. And though the routine of the household proceeded marvellously without apparent hitch or friction, luncheon and dinner degenerated into affairs of emptiest formality. At the latter, indeed, Mrs. Gosnold presided over an oddly balanced board; three-fourths of those present were men—fully half the feminine guests dining from trays in their rooms or else abstaining altogether in order that not one precious moment might be lost to the creation of their improvised disguises. And the talk at table was singularly disconnected, with an average of interest uncommonly low. People were obviously saving themselves up. There was no lingering over tobacco; the last course served, the guests dispersed in all haste compatible with decency.

It was at this meal that Sally got her first glimpse of Savage since his arrival in the course of the afternoon. She had been far too busy to keep watch and unable to invent any plausible excuse for inquiring after him, but the thought of his return had never been far out of mind. However busy, she had been unable to dismiss entirely the consideration that Savage was bringing the first authentic news of whatever activities the police might have inaugurated in connection with the burglary and whatever their progress in pursuit of the clue furnished by the garments discarded in the bath-room. And all the reassurances of Mrs. Gosnold were impotent to counteract apprehensions fostered by such reflections.

But there was the length and the width of the table between them. She had to be content with all that Savage found chance to accord her—a bow, a smile, and a glance down his nose significant of unspeakable intelligence.

She thought he looked a bit pale and worried and betrayed more nervousness than was natural in the man as she had come to know him.

Whether or not he had been accompanied by the threatened insurance adjuster (or detective!) she was unable to surmise; notwithstanding several strange faces in the number at table, she was inclined to believe that a person of such character would have been lodged somewhere in the village which served as the island's main port of entry, rather than brought to Gosnold House— already crowded with guests.

As soon as the company rose Savage manoeuvred to the side of the girl, detaining her long enough to convey a surreptitious message under cover of apparently care-free greetings.

"Must have a talk," he muttered out of the corner of his mouth. "Something you ought to know immediately."

A pang of pure fear shot through her mind, but she retained sufficient command of herself not to betray her emotion or even to seem anxious to make the appointment.

"Oh, there's no chance for that now," she evaded as per instructions, and with so successful a semblance of indifference that Savage was openly and profoundly perplexed. "I've heaps of things yet to do for Mrs. Gosnold—I'm really frightfully pushed for time even to dress."

"Yes—of course. But this talk has got to happen some time soon. However, it ought to be easy enough under our masks. What costume will you be wearing?"

"I don't know. Mrs. Gosnold promised to find something and send it to my room. I presume she must have forgotten—but perhaps it's there now."

"Well, keep an eye bright for me, then. I'll be Harlequin—an old costume I happened by sheer luck to have left here some years ago. Otherwise, I guess, I'd have to wrap up in a sheet and act like a dead one."

She laughed mechanically, murmured "I must fly!" and forthwith dashed up the great staircase and to her room.

Her costume had not yet been delivered; she had still to wait half an hour by the clock; but there was plenty of detail wherewith to occupy her time. On the other hand, the routine of one's toilet is a famous incentive to thoughtfulness, and as she went automatically through the motions of beautifying herself and dressing her hair, Sally's mind took advantage of this, its first real freedom of the day, and focused sharply on her own concerns.

It reminded her, among other things, of the fact that she had not seen Lyttleton since an adventitious glimpse of him going in to breakfast just as she was leaving the house to deliver the invitations.

She wondered idly about him, in an odd humour of tolerant superiority, as one might contemplate the presumption of an ill-bred child. And she wondered dumbly at herself, whom she found able to imagine without flinching an encounter with him of the mildly flirtatious description licensed by the masquerade. Would he know instinctively who she was and avoid her? Or have the impudence to renew his advances? Or would he fail to fathom her identity and so lay himself open to her castigation?

She did not for an instant forget that she was endued, not only by personal right as an injured woman herself at fault, but also by the authority of Mrs. Gosnold, with letters of marque and reprisal.

That she would penetrate at sight his disguise, whatever its character, she hadn't the faintest doubt.

But, then, woman's faith in her vaunted if vaguely comprehended faculty of intuition is a beautiful thing and a joy to her forever.

And she wondered what Savage would have to say to her. But in this phase her thoughts wore a complexion of far less self-assurance, notwithstanding the moral support of her employer. What could have happened in New York that he must seek an early meeting to discuss it with her? What had been the outcome of that terribly incriminating clue, her name on the garments composing that sloughed chrysalis of yesterday? Was it possible that her comrades of the studio (Heavens! how historically remote and almost unreal seemed that well-hated chapter of existence) had become anxious enough to notify the police of her long absence? In such cases, she believed, something called a general alarm was issued—a description of the absentee was read to every member of the metropolitan police force, that it might be on the alert to apprehend or succour the lost, strayed or stolen. Could that possibly have been done in the case of missing Sally Manvers? And, if so, could the police detectives possibly have overlooked the fact that the name of the wanting woman was identical with the name of the woman wanted?

For all the strength of her tower of refuge Sally shivered.

And she realised with a twinge of sincere regret that she would never dare return and share these happier fortunes with those two unhappy partners of her days of suffering and privation.

She wasn't heartless; she had thought frequently of them before, but always with the notion that she would some day, and by happy chance some day not distant, reveal her transfigured self to them and, out of the plenitude of her blessings, lend them a little, and much more than a little, aid and comfort. Something of that sort, indeed, was the least she could do; it was but justice; it was simply repayment of acknowledged indebtedness. And now, it seemed, it might never be!

From this she passed into new wonder and bewilderment at the duplicity of Savage and his sister, and the mystery of their motives and the still deeper mystery of their actions, and the inscrutable mystery of the boat that had landed on the beach of Gosnold House at three o'clock in the morning.

All of which led her suddenly to make sure of the jewel-box.

It was no longer in its place of concealment.

Mrs. Gosnold, she assumed, must have removed it.

But for what purpose? To what end?

A knock on the door announced the arrival of her costume by the hands of Mrs. Gosnold's personal maid.

"And Mrs. Gosnold says please will you come to her boudoir, miss, directly you're dressed?"

"Tell her I'll be there in fifteen minutes."

Moderate disappointment waited upon recognition of the character of her assigned disguise. She had had visions of something very splendid, something almost barbaric in its richness—had nursed a day-dream of herself flaunting radiantly through the chiaroscuro of the moonlight fete like some great jewelled butterfly.

After that vision the modest garb of a Quaker maid seemed something of a come-down, even though the costumer's conception of a Quakeress had been considerably influenced by musical comedy standards.

But her disappointment was fugitive. After all, the dress was of exquisite quality and finish, and it became her wondrous well. She took from the room the memory of a very fetching figure in a gown of dove-grey crepe-de-chine, the bosom crossed by glistening bands of white, the skirt relieved by a little apron of lace and linen, white bands at wrist and throat, a close-fitting cap of lace covering her hair, her feet and ankles disclosed discreetly in stockings of dove-grey silk and suede slippers of the same neutral shade set off by silver buckles—the whole rendered the more tempting by an almost jaunty cloak of grey satin lined with white.

With the addition of the mask (which she wore to pass through the corridor in memory of Mrs. Gosnold's injunction) the effect was quite positively fascinating.

And that mask proved to be far from superfluous, for when she followed her knock into the boudoir of her mistress she was thunderstruck to find nearly two dozen people, men and women, gathered together there, sitting and standing about in a silence which seemed curiously constrained, taken in connection with their festival attire. For they were all in costume and, with the single exception of Mrs. Gosnold, all masked.

This last was very brilliant in the billowy silken skirts, puffed sleeves, tight bodice, and wide ruff of Queen Elizabeth, and carried off well the character of that hot-tempered majesty, making no effort to disguise the fact that she was deeply wounded and profoundly agitated.

She sat regally enthroned upon a spindle-shank chair that matched her escritoire, and betrayed her impatient humour by the quick tapping of one exquisitely shod foot. And the others seemed to wait upon her pleasure in a silence almost of subjugation—a nervous, unnatural, ominous hush.

It was broken on Sally's entrance by the mistress of Gosnold House, who nodded without a sign of recognition and said in a bleak manner thus far in Sally's experience wholly foreign to the nature of the speaker: "Come in, please, shut the door, and find some place to sit down. Retain your mask. There are two guests wanting, and we must wait for them."

There were no chairs vacant, and a majority of the men were already standing, but another (by whose unquestionably authentic cowboy costume Sally was sure she recognised Trego) rose and silently surrendered to her his place.

She accepted it with a stifled murmur of thanks.

The slight stir occasioned by her addition to the company subsided, and the sense of constraint became even more marked. Nobody appeared to care to know his neighbour; there was no whispering, no murmuring, even the indispensable fidgeting was accomplished in an apprehensive and apologetic manner. A few men breathed audibly, a few fans stirred imperceptibly an atmosphere supercharged with radiations from so many human bodies added to the natural heat of a summer's evening; there were no other sounds or movements of any consequence. Sally became uncomfortably susceptible to the undercurrent of high nervous tension, conscious of a slight dew on her hands and forehead, and surprisingly conscious of the sonorous thumping of her heart. Unaccountably, nobody else seemed to hear it.

Perhaps they were all listening to their own hearts. But why …?

She wasted a few moments vainly scrutinising the masks in her immediate neighbourhood. Their eyes gleamed uncannily through the slits in the black silk, and when she intercepted a direct glance, it was hastily lowered or averted, as if there were something indecorous in acknowledging her bewildered appeal.

Again, perhaps, they were as much puzzled by her incognito as she was by theirs.

Those small shapes of black, silk-covered cardboard proved singularly effective, even when they concealed no more than the nose and the cheeks immediately beneath the eyes. She found it surprisingly difficult to fix an identification, even when satisfied she could not be in error; but she was measurably sure of Mrs. Artemas beneath Diana's Grecian draperies, of Trego in his Western guise, of Mercedes Pride in the conventional make-up of a witch. The rest at once provoked and eluded conjecture; she fancied she knew Lyttleton in the doublet and hose of Sir Francis Drake, but could not feel certain; divested of his peculiarly well-tailored personality, he was astonishingly like half a dozen other men among the guests.

Presently Mrs. Gosnold's maid, Marie, appeared in the doorway to the bedroom, holding in her hand a number of envelopes, and at a nod from her mistress began to thread the gathering, presenting one envelope to each guest, together with a small pencil such as is commonly attached to dance-programs.

The incident provided a grateful interruption to a situation that was rapidly assuming in Sally's esteem the grotesqueness of a dream. Remembering that this was Gosnold House, the focal point of America's most self-sufficient summer colony, and that all these subdued and inarticulate masqueraders were personages daily exploited by the press as the brightest stars in the social firmament, the incongruity of this dumb gathering seemed as glaring, as bizarre as anything her fancy could conceive.

And when her envelope was handed her and she had lifted the flap and withdrawn an oblong correspondence-card bearing the monogram A-G and nothing else, the final effect of meaningless mystery seemed to have been consummated.

But this, as it happened, was coincident with the arrival of the last two guests —one of whom was a lithe and shapely Harlequin in party-coloured tights, and the other a bewitchingly blond Columbine— and then the purpose of the meeting was soon exposed.

With no more expression than she had employed in the case of Sally, Mrs. Gosnold saluted the last comers with a request to enter and be seated, then directed her maid to go out into the hall, close the door, and stand guard to prevent eavesdropping. When the door was closed she plunged directly into a prepared address.

"I owe every one an apology," she began with a fugitive, placating smile, "for all this inconvenience and nonsense—as it must seem. But I'm sure you will bear with me when you know the circumstances, which are extraordinary, and my motive, quite a natural one.

"We are now," she pursued with a swift glance that embraced the room, "just twenty-three, including myself; that is to say, everybody who slept here last night, and one or two more. And your masks are a sure screen for any betrayal of emotion when I tell you why I have asked you to oblige me by meeting here. So please retain them whatever happens."

She paused, made a little gesture of deprecation.

"I would rather almost anything than be obliged to say what I must.

"One of us," she announced deliberately, "is a thief. These rooms were entered some time last night, while I was asleep, and all my personal jewelry was stolen. Please no one interrupt. I will answer all the natural questions before I finish.

"The robbery was not difficult to accomplish."

"The Island is well-policed, there has not been a burglary in its history, and I am a careless old woman. When I take my things off at night I leave them on my dressing-table. Marie, my maid, puts them away in the morning. I have three large jewel-cases, none of which is ever locked except when I travel. I have never had a safe. The jewel-cases are stored away in unlocked dresser-drawers. My bedroom and boudoir doors are never locked. And I am a sound sleeper. There is—and was—nothing to prevent the thief from entering after I had turned out my light and, employing ordinary discretion, helping him or her self. Which is precisely what happened last night. Every piece of jewelry was taken from my dressing-table, and the three jewel-cases from their drawers."

"I discovered my loss promptly after waking up this morning. I said nothing, but after setting in motion the machinery for to-night's amusement, which I have long had in mind, devoted the day to a quiet investigation, as a result of which I am convinced that the house servants had no part in the robbery. In short, I am persuaded that the thief is now in this room. I do not, however, wish to know his or her identity. And I am especially anxious to avoid the scandal which must follow if this affair leaks out."

"Finally, I feel so sure you all share my horror of publicity and my aversion to knowing positively who committed this crime that I ask you all silently to pledge yourselves to secrecy—and then to humour my plan for regaining my jewels and covering up the affair completely. I have thought it might be accomplished this way:"

"Marie has given you each a card, an envelope, and a pencil. The cards and envelopes have no distinguishing marks. The pencils are all alike. The authorship of anything you may care to communicate cannot possibly be traced, if you will be careful not to write but to print."

"Please take the cards away with you to your rooms, and please each of you remain there at least five minutes before coming out. Then take the cards in the envelopes, sealed, down-stairs and deposit them in the mail-box. It will not be unlocked until one o'clock. By that time I shall expect the thief to have deposited my jewelry in some hiding-place about the house or grounds—a dozen will suggest themselves on a moment's thought—the spot to be indicated on the card. By this method ample time is granted in which to make restitution with complete immunity from recognition, the secret will be kept, the scandal hushed up, and, best of all, I shall be able to continue considering each and every one of you my very dear friend."

"But"—and her handsome old face darkened with the shadow of the determination that rang in her tone—"if this scheme should fail, and the thief refuse to make restitution, then, though it break my heart, I shall feel without alternative other than to take certain steps—steps which I cannot now contemplate without positive loathing, so repugnant are they to me… ."

"Now I have finished," Mrs. Gosnold said quietly. "I am sorry to have imposed in this way upon your patience, but it seemed, I think you'll grant me, warranted and necessary. I thank you, and hope you'll forgive me. And now will you please return to your rooms, without asking me any questions, and do as I have begged? And I sincerely hope that this wretched business may not interfere with your enjoyment to-night. For my part, I am so confident of the success of this scheme that I mean to consider that I have not been robbed—that everything is as it has always been, and as it will be after the envelopes are opened at one o'clock."

She ceased; there was the stir of a general rising and movement toward the door, amid a hum of excited murmurings.

CHAPTER XIII

MARPLOT

Once sheltered by the privacy of her bedchamber and seated before the little white-enamel desk with its chintz-covered fittings that suited so well the simple, cheerful scheme of decoration, the girl lingered long, an idle pencil caught between fingers infirm of purpose. Her gaze was fixed as if hypnotised to the blank white face of the bit of cardboard that lay before her on the blotting-pad, her thoughts far astray in a dark jungle of horror, doubts, suspicions, fears.

Immediately after shutting herself in she had gone straight to this desk, possessed by the notion that there was a message requiring to be written upon the card, one self-exculpatory sentence which had framed itself in her mind as she sped down the corridor from that remarkable meeting in Mrs. Gosnold's rooms.

"I have not told you everything—but I am innocent," thus ran the words which she felt were demanded of her and a legitimate privilege, her duty to herself in sheer self-preservation. And as they wrote themselves down before her mental vision she saw two heavy strokes of the pen underlining "everything," and her own true name, Sarah Manvers, following in the place of the signature—no more "Sara Manwaring," Mrs. Gosnold's explicit commands to the contrary notwithstanding.

But that had been an impulse, only natural in the first shock of horror inevitably attending the disclosure of the robbery, to clear herself; or, rather, to reaffirm her innocence.

For with second thought had come the consideration: Was she not already cleared, was her innocence not already established?

She was prepared to believe that Mrs. Gosnold knew everything. That extraordinary woman! What had she not known, indeed? Mark how cunningly she had drawn from Sally the admission that she had been up and about the house and grounds long after she had gone to her bedchamber for the night— at the very time, most probably, when the robbery was being done! And that had been by way of preface to the pledge she had made Sally of her protection before startling confession from the girl—a pledge not only given in advance, but by implication at least renewed when the truth was out.

If she had believed Sally guilty, or party to the crime, or even in possession of guilty knowledge of it, would she have made that generous promise?

She was kind of heart, was Mrs. Gosnold, but she was nobody's fool; if she had not been well satisfied in her own mind as to the thief she would never have so committed herself to Sally, for she was no one to give her word lightly or, as she herself had said, to bait a trap with fair words and flattery.

In vain Sally searched her memory for anything to warrant an assumption that her mistress had been in any way ignorant of that black business of the small hours. She had neither denied such knowledge nor asserted it, but had simply permitted Sally to leave out of her account all reference to the overnight adventure.

And all that assorted consistently with her statement that she did not wish to learn the thief's identity, as well as with her invention of a means for obtaining restitution without such intelligence.

So Sally ended by believing it rather more than possible that Mrs. Gosnold knew as well as the girl herself who had consummated the crime—or, at all events, shared the damning suspicions engendered in Sally's mind by circumstantial evidence.

Lyttleton, of course: Sally entertained but the slenderest doubts of his black guilt.

If innocent, what had he been carrying hidden in the hollow of his arm? What had he left down there on the beach? Why had he left it there? Why such anxiety to escape observation as to make the man alert to notice Sally's head peering over the parapet of the landing at the head of the cliff? And if he had been employed in no way to be ashamed of, and had no consequences to fear, why that roundabout way up the cliff again and that ambush of his watcher?

And why those signals between window and yacht, if not to apprise the latter that something had been consummated, that the coast was clear for its tender to come in and take away the plunder?

It would seem, then, that Mr. Lyttleton must have had a confederate in the house, and for that role Mrs. Standish was plainly designated. An understanding of some close sort between her and Lyttleton had been quite evident from the very first day. And whose bedchamber window had shown the signals, if not hers? Not the pretty young widow's—not in any likelihood Mrs. Artemas'. To believe the latter intimate with the affair was to assume an understanding between her and Lyttleton—or else Trego.

Trego!

Sally was conscious of a slight mental start, a flurry of thoughts and sensations, of judgment in conflict with emotions.

Why not Trego? A likelier man than Lyttleton for such a job, indeed. Trego had such force of personality as to excuse the suspicion that what he might desire he would boldly go after and possess himself of. With a nature better adapted to the planning and execution of adventures demanding courage, daring and indifference to ethical considerations, Trego was capable of anything. Lyttleton was of flimsier stuff, or instinct were untrustworthy.

But after a little the girl sighed and shook her head. It was less plausible, this effort of hers, to cast Trego for the role of villain. True, he might have invented that story of the marks on the sands; true again, he might have acted in accord with Mrs. Artemas. But those were far-fetched possibilities. Unless, indeed, professed distrust and dislike of Mrs. Artemas had been altogether ingenious, a mask manufactured in anticipation of just this development.

No, it wasn't likely of Trego. She could not overlook the impression he conveyed of rugged honesty and straightforwardness. However strong the aversion he inspired, Sally could ignore neither that impression nor yet its correlative, that if he was not an over-righteous scorner of lies, he was the sort that would suffer much rather than seek to profit by a lie.

She perceived, with a little qualm of contrition, that she had been eager to condemn the man out of sheer unreasonable prejudice, all too ready to do him injustice in her thoughts. Unpleasant though she found his personality, harshly though his crudities grated upon her sensibilities, she owed him gratitude for an intimate service in an emergency when she had been only too glad of his personal intervention; and it were rank ingratitude to wish him ill, just as it was frankly base of her to be eager to think ill of him.

Repentance had got hold of this girl by the nape of her neck; it shook her roughly, if justly. For a little time she cringed in shame of herself and was torn by desire in some way to make amends to this animal of a Trego, whom she so despised because he refused to play up to the snob in her and ape the manners of his putative betters even as she was keen to ape them.

Perhaps it had needed this ugly happening, or something as unsettling, to reveal the girl to herself in a true light—at least a light less flattering than she found pleasant.

Certainly its aftermath in the way of private communion served well to sober and humble Sally in her own esteem. Outside the immediate field of her reverie she was now conscious of the words "sycophant" and "parasite" buzzing like mosquitoes about the head of some frantic wooer of sleep, elusive, pitiless, exasperating, making it just so much more difficult to concentrate upon this importunate problem of her duty.

If she was not to protest her own innocence, what ought she to say upon that card?

Was it consistent with loyalty to Mrs. Gosnold to keep silence about matters that might clear up the mystery and repair the wrong-doing?

But how could she attack another? How bring herself to point the finger of accusation at Lyttleton?

On the terrace outside her window a stringed orchestra tuned and hummed softly in the perfumed night. Rumour of gay voices and light laughter came to her in ever greater volume. Before her distracted gaze swam a view of the formal garden, a-glimmer like a corner of fairy-land with the hundreds of tiny lamps half concealed amid the foliage of its shrubs and hedges.

She knew that she must rouse herself and be seen below; not only must her message take its place with its twenty-odd fellows in the mail-box, but nothing could seem so incriminating as prolonged and deliberate absence from the fete.

Yet she had little desire now for what two hours since had seemed a prospect of bewitching promise. The music rose and fell in magic measure without its erstwhile power to stir her pulses. There was not one in all that company below for whom she cared or who cared for her, none but whose interest in her presence or absence was as slight as hers; and her mood shrank from the thought of such casual and conventional gallantries as the affair would inevitably bring forth. She was in no humour tonight to dance and banter and coquette with an empty and desolate heart.

Thus it was made clear to her that she had never been, and never would be, in such humour; that in just this circumstance resided all her insuperable dissociation from these people of light-hearted lives; that this was why she was and forever must remain, however long and intimate her life among them, an outsider; because what she needed and demanded, the blind and inarticulate impulse which had made her aspire to their society, was not the need of a wide social life, but the need of a narrow and constricting love.

And all the love that she had thus far found in this earthly paradise had proved a delusion, a mockery and a snare.

Presently she stirred with reluctance, sighed, resigned herself to the prospect of a night of hollow, grinning merriment, and turned back to contemplation of that importunate card. And while still she hesitated, pencil poised, with neither knock nor any sort of announcement whatsoever the door flew open, and through it, like a fury in a fairy's dress, flew Mrs. Standish clothed as Columbine.

She shut the door sharply, put her back to it, and keeping her gaze fixed on the amazed girl, turned the key.

Her passion was as evident as it was senseless. Bare of the mask that swung from silken strings caught in her fingers, her face shone bright with the incandescence of seething agitation. Her eyes were hard, her mouth tight-lipped, her temper patently set on a hair-trigger.

Quite automatically, on this interruption, Sally rose and, standing, slipped the card into its envelope, an action which brought from the older woman a curt, imperative gesture.

"What have you written there?" she demanded brusquely.

Before answering Sally carried the envelope to her lips, moistened its flap, and sealed it. Thus she gained time to collect herself and compose her attitude, which turned out unexpectedly to be something cold and critical.

"Why do you ask?" she returned.

"Because I've a right to know. If it concerns me—"

"Why should it?" Sally cut in.

"You know very well that if you breathe a syllable about last night—"

"But what about last night? You came to my room while I was inexplicably out and waited till I returned. I can't see why you should care if that became known."

"Have you written anything about that?" Mrs. Standish demanded insistently.

"And even if I had, and you were merely afraid of being embarrassed, I couldn't very well drag you in without incriminating myself, now could I?"

"I don't care to bandy words with you, young woman. Tell me—"

"You needn't to please me, you know. And I shan't tell you anything."

"Why—?"

"My business," said Sally with all the insolence she knew how to infuse into her tone. "I think we covered that question rather completely last night—or rather this morning. I imagined it was settled. In fact, it was. I don't care to reopen it; but I will say this—or repeat it, if you prefer: I'm not going to permit you to interfere in my private affairs."

"You refuse to tell me what you've written?"

"For the last time—positively."

"See here," Mrs. Standish ventured, after a baffled moment: "be reasonable. There's no sense in making me lose my temper."

"I'm sure I don't wish you to."

"Then tell me-"

"No."

"Must I threaten you?"

Sally elevated supercilious eyebrows. "If you like."

"I have a way to force you to obey me."

"Oh?" There was an accent in this innocent syllable cunningly calculated to madden.

"Very well. If you will have it. Do you recall a certain letter of introduction?"

"Why—no."

"That you brought me from Mrs. Cornwallis English."

"What do you mean?"

"Don't be stupid. You surely are not prepared to deny that you came to me last Wednesday, looking for work, with what purported to be a letter of recommendation from Mrs. English."

"Please go on."

"Well," Mrs. Standish announced triumphantly, "I kept that letter, of course, and now I've had occasion to look closely, I find it's a forgery."

"Please!" Sally faltered.

"I tell you, I have safe in my possession a letter recommending you to me and signed with the forged signature of Mrs. Cornwallis English. If necessary to protect myself, I shall not scruple to exhibit that letter."

"Oh!" With a gasp of incredulity Sally sat down and stared at this impudent intrigante.

"Now will you tell me what you've written? No. I won't trust you to tell me. Give me that envelope. I'll see for myself."

"It isn't possible," Sally said, "that you would do anything so cruel and unjust and dishonest?"

"Dishonest? I dare say you consider yourself a judge."

"I can't believe it of you, Mrs. Standish."

"That's your personal affair, of course. You've asked me not to interfere... ."

She permitted Sally to think it over, meantime coming closer, holding out her hand with an effect of confident patience.

"Surely you wouldn't show that forgery you've made up to Mrs. Gosnold?"

"I don't know what you mean by 'forgery I've made up.' I shan't hesitate to show the forgery you brought me."

"I guessed all along," Sally told her, "that you were not what you made yourself out to be, neither a good woman nor a kind one. But I never for a moment imagined you would stoop to such infamy."

"Now that's settled, be good enough—"

"But what makes you so afraid I'll tell Mrs. Gosnold about last night?"

"To protect yourself, of course. I don't believe you mean to confess—"

"Confess!"

"Take advantage of this opportunity to restore the jewels—and get off without punishment. Probably you can't. Probably the man you met outside and gave them to is by now so far away that you couldn't, even if you wanted to."

"Wait a minute. Let me get this straight. I don't want to make any mistake."

"Sensible of you, I'm sure."

"You really mean to accuse me of this abominable thing?"

"I know no reason to believe you incapable of it. And you did meet a man out there last night."

"Then why do you hesitate to inform Mrs. Gosnold? Isn't it your duty?"

"I'm willing to give you the benefit of the doubt, providing you—"

"Have you consulted Mr. Lyttleton about this?"

That shot told. Mrs. Standish paused with an open mouth. "Mr. Lyttleton!" she exclaimed, recovering, in a tone that implied complete ignorance of the existence of any such person.

"Mr. Lyttleton," Sally repeated. "You know very well it was he to whom I was talking out there—and I know you know it."

"Say I do, for the sake of the argument; do you imagine Mr. Lyttleton would sacrifice himself—admit that he got up and left the house, for whatever reason, last night after going to bed—to save you?"

"No," Sally conceded; "I don't expect anything from either you or any of your friends. But Mr. Lyttleton will find the facts hard to deny. There was a witness, you must know—though I've no doubt it's news to you. He wouldn't be likely to mention that to you. In fact, I can see from your face he didn't. But there was."

"Who?" the woman stammered.

"That's for you to find out. Why not ask Mr. Lyttleton? It's no good, Mrs. Standish. I don't understand your motive, and I'd rather not guess at it; but I'm not a child to be scared by a bogy. Show your forged letter to Mrs. Gosnold, if you like—or come with me and we'll both show it to her—"

"Are you mad'? Do you want to be exposed?"

"I'm not afraid, Mrs. Standish—and you are!"

After an instant the woman's eyes clouded and fell. "I don't know what you mean," she faltered.

"I mean that this scene has gone on long enough. I'm sick and tired of it—and it isn't getting you anything, either. Good *night*!"

With this Sally marched to the door, turned the knob, and found it locked and the key missing.

"The key, please, Mrs. Standish."

"Not till you tell me—" the other began with a flash of reviving spirit.

Sally advanced a finger toward the push-button. "Must I call one of the maids to let me out?"

Capitulation was signalled with a distracted gesture. "Miss Manwaring, do tell me—"

"Nothing—I'll tell you nothing! Give me that key."

"Promise you haven't written—"

"The key!"

It was surrendered. "Well—but that jewel-case: what have you done with it?"

"I've hidden it."

"Where?"

"I'll tell you to-morrow, perhaps."

Opening the door, Sally strode out with her head high and the light of battle in her eyes.

A hesitant, pleading call followed her, but she wouldn't hear it. Pursuit and continuation of the scene, with or without another specious semblance of apology and reconciliation such as had terminated their previous passage-at-arms, was out of the question; the corridor was lively with young women in gayest plumage, fluttering to and from the dressing-rooms, and Sally was among them even before she remembered to reassume her mask.

At the head of the main staircase she paused, searching narrowly the shifting groupings of the animated scene disclosed by the wide reception-hall. She was looking for Queen Elizabeth's imperious ruff, anxious to find and keep in the shadow of that great lady's sovereign presence; and she was also looking for the leather-banded sombrero of the cowboy and the skull-cap of Harlequin, with a concern keen to avoid those gentlemen.

Considerably to her surprise, still more to her disappointment, not even the first of these was in evidence (as Sally had made sure Mrs. Gosnold would be) waiting to welcome her guests just within the doorway to the porte-cochere.

None the less, the lady must be found, and that without delay; the envelope, with its blank enclosure half crushed in Sally's hand, was an ever-present reminder of her duty first to herself, secondly to her employer. If she had written nothing, and but for Mrs. Standish would have kept her counsel till the last minute, the latter's threat of denunciation had lent the temper of the girl another complexion altogether; as Sally saw it, she no longer had any choice other than to find Mrs. Gosnold as quickly as possible and make complete the revelation of last night's doings. And her mind was fixed to this, with a cast of angry pertinacity that would prove far from easy to oppose or even to modify; whether or not the hostess wished it, she must suffer herself to be informed immediately and completely.

Threading a swift way in and out among the masks clustered upon the broad staircase in groups of twos and threes, laughing, chattering and watching the restless play of life and colour in the hall, she gained the floor and then the letter-box, near the door where she had thought to find her employer.

A distrustful scrutiny of the near-by masks failed to single out one of those she had marked and memorised in the boudoir, and without detecting any overt interest in her actions, she slipped her blameless message into the box, then turned back and, steadfast to her purpose, made her way forward through the throng to the veranda.

After the glare of the hall the dusk of the veranda was as grateful as its coolth and spaciousness. Beyond the rail the purple-and-silver night pressed close and beckoned; its breath was sweet, its pulses throbbed with the rhythmic passion of violins that sobbed and sang in hiding somewhere in the shadows. Up and down that broad, smooth flooring gay couples swayed, eye to eye and breast to breast: anachronisms reconciled by the witchery of the dance. And when Sally darted across and down the steps she found the lawns, the terrace, and the formal garden, too, peopled with paired shadows, murmurous with soft voices and low-pitched laughter.

And she who quartered so swiftly and so diligently that maze of lights and shadows found nowhere the one she wanted, but everywhere the confirmation of her secret thought—that there was no place here for her, no room, no welcome. On every hand love lurked, lingered, languished, but not for her. Whichever way she turned she saw some lover searching for his mistress, but not for her. They crossed her path and paused and stared, sometimes they spoke and looked deep into her eyes and harkened to the voice with which she answered them, giving back jest for jest—and they muttered excuses and hurried on; she was never for them.

It was as if life and fate conspired to humble her spirit and prove her ambitious of place beyond her worth; to persuade her that she was by birth, and must resign herself to remain always, Nobody.

Forlornly haunted, she circled back to the house, and on impulse sought again the boudoir door.

Marie answered, but shook her head; no, she could not say where Mrs. Gosnold might be found.

Impulse again took her out by the door to the drive. Motors were still arriving and departing, to return at a designated hour, but here, at what might be termed the back of Gosnold House—if that mansion could be said to have either back or front—here on the landward side was little light or noise or movement. And after an undecided moment on the steps beneath the porte-cochere the Quakeress stepped down and out into the blackness of the shadow cast by the western wing, a deep shadow, dense and wide from the pale wall of the house to the edge of the moon-pale lawn.

She moved slowly on through this pleasant space of semi-darkness, footfalls muffled by the close-trimmed turf, her emotions calming a little from the agitation which had been waxing ever more high and strong in her with each successive crisis of the night. Here the breeze was warm and bland, the music and the laughter a remote rumour, stars glimmered in a dome of lapis lazuli; peace was to be distilled of such things by the contemplative mind, peace and a sweet, sad sense of the beauty and pain of life. No place more fit than this could one wish wherein to shelter and to nurse bruised illusions.

Insensibly she drew near the corner of the building, in abstraction so deep and still that she was almost upon them when she appreciated the fact that people were talking just beyond that high, white shoulder of stone, and was struck by the personal significance of a phrase that still echoed in ears which it had at first found heedless: "… a Quaker costume, grey and white, with a cloak …"

It never occurred to the girl to stop and eavesdrop; but between that instant of reawakened consciousness and the moment when she came around the corner, three voices sealed an understanding:

"You've simply got to make her listen to reason . .."

"Oh, leave that to my well-known art!"

"She'll see a great light before one o'clock or I'm—"

Silence fell like a thunderclap as the Quaker Girl confronted Harlequin, Columbine, and Sir Francis Drake.

She said coolly: "You were speaking of me, I believe?"

Drake stepped back, swore in his false beard, and disappeared round the corner in a twinkling.

Columbine snapped like the shrew she masked: "You little sneak!"

And Harlequin capped that with an easy laugh: "Oh, do keep your temper, Adele. You've less tact than any woman that ever breathed, I verily believe. Cut along now; I'll square matters for you with Miss Manwaring—if it's possible."

With a stifled exclamation Columbine caught her cloak round her and followed Drake.

The accent of the comic was not lost upon the girl. She could not but laugh a little at Harlequin's undisguised discomfiture.

"So you're nominated for the office of peace-maker, Mr. Savage?"

"I'm afraid so." He shuffled, nervously slapping his well-turned calves with Harlequin's lath-sword. "I swear," he complained, "I do believe Adele is crazier than most women most of the time. She's just been telling me what a fool she made of herself with you. I'm awfully glad you turned up when you did."

"I noticed that, believe me!"

"Oh, I mean it. Ever since dinner I've been looking for an opportunity to explain things to you, but until Adele told me your costume just now—"

"Well?" Sally inquired in a patient tone as he broke off.

"We can't talk here. It's no good place—as you've just proved. Besides, I've got an appointment with another lady." He grinned gracelessly. "No, not what you think—not philandering—but in connection with this same business. I've got to butter thick with diplomacy an awful lot of mistaken apprehensions before I can set Don and Adele right, after that confounded foolishness of theirs last night—and this rotten robbery coming on top of it, to make things look black! It's a frightful, awful mixup, really, but as innocent as daylight if you only understand it. Look here, won't you give me a show to explain?"

"Why, I'm here, and I can't help listening."

"No. I mean later. I can't stop now, really."

"How much later?"

"Let's see. It's nearly midnight, and all this has got to be cleared up and set straight before one. Do be patient with me until a quarter to one, now won't you please?"

"I may be busy then."

"Oh, come! That's all swank, and you know it. Besides, you do owe me, at least, some little consideration. I don't mean that, exactly—our account's pretty well squared, the way I see it. But, after all, life's a give-and-take affair. Say you'll meet me at a quarter to one."

"Well. Where?"

He appeared to take thought. "It's got to be somewhere off the beaten track.

And you're not afraid of the dark. Would you mind coming as far as the gate on the drive?"

"Back there, beyond the trees?"

"I mean the gateway to the main road."

"I wonder why you want me there, of all places. Oh, never mind!" She forestalled a protest of injured innocence. "I'm not in the least afraid to find out. Yes; I'll be there at a quarter to one."

"You're a brick!" Savage declared fervently. "You won't regret being so decent to me. Now I'll run along and be a diplomatist."

He cut a light-hearted caper, just to prove he could, slashed the air gaily with his wooden sword, bowed low and skipped round the corner, leaving Sally even more puzzled than before but somehow placated—comforted by a sense of her own consequence conjured up by the way in which apparently she could manage people …

Savage, for instance.

CHAPTER XIV

MAGIC

For several seconds after Savage had made off Sally delayed there, alone on the empty lawn in the westerly shadow of Gosnold House, doubting what next to do, where next to turn in quest of Mrs. Gosnold; questioning the motive for that furtive meeting which she had surprised, wondering at Savage's insistence on a spot so remote and inconvenient for their appointment, and why it must needs be kept in so underhand a fashion, and whether she had been wise to consent to it and would be wise to keep it. She was at a loss how to fill in the time until the hour nominated, shrinking alike from the lights and gaiety of the hall, the supper-room and the veranda, and the romantic, love- sick peace of moonlit lawns and gardens. Altogether she was in a most complicated, distracted, uncertain and unhappy frame of mind.

Then a latch clicked softly, the hinges of a shutter whined, and the startled young woman found herself staring up into the face of Mrs. Gosnold—a pallid oval against the dark background of an unlighted window not two feet above Sally's head.

She gasped, but respected the admonition of a finger pressed lightly upon the lady's smiling lips.

"S-s-s-sh!" said Mrs. Gosnold mysteriously, with cautious glances right and left.

"There's no one here," Sally assured her in tones appropriately guarded. "You've been listening—" Mrs. Gosnold nodded with a mischievous twinkle: "I have that!"

"You heard—?"

"Something—not much—not enough. If you had only been a few minutes later..."

"I'm sorry, but I've been looking for you everywhere. Please, may I come in and tell you something?"

"Not now."

"It's very important—something you ought to know at once."

"Oh, my dear!" the woman sighed with genuine regret: "I know already far more than I care to know!"

"But this—"

"Not now, I say. I've been too frequently and too long away from my guests as it is. I'll have to show myself for a little while. Then, come to my room in half an hour."

"At half past twelve?"

"Yes, and don't be late. Now do run along and have a good time."

The shutter was drawn gently to, and Sally, with an embittered smile for the unconscious irony of that parting injunction, moved slowly on toward the front of the house.

But it was true that she felt a little less disconsolate now than she had two minutes ago; after all, it seemed, she wasn't altogether friendless and forsaken; and as for those doubts and questions which so perplexed her, they would all be resolved and answered once she had opportunity to lay them, together with the story of last night, before the judgment of her benefactress.... .

Still, if she reckoned confidently upon her hostess, she reckoned not wisely without her host, whose mask to-night was that of a sardonic destiny. And when a tentative venture into the throngs on the veranda had been discouraged by the spirited advances of a forward young Cavalier who chose to consider his honour piqued, first by her demure Quaker garb, then by her unresponsiveness, Sally was glad enough to fall back upon the comparative quiet and solitude of the moon-drenched gardens. Whereupon her destiny grinned a heartless grin and arranged to throw her to the lions that, all unsuspected, raged in the maiden bosom of Mercedes Pride.

The tireless ingenuity with which that rampant spinster devised ways and means of rendering herself a peripatetic pest had long since won the ungrudged admiration of Sally, who elected to be amused more than annoyed by the impertinences, the pretentiousness, the fawning adulation and the corrosive jealousy of Mrs. Gosnold's licensed pick-thank. And when she had first divined the woman beneath the disguise of the witch Sally had wondered what new method of making a sprightly nuisance of herself Miss Pride had invented to go with her impersonation.

It proved, naturally enough, remembering the limitations of a New England maiden's imagination, to be compulsory fortune-telling with the aid of cards, a crystal ball, the palm of the victim's hand, unlimited effrontery, and a "den" rigged up in a corner of a hedge with a Navajo blanket for a canopy and for properties two wooden stools, a small folding table, a papier-mache skull, a jointed wooden snake, an artificial pumpkin-head with a candle in it, and a black cat tethered by a string to a stake in the ground and wishing he had never been born.

Within this noisome lair the sorceress squatted and practised her unholy arts upon all comers without mercy or distinction as to race, caste, sex, age, colour, or previous condition of servitude. And when trade slackened (as inevitably it did when "the young people" for whose "amusement" this mummery ostensibly was staged asserted their ennui by avoiding the neighbourhood) Ecstatica, nothing daunted, would rise up and go forth and stalk her prey among the more mature, dragging them off forcibly by the hand, when needs must, to sit at her table and sympathise with the unfortunate cat and humour her nonsense.

Thus she inveigled Sally when the latter unwarily wandered her way.

Miss Pride knew her victim perfectly, but for the sake of appearances kept up the semblance of mystification.

"Sit you there, my pretty," she grabbed vivaciously, two hands on Sally's shoulders urging her to rest on one of the stools. "Don't be afraid of my simple magic; the black art has nothing to do with the lore of the wise old woman. Just show me your rosy palm, and I will tell you your fortune. No, you needn't cross my palm with silver; I will ply my mystic trade and tell your future all for the sake of your pretty eyes."

She peered, blinking with make-believe myopia, into the hollow of Sally's hand.

"Ah, yes, yes!" she grunted, "you have an amiable and affectionate disposition; you love pretty things to wear and every sort of pleasure. There is your gravest fault and greatest danger, pretty: love of clothes and pleasure and—forgive the wise old woman's plain speaking—false ambitions. Beware of the sin of vain ambition; only wrong and unhappiness can come of that. No, no; don't draw your hand away. I have not finished. Let me look closer. There is much written here that you should know and none but my wise old eyes can read, pretty."

Effrontery battened on indulgence:

"The past has been unfortunate. The present is bright with misleading glamour—beware of the vanities of the flesh! The future—I see a shadow. It is dark. It is difficult to read. I see a journey before you—a long journey; you will cross water and travel by the steam-cars. And there is a lover waiting for you at the journey's end—not here, but far away. I cannot see him clearly, but he waits. Perhaps later, when I consult my magic sphere of crystal. But wait!"

She breathed hard for a moment, perhaps appreciating her temerity; but she was as little capable of reading Sally's character as her palm.

"I see danger in your path," she resumed in accents of awe; "the shadow of something evil—and a window barred with iron. I cannot say what this means, but you should know. Look into your heart, my pretty; think. If perhaps you have done something you should not have done, and if you would not suffer shame for it, you must make all haste to undo that which you have done—"

"Miss Pride!" Sally interrupted hotly, snatching her hand away. "You—"

"No, no. I have no name!" the other protested in the falsetto she had adopted to suit her impersonation; "I am only the wise old woman who tells the future and the past and reads the secrets ..."

But the white anger that glowed in Sally's countenance abashed her. The shrill tones trailed off into a mumble. She looked uneasily aside.

"You must not be angry with the poor old wise woman," she stammered uncertainly.

"You know very well what you have said," Sally told her in a low voice vibrant with indignation. "You know very well you have deliberately insulted me."

"No, no!"

"You know who I am and what your insinuation means, after what has happened here to-night. Miss Pride! Do you dare accuse me—?"

"Oh, no-please!" Mercedes begged, aghast, quaking in realisation of the enormity of her mistake. "I didn't think—I didn't know you—I didn't mean —"

"That," Sally cut in tensely, "is a deliberate falsehood. You inveigled me into this for the sole purpose of insulting me. Now I mean to have you repeat your accusation before witnesses. I shall inform Mrs. Gosnold—"

"Oh, no, Miss Manwaring! I beg of you, no! I didn't mean what you think, indeed I didn't!"

Sally made to speak, choked upon her indignation, and gulped.

"That's a lie!" she declared huskily; and rising fled the place.

She went a few hasty paces blindly, then remembering she mustn't make an exhibition of herself, however great the provocation, checked her steps and went on at a less conspicuous and precipitate rate.

But still her vision was dark with tears of rage and mortification, and still her bosom heaved convulsively. Now and again she stumbled.

Twice since nightfall the abominable accusation had been flung into her face, the unthinkable thing imputed to her, and this last time out of sheer, gratuitous spleen, the jealous spite of a mean-minded old maid. For Miss Pride had no such excuse as Adele Standish had for thinking Sally capable of infamy— unless indeed, Mrs. Standish had proved false to her pledge and had told people. But no; she'd never do that; not, at least, while the settlement of her insurance claim remained in abeyance.

The brutality of it!

A strong hand closing unceremoniously on her wrist brought Sally to a standstill within two paces of the low stone wall that guarded the brink of the cliff.

"Look where you're going, Miss; Manwaring!" Trego's voice counselled her quietly. Then, seeing that she yielded readily, he released her. "I beg your pardon," he said, "but in another minute if I hadn't taken the liberty of stopping you, you might have hurt yourself."

She managed to mutter an ungracious "Thank you."

"It's none of my business," Trego volunteered with some heat, "but I'd like to know what that vicious old vixen found to say to upset you this way."

"Oh, you were watching."

"No; I just happened to be sticking round when you flew out of that fool sideshow of hers like you were possessed. And then I saw you weren't paying much attention where you were going, and I was afraid. Hope you don't mind my butting in."

"Not at all," she gulped. "I suppose I ought to be grateful."

"That's just as you feel about it," he allowed reasonably.

She made an effort to collect herself. "But I am grateful," she asserted. "Please don't think I mean to be rude. Only," she gulped again, overcome by the stinging memory of that woman's insolence, "I'd almost as lief you hadn't stopped me—and that wall wasn't there!"

"Now, now!" he reminded her. "It can't be as bad as all that, you know."

"Well, but think how you would feel if you'd been twice accused of stealing Mrs. Gosnold's jewels last night!"

"Once would be plenty," he said gravely. "I don't reckon anybody would say that twice to my bare face."

"Yes—but you can resent insults like a man."

"That's right, too. But then it's the only way I know to resent 'em—with my fists. That's where you women put it all over us men; you know a hundred different ways of sinking the poisoned barb subtly. I wouldn't like to be that Pride critter when you get through with her."

There was unquestionably a certain amount of comfort to be gained by viewing the case from this angle. Sally became calmer and brightened perceptibly.

"Perhaps," she murmured in an enigmatic manner becoming in the putative mistress of unutterable arts.

"It's just like that shrivelled old shrew. What you might expect. If I had thought of it in time, I'd've been willing to make a book on her laying it to you."

"But why?" Sally protested perplexedly.

"Sure, I don't have to tell you why," he said diplomatically. "You know as well as I do she's plumb corroded with jealousy of you for winning out with her dear Abigail just when she thought she had things fixed. I don't suppose you know the inside story of how your predecessor got the sack? The Pride person was responsible. Miss Matring was in her way, and a good deal of her own disposition to boot. It was a merry war, all right, while it lasted—scheming and squabbling and backbiting and tattling and corrupting servants to carry tales—all that sort of thing. To be honest about it, I don't just know which was the worse of the two; they didn't either of them stick at much of anything noticeable. But, of course, Miss Matring was handicapped, not being blood-kin, and the upshot was she had to go—and until you showed up the old maid was actually miserable for want of somebody to hate. I noticed the light of battle in those beady little eyes of hers the minute she laid 'em on you. I'd have warned you, only ..."

He stumbled. She encouraged him: "Why didn't you?"

She didn't like Trego—that was understood—but sympathy was very sweet to her just then, whatever its source, and she had no real objection to disparagement of her slanderer, either.

"Well, it wasn't my fight. And I didn't know how you'd take interference. You looked pretty well able to take care of yourself—in fact, you are. And then—I don't reckon it's going to do me any good to say this; but I might as well make a clean breast of it—I was just selfish enough to have a sneaking sort of hope, deep down, that maybe you'd find it so unpleasant you'd quit."

"Mr. Trego!" No more than that; he had taken her breath away.

"I guess that does sound funny," he admitted, evading her indignant eye. "You can't trust me, ever. I always say things the wrong way; that's the best thing I do."

"If it's possible for you to explain ..."

"It's possible, all right, but it's anything but easy. What I meant was ... Well, any fool could see that as long as you were so strong for this society racket I didn't stand much show."

"Show?"

"Of making good with you. Oh, look here, what's the use of beating about the bush? I'm a rude, two-fisted animal, and that's all against me. I never could flummux up my meaning successfully with a lot of words like—well, name no names. All the same, it's pretty hard for a fellow who knows the girl he's sweet on isn't crazy about him to come out in plain talk and say he loves her."

She was dumb. She stared incredulously at his heavy, sincere, embarrassed face, as if it were something abnormal, almost supernatural, a hallucination.

"Meaning" he faltered, "I mean to say—of course—I love you, Sar—er—ah —Miss Manwaring—and I think I can make you happy—"

He was making heavy weather of his simple declaration, labouring like an old-fashioned square-rigger in a beam sea.

"If you'll marry me, that is," he concluded in a breath, with obvious relief if with a countenance oddly shadowed in the staring moonlight by the heat of his distress.

She tried, she meant to give him his answer without delay; it were kinder. But she found it impossible; the negative stuck stubbornly in her throat. She knew it would stab him deep. He wasn't the man to take love lightly; his emotions were anything but on the surface; their wounds would be slow to heal.

And in spite of the positive animus she had all along entertained toward him, she didn't want to hurt him now; perhaps not strangely, remembering that this proposal of marriage was a direct, down-right protestation of implicit faith in her, uttered squarely on top of a most damnable indictment—remembering, too, that it was barely two hours since Sally herself had been ready, almost eager, to believe him capable of committing the very crime of implication in which he exonerated her without an instant's hesitation.

True, she had been quick to exonerate him in her thoughts as soon as the suspicion was engendered in them, but she had done so almost reluctantly, ungenerously, not because she wanted to believe him innocent, but because the burden of the evidence, together with the counsel of instinct, had been too strong in his favour to permit more than a moment's doubt. And she had repented; but that, it appeared, was not enough; she must be punished in this unique way, have her own unworthiness demonstrated by this artless manifestation of his worth. And however much she might long to make amends to him, she couldn't.

The pain and the pity of it! He was a far better man than she a woman, and he honoured her with his love—and she couldn't requite him, she couldn't love him; he was still too far from the mirage of her ideal.

"Oh!" she sighed. "Why?"

He misconstrued. "I've told you heaps of times—because you're a woman, not a manikin. Marriage would mean something more to you than clothes, Europe, idleness, and flirting with other women's husbands, just as it would have to mean more to me than hiring a woman to live with me and entertain my friends."

"How do you know? How can you tell? What do you know about me?" she protested almost passionately, and answered herself. "You don't know; you can't tell; you know nothing about me. You assert things—I only wish they were true—"

"Oh, they're true enough," he interrupted unceremoniously. "It's no use trying to run yourself down to me. I couldn't feel the way I do about you if you were not at heart as sound as an apple, no matter what nonsense you may have been guilty of at one time or another, as every human being's got to be."

"Has nobody told you anything about me? Mrs. Gosnold—?"

"Mrs. Gosnold 'tends to her own knitting. And nobody has told me anything —except yourself. More than that, I don't go by other folks' opinions when I make up my mind about a matter as vital to me as marrying a wife."

"Then I must tell you—"

"Not until you give me some legitimate title to your confidence. You've got no right to confide in me unless you mean to marry me—and you haven't said you would yet."

"I can't—I couldn't without telling you—please let me speak!" She drew a long breath of desperation and grasped the nettle firmly. "I stole the clothes I came here in. My name isn't Manwaring—it's Sally Manvers. I was a shop-girl—"

"Half a minute. Mrs. Gosnold knows all this, doesn't she?"

"Yes—"

"You told her everything, and still she stood for you?"

"Yes, but—"

"That's enough for me. I don't want to hear anything more until you're my wife. After that you'll have to tell me—and if there's any trouble remaining to be straightened out then, why, it'll be my natural job as a husband to fix it up for you. Till then I won't listen to any more of your confidences that have nothing whatever to do with the fact that I love you and believe in you and want to make you happy."

"But don't you understand that a girl who would steal and lie in order to get into society—"

"Oh, everybody's got to be foolish about something or other. You'll get over this social craze. The more you see of it the more sure your cure. Now don't mistake me; I'm not for an instant implying that some of the finest people that ever walked God's green earth don't figure in what we call Society; and there are more of them on this little island, perhaps, than anywhere else in America; and I'd be the last to cry them down or pretend I'm not glad and proud of their acquaintance and friendship. The trouble is, they can't in the nature of things keep up their social order without attracting a cloud of parasites, snobs, and toadies—and that's what makes me sick of the whole social game as practised to-day."

"And you can't understand that I am precisely what you've described—a parasite!"

"You couldn't be if you wanted to. Maybe you think you could, but you're wrong; you haven't got it in you."

Against such infatuation candour was powerless. She retreated to the last ditch. "But you told me your father's heart was set on your marrying a society woman!"

"Well, what of that? You don't suppose I think any of them have got anything on you, do you? Besides, dad isn't altogether an old idiot, and if the kind of society woman he wants me to marry wouldn't look at me, and if my happiness is at stake ... Well, even if he did want to ruin my life by hitching me up in double harness to a clothes-horse, I wouldn't let him!"

"But if I want—"

"There isn't anything you want that I can't get you. If you like this sort of thing, you shall have it. And don't run away with the idea that I'm not strong for society myself—the right sort."

Her gesture was hopeless. "What can I say to you?"

He suggested quietly, not without humour: "If you don't mind, say yes."

"You don't know what you're doing, making me such an offer. Suppose I married you for your money ..."

"You won't do that. You can't."

"What do you mean?"

"You've got to love me first. And you're too fine and honest to pretend that for the sake of my money."

Of a sudden his tone changed. "Oh, forgive me!" he pleaded. "I was a fool to ask. I might have known—I did know you didn't care for me. Only, I hoped, and I guess a man in love can't help letting his hopes make him foolish, especially when he sees the girl in trouble of some sort, needing what he can give her, love and protection—and when it's moonlight and there's music in the air!"

He checked himself with a lifted hand and stood for a moment, half smiling, as if made suddenly conscious of the pulsing rapture of those remote violins.

"*That's* what's made all the mischief," he complained: "that, and the way you look. It isn't a fair combination to work on a fellow, you know. Please don't say anything; you've said enough. I know very well what you mean, but I'd rather not hear it in one word of two letters—not to-night. I'm just foolish enough to prefer to go on hoping for a while, believing there was a bare chance I had misunderstood you."

He laughed half-heartedly, said "Good night" with an admirable air of accepting his dismissal as a matter of course, and marched off as abruptly as if reminded of an overdue appointment.

No other manoeuvre could have been more shrewdly calculated to advance his cause; nothing makes so compelling an appeal to feminine sympathies as a rejected suitor taking his punishment like a man; the emotional affinity of pity has been established ever since the invention of love.

Sally sank down mechanically upon a little marble seat near the spot where they had stood talking and stared without conscious vision out over the silvered sea.

Her thoughts were vastly unconcerned with the mysterious behaviour of Mrs. Standish and her brother, the inexplicable insolence of Mercedes Pride, the shattered bubble of her affair with Donald Lyttleton, the kindness of Mrs. Gosnold, or the riddle of the vanished jewelry.

Now and again people passed her and gave her curious glances. She paid them no heed. The fact that they went in pairs, male and female after their kind, failed to re-excite envy in her bosom.

There is deep satisfaction to be distilled from consciousness of the love of even an unwelcome lover.

She thought no longer unkindly but rather pitifully of poor, tactless, rough-shod Mr. Trego.

When at length she stirred and rose it was with a regretful sigh that, matters being as they were with her, she was unable to reward his devotion with something warmer than friendship only.

Friendship, of course, she could no more deny the poor man... .

CHAPTER XV

FALSE WITNESS

Sally failed, however, fully to appreciate how long it was that she had rested there, moveless upon that secluded marble seat, spellbound in the preoccupation of those thoughts, at once long and sweet with the comfort of a solaced self-esteem, for which she had to thank the author of her first proposal of marriage.

She rose and turned back to Gosnold House only on the prompting of instinct, vaguely conscious that the night had now turned its nadir and the time was drawing near when she must present herself first to her employer with the tale of last night's doings, then to Savage to learn his version of the happenings in New York.

But by the time she reminded herself of these two matters she found that they had receded to a status of strangely diminished importance in her understanding. It was her duty, of course, a duty imposed upon her by her dependent position as much as by her affection for the lady, to tell Mrs. Gosnold all she knew without any reservation whatever; and it was equally her duty to herself, as a matter of common self-protection, to hear what Savage professed such anxiety to communicate. And not quite definitely realising that it was Mr. Trego's passion which overshadowed both of these businesses, she wondered mildly at her unconcern with either. Somehow she would gladly have sealed both lips and ears to them and gone on basking uninterruptedly in the warmth of her sudden self-complacence.

By no means the least remarkable property of the common phenomenon of love is the contentment which it never fails to kindle in the bosom of its object, regardless of its source. In a world where love is far more general than aversion, wherein the most hateful and hideous is frequently the most beloved, it remains true that even a king will strut with added arrogance because of the ardent glance of a serving-wench.

And so, failing to realise her tardiness, it was not unnatural that Sally, entering the house by that historic side door and ascending the staircase that led directly to her bedchamber, should think to stop a moment and consult the mirror for confirmation of Mr. Trego's implicit compliments.

As one result of this action, instigated in the first instance less by vanity than by desire to avoid the crowds at the main entrances, Sally uncovered another facet of mystery.

On entering, she left the side door heedlessly ajar, and there was enough air astir to shut it with a bang as she turned up the staircase. Two seconds later that bang was echoed by a door above, and a quick patter of light footfalls followed. But by the time Sally gained the landing there was no one visible in the length of the corridor from end to end of that wing.

Now the door of the room opposite her was wide open on a dark interior. And the room adjoining was untenanted, as she knew. It seemed impossible that the second slam could have been caused by any door other than that of her own bedchamber. Yet why should anyone have trespassed there but one of the housemaids? And if the trespasser had been a housemaid, why that sudden and furtive flight and swift disappearance from the corridor?

Her speculations on this point were both indefinite and short-lived. She thought her hearing must have deceived her; a hasty look round the room discovered nothing superficially out of place, and the little gilt clock on her dressing-table told her that she was already seven minutes behind time. She delayed only for one hasty survey of the flushed face with star-bright eyes that the mirror revealed, and then with an inarticulate reflection that, after all, one could hardly blame Mr. Trego very severely, Sally caught up her long dark cloak and made off down the corridor, past the head of the main staircase, to the door of Mrs. Gosnold's boudoir.

A voice sharp with vexation answered her knock; she entered to find its owner fuming, and not only that, but surprisingly *en déshabillé*. The dress of Queen Elizabeth was gone, and Mrs. Gosnold stood on the threshold of her bedchamber clothed simply in undergarments and impatience.

"Why are you so late?" she demanded. "I was beginning to be afraid … But thank Heaven you're here! You very nearly spoiled everything, but there's still time. Come in."

She led the way into her bedchamber, and without acknowledging Sally's murmur of startled apology, waved an impetuous hand at her.

"Quick!" she demanded. "Get out of that costume at once!"

Her maid was already at Sally's side, fumbling with pins and hooks, before the girl recovered from her astonishment sufficiently to seek enlightenment.

"But what's the matter? What have I done? What—?"

"Nothing much—merely almost upset the applecart for me!" Mrs. Gosnold laughed in grim humour, her own fingers busily aiding the maid's. "Come, step out of that skirt, please. If you'd been two minutes later … I'm simply going to pretend I'm you for ten minutes or so," she explained, lowering the shimmering gray Quaker skirt over her own shoulders. "I'm going to meet Walter Savage in your stead."

"But—"

"But me no buts. I heard enough there at the window, before you came on the scene, to make me very suspicious of that young rascal, even more so than I had every right to be from what you had told me. Now I mean to learn the rest, find out precisely what devilment he's up to."

"He only wants to tell me—"

"There's nothing he can possibly have to say to you that he couldn't have said a hundred times tonight in as many corners of the house and grounds without a soul hearing a word or thinking it odd that two young people should be exchanging confidences—and both of you masked into the bargain."

Sally, now entirely divested of her masquerade, resignedly shrugged herself into the black silk cloak for lack of a better negligee.

"I don't understand what you can suspect," she said dubiously.

"I don't suspect anything; but I'm going to find out everything."

"But aren't you afraid—"

"Of what, pray'?" Mrs. Gosnold demanded with appropriate asperity.

"I mean, don't you think he'll know?"

"Nothing in the shadow of those trees, with my mask and that cape to disguise the fact that I'm a bit more matronly than yourself—worse luck!"

"But your voice—"

"Haven't you ever read about 'guarded accents' in novels? Those will be mine, precisely, when I talk to my graceless nephew. I shan't speak once above a whisper—and I defy any man to tell my whisper from yours or any other woman's for that matter. Don't flatter yourself, my dear! I shall fool him perfectly; there's precious little to choose between any two women in the dark!"

Already she was almost finished dressing, and as yet Sally hadn't had a chance to breathe a word about her own information.

"But there's something I must tell you," she insisted, suddenly reminded.

"About what?"

"Last night—things that happened after everybody had gone to bed. You knew I was restless. I saw several things I haven't told you about. You ought to know. They may clear up the mystery of the theft."

"I already know all about that," Mrs. Gosnold declared calmly.

"About Mr. Lyttleton and the boat and the signals—"

Mrs. Gosnold turned sharply from her mirror. "What's this? Why didn't you tell me before?"

"I didn't know about the robbery, and I thought it was none of my affair—"

"It doesn't matter." Mrs. Gosnold caught up her cloak and threw it to the maid to adjust on her shoulders. "Whatever you saw had nothing to do with the robbery. Don Lyttleton's a bad lot in more ways than one, but he didn't steal my jewels last night—that I know."

"But who did?"

"I hope you may never find out."

"You know, then?"

"Positively." The lady adjusted her mask and caught her cloak about her. "Wait here till I come back. Then you may tell me about Don Lyttleton and the boat and the signals. I'll be as quick as I can."

She darted hurriedly away.

The wonder excited by Mrs. Gosnold's declaration that she knew the identity of the thief—even though, the girl told herself, she had all along suspected as much—kept Sally quiet for the next several minutes. She was sorely tempted to question the maid, but one look at that quiet, impassive countenance assured her that this would be wasted breath.

Insensibly the tempo of a haunting waltz that sang clear in the night beyond the open windows wove itself into the texture of Sally's thoughts and set her blood tingling in response.

She recalled Trego with a recurrent glow of gratification.

Poor fellow!

One foot began to tap the floor in time to the music. She hadn't danced once that night, had purposely avoided every chance of an invitation to dance. And now, of a sudden, she wanted to, without reason or excuse.

It was very curious. She wondered at herself. What had worked this change? Was it really nothing more nor less than a declaration of love on the part of a man she—didn't altogether like?

Though, of course, she hadn't ever been quite fair to him. He had admirable qualities. His honesty. His scorn of pretence and subterfuge. His simple faith in Sally Manvers, however misplaced.

If he were to beg a dance when Mrs. Gosnold had returned and Sally, recostumed, had rejoined the maskers, she hardly knew how she could in decency refuse him now... .

147

The clock on the mantelpiece struck a single stroke.

Sally started and looked up, to meet Marie's questioning glance.

"One o' clock?"

"Yes, Miss Manwaring."

"Then—why, she's been gone over fifteen minutes."

"Yes, miss."

What could Savage have found to say to Sally that her substitute need delay so long to hear it?

Sally frowned.

At the end of another five minutes the maid volunteered uneasily: "It's very odd. Mrs. Gosnold didn't expect to be away more than five or ten minutes, I know. She said as much before you came in."

Sally got up and went to a window which overlooked the driveway and lawn. Parting the curtains, she glanced out. The lawn was fair with moonlight, the driveway silver-blue, the woods behind dark and still. There was a closed car waiting at one side of the porte-cochère. The others—all those belonging to Gosnold House, as well as those of guests for the fete—were hidden among the trees bordering the road or parked in the open spaces around the garage and stables at a considerable remove from the house.

There was no one to be seen on the lawn or drive, no hurrying figure cloaked in Quaker grey.

After some minutes of fruitless watching Sally ventured doubtfully: "What time is it?"

"Ten past one, miss."

"Nearly half an hour—"

"Yes, miss."

"Do you think Mrs. Gosnold would mind if you went to make sure she was all right?"

"I don't know, Miss Manwaring. She doesn't like interference, if I may make so bold as to say so."

A little later, however, the woman added tentatively: "I wouldn't care to take the responsibility, myself, of going to see."

"But if I order you to go—"

"Yes, miss," Marie smiled.

"Then I do order you to go. But don't be long."

"No, miss."

Sally waited in a mood of constantly increasing anxiety. It was absurd to think that anything untoward could have happened to Mrs. Gosnold on her own grounds, meeting her own nephew for a clandestine talk. And of course she might have learned something from Savage which had induced her, for her own ends, to maintain her masquerade for a longer time. She was quite possibly somewhere on the terrace or in the formal garden.

Marie was back within five minutes, wearing an apprehensive countenance.

"There's nobody out back, miss, near the road, where she said she was to meet Mr. Savage, and I asked Thomas and some of the waiters, and they all said they hadn't seen her."

"But in my costume and masked ..."

"It's past one, miss, already, and everybody has unmasked."

"To be sure. I'm going to my room and get into another dress. Then I'll look round for her myself."

"If you'll be so kind, miss—without letting on—"

"Of course."

"Mrs. Gosnold would be very indignant if any mistake was made."

Sally caught her cloak tightly about her, and because of its unconventionality as a costume, resumed her mask against the chance of meeting anybody in her passage through the corridor to the far wing of the building.

She fairly ran in her impatience, and through this haste was brought to the head of the main staircase at the precise moment when an unmasked Harlequin was about to set foot upon the upper landing.

Mr. Savage was smiling quietly to himself and slapping his calves lightly with his lath-sword; nothing in his manner excused the suspicion that he was not perfectly satisfied with himself and all his circumstances.

Somewhat reassured by the vision of this amiable countenance, Sally paused, and won a glance of quizzical inquiry, with especial application to the mask which she still wore in defiance of the rule.

But when she spoke in her natural voice that look was erased from the features of Mr. Savage as chalk-marks may be erased from a blackboard.

"Oh, Mr. Savage, if you please—"

"Wha-at!" the man ejaculated blankly, stopping short and dropping his make-believe weapon.

"I'm looking for Mrs. Gosnold. Have you seen her anywhere about?"

"Mrs. Gos—! Aunt Abby!" He choked and gasped. "But you—who are you?"

"I thought you must know my voice."

Sally removed her mask, and incontinently Savage fell back against the banister-rail and grasped it for support.

"Miss Manvers! But—what—how the devil did you get back here?"

"I haven't been out."

She pulled up on the verge of frank explanation; it was quite possible that Mrs. Gosnold might furiously resent betrayal of her stratagem. And yet Savage's look of pure fright only augmented Sally's solicitude for her employer.

"You haven't been out! But ten minutes ago—out there—behind the trees—"

She shook her head and tried to smile a superior sort of a smile: "It wasn't I who met you."

The man made a gesture of hopeless confusion, and she could not but remark his surprising loss of colour. Suddenly he stepped to her side and seized her roughly by the arm.

"Then who was it'?" he demanded furiously. "If it wasn't you—who then? Damn it, you'd better tell me—!"

"Let go my arm!" she demanded with a flash of temper that was instantly respected. "If you must know," she went on, reckless at consequences, "it was your aunt who met and talked to you out there. Don't you understand? She borrowed my costume and went to meet you in my place."

"Oh, my God!"

Savage was now chalky pale. He seemed to strive, to say more, but failed for the constriction of his throat. For another instant he stared incredulously, then, without a word of explanation or apology, he turned and flung himself headlong down the steps!

Before reaching the middle landing, however, he checked himself on the reflection that he must avoid attracting attention, and went on more slowly, if still with many a symptom of nervous haste.

At the bottom he turned aside and was quickly lost in, the crowd.

Unable to pursue, dressed as she was, Sally went on to her room in a mood of dark perplexity.

Surely it would seem that Savage must have been engaged in some very damnable business indeed, and have given himself away irremediably to Mrs. Gosnold, thinking her Sally, to exhibit such unmitigated consternation on discovery of his error.

But what could it have been? Sally could imagine nothing in their admittedly singular relations which, being disclosed to the aunt, should so completely confound the nephew.

Mrs. Gosnold had suggested no insufferable resentment of the deception practised upon her, when informed of it by Sally. And why, therefore, Mr. Savage should comport himself as if the heavens had fallen on learning that he had betrayed himself unconsciously to his aunt, was something that passed Sally's comprehension.

And the strange flavour of the affair alarmed her: first, Mrs. Gosnold's unexplained (but, after all, not inexplicable) failure to return to her room on time; then this panic of Savage's.

It was patently the girl's immediate business to find one or the other or both of them and make sure that nothing was radically wrong after all.

By happy chance her very prettiest evening frock didn't hook up the back; she was able to struggle into it not only without assistance, but within a very few minutes.

Then, scurrying back to Mrs. Gosnold's room, she read in the apprehensive eyes of the maid, even before this last could speak, the news that the mistress was still missing, and so, darting down-stairs, began industriously to search the house and grounds.

By this hour few signs were wanting that the festival was on its wane; already cars were arriving and departing, laden with the very youngest and the oldest people; there was perceptibly more room on the dancing-floor of the veranda, which was populated chiefly by the younger set; in the supper-room the more rowdy crowd hung on with numbers undiminished and enthusiasm unabated if liberally dampened; about the grounds there was far less movement, far more lingering in sequestered nooks and shadows. Ecstatica, for one, had folded her tent, liberated her black cat to the life of a convinced misogynist, and vanished into the shades of night.

But nowhere was any sign to be found of anyone of those three whom Sally sought—Mrs. Gosnold or Savage or, failing these, Mrs. Standish.

Now when she had nearly completed one exhaustive round of the grounds and was wondering where next to turn, with neither warning nor expectation she came around one end of a screen of shrubbery and stopped just short of surprising another sentimental tableau, staged in the identical setting used for Mr. Trego's declaration and cast with a change of but one mummer.

And in the instant marked by recognition of that selfsame marble seat commanding that same view of silvered sea and bathed in the light of that same heartless moon, Sally seemed to hear the echo of her destiny's sardonic laughter.

The gentleman was Mr. Trego, the lady Mrs. Artemas; and they were ignorant of Sally's observation for the simple reason that Mr. Trego's back was toward her and the head of Mrs. Artemas was pillowed on his shoulder—her arms white bonds around his neck.

And as if this were not enough, Sally's discovery of them anticipated by the barest moment the appearance of another couple around the farther end of the clump of shrubbery—two people who happened to be husband and wife and known to Sally as recent additions to the house-party.

These, too, stopped sharply and would have considerately withdrawn but for the fact that, standing as he did, Trego could not help seeing them. He spoke a word, presumably, in the ear so near his lips. The woman swung away in a twinkling, breaking from his arms but retaining one of his hands, and faced the two with a little excited laugh that sounded almost hysterical; and Sally noted that her eyes were bright with tears—of happiness, of course.

"Oh!" she cried, laughing and confused, "is it you, Mrs. Warrenden? No, please don't run. It's too late now—isn't it—when you've caught us in the act! You and Mr. Warrenden will be the first to know of our happiness …"

Sally heard no more. The scene vanished from her vision as if the moonlight had been extinguished. It was some moments before she realised that she was running madly, as if hoping flight might help her exorcise that ironic vision. But when she did realise what she was doing, she but ran the faster; let people think what they would; she no longer cared; their esteem no more mattered, for she was finished with them one and all—yes, even with Mrs. Gosnold!

Blindly instinct led her back to her room, again via that side door.

She flung tempestuously into its friendly darkness, locked herself in, and dropped, spent and racked, upon the edge of the bed, clenching her hands into two hard, tight fists, gritting her teeth, and fighting with all her strength to keep back the storm that threatened of sobs and tears and nervous laughter.

It wasn't as if she had really cared for the man—it was worse. It was the sum of all the blows her poor, struggling pride had suffered in the course of the last twenty-four hours, beginning with her awakening to the worthlessness of Lyttleton and realisation of the low esteem in which he held her, and culminating in this facer from one whose love she had refused but none the less prized for the comfort it gave her.

Nor was this all. In addition to the writhings of an exacerbated vanity, she was conscious of a sense of personal loss, as if a landmark had been razed in the perspective of her life. In spite of those faults and shortcomings, so unduly emphasised through the man's own deliberate intent and so inexcusable in one who appreciated so well what was expected of a man in his position, Sally had subconsciously from the very first felt Trego to be one whose faith and loyalty were as a rock, whose friendship might be counted upon as an enduring tower of refuge.

And to have him go from her, protesting passionate patience, leaving her exalted with the consciousness that she was wanted—to have him go thus from her and straightway fall into the trap which Mrs. Artemas unaffectedly baited—the trap of which he had not once but many times obliquely alluded to in half-humorous, half-genuine terms of fear—it was, or seemed to be, intolerable.

The waves of burning emotion that swept and scorched her were alternately of rage and chagrin.

Granted the opportunity, she could easily conceive herself as dealing very vigorously with the mantrap.

Some one rattled the knob of her door. Startled, Sally jumped up, and with her wadded handkerchief dabbed hastily and superfluously at her eyes, which were quite dry as yet.

She did not answer, but eyed apprehensively the dark recess in which the door was set at the end of her unlighted room.

A knock followed the noise of the knob. Still she hesitated to reply. Uncertainly she moved toward the nearest wall-sconce and lifted her hand to the switch. She was sadly confused and unstrung, her thoughts awhirl and nerves ajangle. The last thing she wished just then was to meet and talk to anybody.

Still it might be Mrs. Gosnold or her messenger. And that lady was Sally's one remaining friend on earth. She swallowed hard, took herself firmly in hand, and when the knock was repeated was able to answer in a tolerably even voice:

"Well? Who is it?"

"Miss Manwaring, are you there?" Heartfelt relief informed the voice of Mrs. Standish. "Please let me in. I must speak with you immediately."

Sullenly, without replying, Sally turned on the light, moved to the door, unlocked and opened it.

"Come in," she said ungraciously.

Mrs. Standish swept in, gay crimson domino over fluffy skirts and slim, pink legs assorting oddly with the agitation betrayed by her unsmiling eyes, her pallor accentuating the rouge on her cheeks like rose-petals against snow.

"Thank God!" she whispered, "I've found you at last. I've looked everywhere for the last half-hour. This is the second time I've been here. You just got in, of course. Where *have* you been?"

"Does it matter?" Sally fenced, maintaining a stony countenance. "I mean, I don't think it does, now you've run me to earth at last. What's the trouble?"

"You haven't seen Walter? He hasn't told you?"

"No; I tried to speak to him half an hour ago, but he ran from me as if I were a ghost!"

"You know why!" The woman's voice trembled with restrained rage. "You impossible girl! Why, why did you let Aunt Abby go to meet him instead of you? It was fatal, it was criminal. Of course, he gave the whole show away to her, never guessing. Now it's all up with us; we'll never be asked here again; and the chances are she'll cut us out of her will as well. Why did you do it? Oh, I could shake you!"

"I know well you would if you could," Sally admitted calmly. "Only-better not try."

"But why—?"

"Well, if you must know, Mrs. Gosnold overheard you three plotting together out there just before I came on the scene. She was at the window overhead, listening through the shutters. I don't know what you were talking about—she didn't tell me—but it was enough to make her insist on my giving her my costume so that she might go and hear the rest of it."

Mrs. Standish bit her lip. And her eyes shifted uneasily from Sally's face.

"You haven't seen her since—"

"No," Sally answered bluntly. "Have you?"

"No. Walter and I have both been looking for her as well as you. That's why he ran when he knew about this terrible mistake; he wanted to find her and set things straight if he could. But she"—the woman stumbled and her eyes shifted again—"she's gone and hidden herself—plotting our humiliation and punishment, I dare say. I only wish I knew. Walter is still hunting everywhere for her. See here: I presume you understand you've got to go now?"

"Why?"

"For one good reason—if what has happened isn't enough to persuade you— because there will be a man here from New York by the first boat—seven o'clock to-morrow morning—with a warrant for the arrest of Sarah Manvers."

"Are you telling the truth, Mrs. Standish?"

"How dare you! No, I won't let you make me lose my temper with your insolence. The matter is too serious, and I've no wish to see you suffer, even if you have ruined everything for us. You must listen to me, Miss Manvers: be advised and go. I don't know what put them on your trail, what made them suspect you were here, but the burglary-insurance people had the warrant sworn out yesterday afternoon and started a man up by the evening boat. Walter got a telegram to that effect about ten o'clock. That's what he wanted to say to you—that, and to give you some money and directions for getting away."

"But why should I leave?"

"Do you want to go to jail?"

"Not much. But I don't see why I need. You can easily explain that my things in the bath-room were left there with your knowledge at the time when you took pity on me and gave me a change of clothing to travel in."

"It's too late. If we had explained it that way, to begin with, it would have been all right. But neither of us thought. And Walter bungled things frightfully in New York. Now if we come forward with any such story they'll think we're all in a conspiracy to defraud the company."

"Oh!" Sally exclaimed abruptly, with an accent of enlightenment that discountenanced the older woman.

With an effort, recovering, she sought to distract the girl.

"Surely you must see now, you have got to go! There's a boat to the mainland at six thirty. If you catch that, you'll have three hours' start; for the detective won't be able to get off the island before half past nine. And you ought to be able to lose yourself in that time somehow. Hurry; I'll help you pack a satchel. You'd better wear that blue serge; everybody wears blue serge, so it's inconspicuous. And here's some money for travelling expenses."

Sally ignored the little fold of bills held out to her.

"I'm not going," she declared firmly.

"Are you mad?"

"I would be to go with the situation what it is here. Don't you see that, unless those jewels are returned to Mrs. Gosnold to-night—yes, I mean the jewels you were so ready to accuse me of stealing a little while ago; but you seem to have forgotten that now—"

"I wish you would," Mrs. Standish replied, schooling her voice to accents of dulcet entreaty. "I was beside myself with anxiety—"

"Wait. If I go before those jewels are recovered—disappear, as you want me to—it will be equivalent to a confession that I myself stole them. And suppose I did."

"What!"

"I say, suppose I did, for the sake of argument. What right have you to assume that I didn't commit the theft? No more than you had to accuse me as you did. And until the theft is made good, what right have you to let me go and, possibly, get away with my loot? No!" Sally shook her head. "You're not logical, you're not honest with me. There's something behind all this. I'm not going to be made a scapegoat for you. I'm not going to run away now and hide simply to further your plans for swindling the burglary-insurance company. I'll see Mrs. Gosnold and advise with her before I stir a step."

"Oh, you are insufferable!" Mrs. Standish cried.

In a flash she lost control of her temper altogether. Her face grew ghastly with the pallor of her rage. And she trembled visibly.

But what else she might have said to the defiant girl was cut short by the sudden and unceremonious opening of the door to admit three persons.

The first and last of these were Mercedes Pride and Mr. Lyttleton. Between them entered a man unknown to Sally—a hard-featured citizen in very ordinary business clothing, cold of eye, uncompromising of manner.

Jubilation glowed in the witch's glance; anticipative relish of the flavour of triumph lent her voice a shriller note. She struck an attitude, singling out Sally with a denunciatory arm.

"There she is! That's the woman who calls herself Sara Manwaring. Now arrest her—make her confess what she's done with those jewels—pack her off to jail!"

CHAPTER XVI

THE PLANT

The very sharpness of the attack shocked Sally into such apparent calm as she might not have been able even to simulate had she been given more time to prepare herself.

After that first involuntary start of surprise and indignation she stood quite still, but with a defiant chin well elevated and her shoulders back, and if she had in her turn grown pale, it was less with fright than with the contained exasperation that lighted the fires in her eyes as they ranged from face to face of the four.

Lyttleton, she noticed, lingered uneasily near the door, hanging his head, avoiding her glance, almost frankly shamefaced.

The spinster posed herself with arms akimbo and smirked superciliously at the badgered girl, malicious spite agleam in her little black eyes.

Mrs. Standish had fallen back on the interruption and now half stood, half rested against the dressing-table, her passion of a moment ago sedulously dissembled. She arched an inquiring eyebrow and smiled an inscrutable smile, questioning the proceedings without altogether disapproving them.

Nearer Sally than any of these, the strange man confronted the girl squarely, appraising her with an unprejudiced gaze.

"If you please—" she appealed directly to him.

"Miss Manwaring, I believe?" he responded with a slight, semi-diffident nod.

Silently Sally inclined her head.

"That's the name she gave when she came here, at least," Mercedes commented.

Sally addressed Lyttleton. "Please shut the door," she said quietly, and as he obliged her, looked back to the stranger.

"Mason's my name, miss," he went on: "operative from Webb's Private Investigation Agency, Boston. Mrs. Gosnold sent for me by long-distance telephone this morning. I've been here all evening, working up this case on the quiet. The understanding was that I wasn't to take any steps without her permission; but she left it to me to use my best judgment in case her little plan for getting a confession didn't work. So I thought I'd better not wait any longer, seeing how late it is and how long after the time limit she set—and all."

"Do I understand Mrs. Gosnold gave you permission to break into my room with—these people?" Sally demanded.

"No, miss—not exactly. As I say, she told me to use my best judgment in case the jewels weren't returned. And, as I've said, it was getting late, and Mrs. Gosnold nowhere to be found, and I thought I'd better get busy."

"Mrs. Gosnold has disappeared?"

"Well, you might call it that. Anyway, we can't seem to find any trace of her. I've got an idea that maid of hers knows something, but if she does she won't talk to me. And considering that, and everything—the circumstances being so unusual all around—it seemed to be up to me to take some steps to make sure nothing was wrong."

He faltered, patently embarrassed by a distasteful task.

"Well?" Sally insisted coolly. "Still you've given me no reason for this outrageous intrusion and accusation."

"No, miss; I'm coming to that. You see, the first thing was to get that letter-box opened and examine those envelopes. I got several of the gentlemen to act as a sort of a committee, so as nobody could kick on the ground that everything wasn't done open and aboveboard."

"You found no confession, I gather?" Mrs. Standish interpolated.

"No, ma'am—no confession. All but two of the cards were blank. The two had something written on them—anonymous information, so to speak. I brought them along so that Miss Manwaring would understand, in case there was any mistake, it wasn't my fault."

He fumbled in a pocket, brought forth the cards, and with some hesitation handed them over to Sally.

Both bore messages laboriously printed in pencil, of much the same tenor:

"Suggest you look into Miss Manwaring's antecedents—also her actions between one and three o'clock last night."

"Ask Miss Manwaring what she was doing out of bed after one last night—search of her room might prove helpful."

Silently Sally returned the cards.

"You see," the detective apologised heavily, "after that, there wasn't anything for it but to ask you to explain."

"There is nothing to explain; the charge is preposterous."

"Yes, miss—that is, I hope so, for your sake. All the same, I had to ask you. Most of the gentlemen present when I opened the envelopes seemed to think I ought to do something at once. Personally, I'd rather have consulted Mrs. Gosnold before putting it up to you this way."

"I'm afraid you will find that would have been wiser."

"Yes, miss, perhaps. But she being absent and no way of finding out when she was liable to be back and the case left in my hands, to act on my discretion, providing no confession was made—"

"Still, I advise you to wait. If you think you must do something, why not employ your talents to find Mrs. Gosnold?"

"Well—that's so, too; and I would, only it was suggested that maybe she hadn't disappeared really, but was just keeping out of sight until this business was settled, preferring not to be around when anything unpleasant was pulled off. Like this."

Sally shrugged.

"Very well," she said indifferently. "What then?"

"I'd like to ask you some questions."

"Spare yourself the trouble. I shan't answer."

"You might make things easier for all of us, miss, yourself included."

"I promise faithfully," Sally said, "to answer any questions you may care to ask fully, freely, truthfully—in the presence of Mrs. Gosnold. Find her first. Until you do, I refuse to say a word."

"I don't suppose you'd mind telling me how you came to get your job as secretary to Mrs. Gosnold."

True to her word, Sally kept her lips tight shut.

At this, Miss Pride felt called upon to volunteer: "Mrs. Standish ought to be able to tell you that, Mr. Mason. She brought Miss—Manwaring here."

"I'm sure," Mrs. Standish said with an elaborate air of indifference, "I know little or nothing about Miss Manwaring." But Sally's regard was ominous. She hesitated, apparently revising what she had at first intended to say. "She came to me last week—the day we left New York—with a letter of recommendation purporting to be from Mrs. English—Mrs. Cornwallis

English, the social worker, who is now in Italy."

"Purporting?" iterated the detective.

"Oh, I have no reason to believe it wasn't genuine, I'm sure."

"Have you the letter handy'?"

"I don't think I have," Mrs. Standish replied dubiously. "Perhaps. I can't say. I'll have to look. I'm careless about such matters."

"That's all you know about her?"

"Practically. She seemed pleasant-spoken and intelligent. I took a fancy to her, gave her an outfit of clothing, brought her here and introduced her to my aunt, who personally engaged her, understanding all the circumstances. That is the limit of my responsibility for Miss Manwaring."

Sally drew a deep breath; at all events, the woman had not dared repeat any of her former abominable accusations; if she was unfriendly, she was also committed to a neutral attitude: no more talk of a forged letter, no more innuendo concerning Sally's "accomplice" of the night before.

There was a pause. The detective scratched his head in doubt.

"All this is very irregular," he deprecated vaguely.

Miss Pride opened her mouth to speak, but Lyttleton silenced her with a murmured word or two. She sniffed resentfully but held her peace.

"I can't accept your apology;" Sally returned with dignity. "But I'm sure you have no longer any excuse for annoying me."

But Mr. Mason held his ground. "The trouble is," he insisted, "after those cards had been read, one of the gentlemen said he had seen you out in the garden between two and three o'clock."

"Mr. Lyttleton!" Sally accused with a lip of scorn.

"Why, yes," the detective admitted.

Mrs. Standish made a furious gesture, but contrived to refrain from speech.

"I suppose I shouldn't have mentioned it," Lyttleton said blandly, looking Sally straight in the face. "But the circumstances were peculiar, to say the least, if not incriminating. I saw this cloaked figure from my window. I thought its actions suspicious. I dressed hurriedly and ran down in time to intercept Miss Manwaring at an appointment with a strange man. I didn't see his face. He turned and ran. While I was questioning Miss Manwaring Mr. Trego came up and misconstrued the situation. We had a bit of a row, and before it was cleared up Miss Manwaring had escaped."

Sally's sole comment was an "Oh!" that quivered with its burden of loathing.

"Sorry," Lyttleton finished cheerfully; "but I felt I had to mention it. I dare say the matter was innocent enough, but still Miss Manwaring hasn't explained it, so far as I know; I felt it my duty to speak."

To the inquiring attitude of the detective Sally responded simply: "Find Mrs. Gosnold."

"Yes, miss," he returned with the obstinacy of a slow-witted man. "Meantime, I guess you won't mind my looking round a bit, will you?"

"Looking round?"

"Your room, miss."

Sally gasped. "You have the insolence to suggest searching my room?"

"Well, miss—"

"I forbid you positively to do anything of sort without Mrs. Gosnold's permission."

"There!" Miss Pride interpolated with sour satisfaction. "If she has nothing to fear, why should she object?"

"Do be quiet, Mercedes," Mrs. Standish advised sweetly. "Miss Manwaring is quite right to object, even if innocent."

"You see, miss," Mason persisted, "I have Mrs. Gosnold's authority to make such investigation as I see fit."

"I forbid you to touch anything in this room."

"I'm sorry. I'd rather not. But it looks to me like my duty."

She perceived at length that he was stubbornly bent on this outrageous thing. For a breath she contemplated dashing madly from the place, seeking Trego, and demanding his protection.

But immediately, with a sharp pang, she was reminded that she might no longer depend even on Trego.

As the detective tentatively approached her dressing-table the girl swung a wicker armchair about so that it faced a corner of the room and threw herself angrily into it, her back to the four.

Immediately, as if nothing but her eye had prevented it theretofore, the search was instituted.

She heard drawers opened and closed, sounds of rummaging. She trembled violently with impotent exasperation. It was intolerable, yet it must be endured. There was one satisfaction: they would find nothing, and presently Mrs. Gosnold would reappear and their insolence be properly punished.

She could not believe that Mrs. Gosnold would let it pass unrebuked. And yet …

Of a sudden it was borne in upon the girl that she had found this little island world a heartless, selfish place, that she had yet to meet one of its inhabitants by whom her faith and affection had not been betrayed, deceived and despised.

Remembering this, dared she count upon even Mrs. Gosnold in this hour of greatest need?

Had that lady not, indeed, already failed her protegee by indulging in the whim of this unaccountable disappearance?

Must one believe what had been suggested, that she, believing her confidence misplaced in Sally, was merely keeping out of the way until the unhappy business had been accomplished and the putative cause of it all removed from Gosnold House?

Behind her back the futile business of searching her room, so inevitably predestined to failure and confusion, was being vigorously prosecuted, to judge by the sounds that marked its progress. And from the shifting play of shadows upon the walls she had every reason to believe that Miss Pride was lending the detective a willing hand. If so, it was well in character; nothing could be more consistent with the spinster's disposition than this eagerness to believe the worst of the woman she chose to consider her rival in the affections of Mrs. Gosnold. A pitiful, impotent, jealousy-bitten creature: Sally was almost sorry for her, picturing the abashment of the woman when her hopes proved fruitless, her, fawning overtures toward forgiveness and reconciliation. Possibly she had been one of the two to accuse Sally on the cards.

The other? Not Mrs. Standish. She would hardly direct suspicion against the girl she despised when by so doing she would imperil her own schemes. She was too keenly selfish to cut off her nose to spite her face. Sally could imagine Mrs. Standish as remaining all this while conspicuously aloof, overseeing the search with her habitual manner of weary toleration, but inwardly more than a little tremulous with fear lest the detective or Mercedes chance upon that jewel-case and so upset her claim against the burglary-insurance concern.

Lyttleton, too, would in all likelihood be standing aside, posing with a nonchalant shoulder against the wall, his slender, nicely manicured fingers stroking his scrubby moustache (now that he had discarded the beard of Sir Francis, together with his mask) and not quite hiding the smirk of his contemptible satisfaction—the satisfaction of one who had lied needlessly, meanly, out of sheer spite, and successfully, since his lie, being manufactured out of whole cloth, could never be controverted save by the worthless word of the woman libelled.

More than probably Lyttleton had been the other anonymous informant.

And whatever the outcome of this sickening affair (Sally told herself with a shudder of disgust) she might thank her lucky stars for this blessing, that she had been spared the unspeakable ignominy of not finding Mr. Lyttleton out before it was too late.

Trego, too; though she could consider a little more compassionately the poor figure Trego cut, with his pretensions to sturdy common sense dissipated and exposing the sentimentalist so susceptible that he was unable to resist the blandishments of the first woman who chose to set her cap for him. Poor thing: he would suffer a punishment even beyond his deserts when Mrs. Artemas had consummated her purpose and bound him legally to her.

For all that, Sally felt constrained to admit, Trego had been in a measure right in his contention, though it had needed his folly to persuade her of his wisdom. She was out of her element here. And now she began to despair of ever learning to breathe with ease the rarefied atmosphere of the socially elect. The stifling midsummer air that stagnated in Huckster's Bargain Basement was preferable, heavy though it was with the smell of those to whom soap is a luxury and frequently a luxury uncoveted; there, at least, sincerity and charity did not suffocate and humbler virtues flourished.

Bitterly Sally begrudged the concession that she had been wrong. All along she had nourished her ambition for the society of her betters on the conviction that, with all her virtues, she was as good as anybody. To find that with all her faults she was better, struck a cruel blow at her pride.

A low whistle interrupted at once her morose reflections and the mute activity of the search.

Immediately she heard the detective exclaim: "What's this?"

Miss Pride uttered a shrill cry of satisfaction; Mrs. Standish said sharply: "Aunt Abby's solitaire!"

To this chorus Mr. Lyttleton added a drawl: "Well, I'm damned!"

Unable longer to contain her alarm and curiosity, Sally sprang from her chair and confronted four accusing countenances.

"What do you know about this?" the detective demanded.

Clipped between his thumb and forefinger a huge diamond coruscated in the light of the electrics.

Momentarily the earth quaked beneath Sally's feet.

Her eyes were fixed on the ring and blank with terror; her mouth dropped witlessly ajar; there was no more colour in her face than in this paper; never a countenance spelled guilt more damningly than hers.

"Yes!" Miss Pride chimed in triumphantly.

"*What* have you to say to this, young woman?"

Sally heard, as if remotely, her own voice ask hoarsely: "What—what is it'?"

"A diamond ring," Mason responded obviously.

"Aunt Abby's," Mrs. Standish repeated.

Mason glanced at this last: "You recognise it?"

The woman nodded.

"Where did you find the thing?" Sally demanded.

"Rolled up inside this pair of stockings." Mason indicated the limp, black silk affairs which he had taken from a dresser-drawer. "Well, how about it?"

"I don't know anything about it. I tell you I never saw it before."

The detective grinned incredulously. "Not even on Mrs. Gosnold's finger?"

"No—never anywhere."

"Mrs. Gosnold seldom wears the ring." Mrs. Standish put in; "but it is none the less hers."

"Well, where's the rest of the stuff'?" Mason insisted.

"I don't know. I tell you, I know nothing about that ring. I have no idea how it got where you found it. Somebody must have put it there." Sally caught her distracted head between her hands and tried her best to compose herself. But it was useless; the evidence was too frightfully clear against her; hysteria threatened.

"Mrs. Standish gave me the stockings," she stammered wildly, "rolled up as you found them. Ask her."

"Oh, come, Miss Manwaring; you go too far!" Mrs. Standish told her coldly. "If you are possibly innocent, compose yourself and prove it. If you are guilty, you may as well confess and not strain our patience any longer. But don't try to drag me into the affair; I won't have it."

"I guess there isn't much question of innocence or guilt," Mason commented. "Here's evidence enough. It only remains to locate the rest of the loot. It'll be easier for you," he addressed Sally directly, "if you own up—come through with a straight story and save Mrs. Gosnold trouble and expense."

He paused encouragingly, but Sally shook her head.

"I can't tell you anything," she protested. "I don't know anything. It's some horrible mistake. Or else—it's a plant to throw suspicion on me and divert it from the real thief."

"Plant?" Miss Pride queried with a specious air of bewilderment.

"Thieves' jargon—manufactured evidence," Lyttleton explained.

"Ah, yes," said the old maid with a nod of satisfaction.

"If it's a plant, it's up to you to show us," Mason came back. "If it isn't, you may as well lead us to the rest of it quick."

"You've looked everywhere, I presume?" Lyttleton inquired casually.

"Everywhere I can think of in this room and the bath-room," the detective averred; "and I'm a pretty good little looker. That's my business, of course. I'm willing to swear there's no more jewelry concealed anywhere hereabouts."

"Unless, perhaps, she's got it on her person."

"That might be, of course," Mason allowed, eying the girl critically. "But somehow I don't think so. If she had, why would she have left this one piece buried here? No; you'll find she's hidden the rest of the stuff somewhere— about the house or grounds, maybe—or passed it on to a confederate, the guy you saw her talking to last night, as like as not and held out this ring to make sure of her bit when it comes to a split-up."

"Still," Lyttleton persisted, "ought you to take any chances?"

"Well ..." The detective shuffled with embarrassment. "Of course," he said with brilliant inspiration, "if these ladies will undertake the job ..."

Miss Pride stirred smartly. "It's not what I want to do," she insisted, "but if you insist, and on dear Abigail's account ..."

With a tremendous effort Sally whipped her faculties together and temporarily reasserted the normal outward aspect of her forceful self.

"I will not be searched," she said with determination. "With Mrs. Gosnold present—yes, anything. Find her, and I'll submit to any indignity you can

165

think of. But if Mrs. Standish and Miss Pride think I will permit them to search me in her absence ..."

She laughed shortly. "They'd better not try it—that's all!" and on this vague threat turned away and threw herself back into the chair.

"I'm sure," Miss Pride agreed, "I'd much rather not, for my part. And dear Abigail is so peculiar. Perhaps it would be best to wait till she gets back."

"Or hunt her up," Lyttleton amended.

"I guess you're right," Mason agreed, a trace dubiously.

"But what will you do with the girl in the meantime? Take her to jail?"

"No; I guess not yet—not until we see what Mrs. Gosnold thinks, anyway. She ought to be safe enough here. That door locks; we'll take the key. She can't get out of the window without risking her neck—and if she did make a getaway uninjured, she can't leave the Island before morning. Let's move along, as you say, and see if we can't find Mrs. Gosnold."

Skirts rustled behind Sally's sullen back and feet shuffled. Then the door closed softly and she heard the key rattle in the lock.

She sat moveless, stunned, aghast.

Strangely, she did not weep; her spirit was bruised beyond the consolation of tears.

The wall upon which her vacant vision focused was not more blankly white than her despair was blankly black. She was utterly bereft of hope; no ray penetrated that bleak darkness which circumscribed her understanding.

Now the last frail prop had been knocked from under her precarious foothold in the faith and favour of Mrs. Gosnold.

As to the identity of the enemy who had done this thing Sally entertained not a shadow of doubt, though lacking this proof she could not have believed she owned one so vindictive, ruthless and fiendishly ingenious.

But after what had happened it seemed most indisputable that Lyttleton, not content with avenging his overnight discomfiture by an unscrupulous lie, had deliberately plotted and planted this additional false evidence against the girl to the end that she might beat out her life against the stone walls of a penitentiary.

For who would not believe his word against hers? Lyttleton had stolen the jewels: what else had he carried so stealthily down to the beach? What else had those signals meant but that they had been left there in a prearranged spot? For what else had the boat put in from the yacht to the beach? As for the window of the signals, it might well have been Lyttleton's, which adjoined the row of three which Sally had settled upon; and she had delayed so long after seeing him disappear on the beach that he must have had ample time to return to his room, flash the electric lights, and come out again to trap the one he knew had been watching him.

And if he hadn't stolen the jewels, what else was that "private matter" which he had been so anxious to keep quiet that he was resigned to purchase Sally's silence even at the cost of making love to her? And if not he, who had been the thief whose identity Mrs. Gosnold was so anxious to conceal that she had invented her silly scheme for extracting an anonymous confession?—her statement to the contrary notwithstanding that Lyttleton had not stolen the jewels and that she knew positively who had! The man was a favourite of Mrs. Gosnold's; she had proved it too often by open indulgence of his nonsense. He amused her. And it seemed that in this milieu the virtue of being amusing outweighed all vices.

Why else had Mrs. Gosnold refused to listen to the story Sally was so anxious to tell her about her precious Don Lyttleton? She must have known, then, that Sally was under suspicion. Miss Pride had known it, or she would not have found the courage to accuse the girl under the guise of fortune-telling; and what Mercedes knew her dear Abigail unfailingly was made a party to. And knowing all this, still she had sought to protect the man at the girl's expense.

And all the while pretending to favour and protect the latter!

Now, doubtless, the truth of the matter would never come out.

In panic terror Sally envisaged the barred window of the spinster's prophecy.

To this, then, had discontent with her lowly lot in life brought her, to the threshold of a felon's cell.

Surely she was well paid out for her foolishness... .

After some time she found that she had left her chair and was ranging wildly to and fro between the door and window. She halted, and the mirror of her dressing-table mocked her with the counterfeit presentment of herself, pallid and distraught in all the petty prettiness of her borrowed finery.

In a sudden seizure of passion she fairly tore the frock from her body, wrecking it beyond repair.

Then, calmed somewhat by reaction from this transport, she reflected that presently they would be coming to drag her off to jail, and she must be dressed and ready.

Turning to her wardrobe, she selected its soberest garments—the blue serge tailleur advised by Mrs. Standish—and donned them.

This done, she packed a hand-bag with a few necessities, sat down, and waited.

The minutes of that vigil dragged like hours.

She began to realise that it was growing very late. The guests of the fete had all departed. The music had long since been silenced. Looking from her window, she saw the terrace and gardens cold and empty in the moonlight.

And at this sight temptation to folly assailed her and the counsels of despair prevailed.

There was none to prevent the attempt, and the drop from window-sill to turf was not more than twelve feet. She risked, it was true, a sprained ankle, but she ran a chance of escaping. And even if she had to limp down to the beach, there were boats to be found there—rowboats drawn up on the sand—and there was the bare possibility that she might be able to row across the strait to the mainland before her flight was discovered.

And even if overtaken, she could be no worse off than she was. Everyone believed her guilty; there was no way for her to prove her innocence.

She might better chance the adventure.

On frantic impulse, without giving herself time to weigh the dangers, Sally switched off her light, sat down on the window-sill, swung her legs over, and let herself down until she hung by both hands from the sill.

And then she repented. She was of a sudden terribly afraid. Remembering too late the high heels of her slippers, she discounted the certainty of a turned ankle—which would hurt frightfully even if it failed to incapacitate her totally. For the life of her she could not release her grasp, though all ready the drag of her weight was beginning to cause most perceptible aches in the muscles of her arms.

She panted with fright—and caught her breath on a sob to hear herself called softly from below.

"Miss Manwaring! For the love of Mike—!"

Trego!

She looked down and confirmed recognition of his voice with the sight of his upturned face of amazement. He stood almost immediately beneath her. Heaven—or the hell that had brewed her misadventures—alone knew where he had come from so inopportunely. Still, there he was.

"What are you doing? What's the matter?" he called again—and again softly, so that his voice did not carry far.

She wouldn't answer. For one thing, she couldn't think what to say. The explanation was at once obvious and unspeakably foolish.

Her hands were slipping. She ground her teeth and kicked convulsively, but decorously, seeking a foothold that wasn't there on the smooth face of the wall.

At this his tone changed. He came more nearly under and planted himself with wide-spread feet and outstretched arms.

"You can't hold on there any longer," he insisted. "Let go. Drop. I'll catch you."

Only the mortification of that prospect nerved her aching fingers to retain their grip as long as they did—which, however, was not overlong.

She felt herself slipping, remembered that she mustn't scream, whatever happened, experienced an instant of shuddering suspense, then an instantaneous eternity wherein, paradoxically, part of her seemed still to be clinging to the window-ledge while most of her was spinning giddily down through a bottomless pit, saw the grinning moon reel dizzily in the blue vault of heaven—and with a little shock landed squarely in the arms of Mr. Trego.

He staggered widely, for she was a solidly constructed young person, but he recovered cleverly—and had the impudence to seem amused. Sally's first impression on regaining grasp of her wits was of his smiling face, bent over hers, of a low chuckle, and then—to her complete stupefaction—that she was being kissed.

He went about that business, having committed himself to it, in a most business-like fashion; he kissed (as he would have said) for keeps, kissed her lips hungrily, ardently, and most thoroughly; he had been wanting to for a long time, and now that his time was come he made the most of it.

She was at first too stunned and shocked to resist. And for another moment a curious medley of emotions kept her inert in his arms, of which the most coherent was a lunatic notion that she, too, had been wanting just this to happen, just this way, for the longest time. And when at length she remembered and felt her anger mounting and was ready to struggle, he disappointingly set her down upon her feet.

"There!" he said with satisfaction. "Now that's settled—and a good job, too!"

She turned on him furiously.

"How dared you-!"

169

"Didn't I deserve it, catching you the way I did?" he asked, opening his eyes in mock wonder. "And didn't you deserve it for being so silly as to try anything like that?" He jerked his head too ward that window. "What on earth possessed you—?"

"Don't you know? Don't you understand?" she stormed. "I'm accused of stealing Mrs. Gosnold's jewels—locked up. You knew that surely!"

"What an infernal outrage!" he cried indignantly. "No, I didn't know it. How would I? I"—he faltered—"I've been having troubles of my own."

That drove in like a knife-thrust the memory of the scene in the garden with Mrs. Artemas. The girl recoiled from him as from something indescribably loathsome.

"Oh!" she cried in disgust, "you are too contemptible!"

A third voice cut short his retort, a hail from above. "Hello, down there!"

With a start Sally looked up. Her window was alight again, and somebody was leaning head and shoulders out.

"Hello, I say! Is that the Manwaring woman '? Stop her; she's escaping arrest!"

Trego barred the way to the gardens; and that was as well (she thought in a flash) for now the only hope for her was to lose herself temporarily in the shadows of the shrubbery.

The thought of the trees that stood between the grounds and the highway was vaguely in her mind with its invitation to shelter when she turned and darted like a hunted rabbit around the corner of the house.

Before Trego regained sight of her she was on the lawns. Crossing them like the shadow of a wind-sped cloud, she darted into the obscurity of the trees and vanished. And Mr. Trego, observing Mr. Lyttleton emerge from under the porte-cochere and start in pursuit, paused long enough deftly to trip up that gentleman with all the good will imaginable and sent him sprawling.

Frantic with fright, her being wholly obsessed by the one thought of escape, Sally flew on down the drive until, on the point of leaving the grounds by the gate to the highway, she pulled up perforce and jumped back in the nick of time to avoid disaster beneath the wheels of a motor-car swinging inward at a reckless pace.

Involuntarily she threw a forearm across her eyes to shield them from the blinding glare of the headlamps. In spite of this she was recognised and heard Mrs. Gosnold's startled voice crying out: "Miss Manwaring! Stop! Stop, I say!"

With grinding brakes the car lurched to a sudden halt.

Weak, spent, and weary, the girl made no effort to consummate her escape, realising that it had been a forlorn hope at best.

CHAPTER XVII

EXPOSE

Some little time later there filed into the boudoir of the hostess of Gosnold House a small but select troupe of strangely various tempers.

Mrs. Gosnold herself led the way, portentous countenance matching well her tread of inexorable purpose but in odd contrast to the demure frivolity of her Quaker costume.

Sally followed, nervously sullen of bearing toward all save her employer.

Mr. Walter Arden Savage came next, but at a respectable distance, a very hang-dog Harlequin indeed, a cigarette drooping disconsolately from the corner of his mouth.

At the door he stood aside to give precedence to his sister, no longer Columbine, but a profoundly distressed and apprehensive blonde person in a particularly fetching negligee.

Miss Pride alone wore her accustomed mien—of sprightly spinsterhood—unruffled.

Mr. Lyttleton was almost too much at ease; Mr. Mason was exceedingly dubious; Mr. Trego was, for him, almost abnormally grave.

This last, bringing up the rear of the procession, closed the hall door at a sign from Mrs. Gosnold. The company found seats conspicuously apart, with the exception of Mrs. Standish and Savage, likewise Mercedes, who stuck to her dear Abigail as per invariable custom. Sally, on her part, found an aloof corner where she could observe without being conspicuous.

"So," said Mrs. Gosnold, taking her place beside the desk and raking the gathering with a forbidding eye. "Now if you will all be good enough to humour me without interruption, I have some announcements to make, some news to impart, and perhaps a question or two to ask. It's late, and I'm tired and short of temper, so you needn't be afraid I won't make the proceedings as brief as possible. But there are certain matters that must be settled before we go to bed to-night."

She managed a dramatic pause very effectively, and then: "I've been kidnapped," she announced.

Murmurs of astonishment rewarding her, she smiled grimly.

"Kidnapped," she iterated with a sort of ferocious relish. "At my age, too. I don't wonder you're surprised. I was. So were my kidnappers, when they found out who they were making off with. For, of course, it was a mistake. They were conventional kidnappers, with not. an ounce of originality to bless themselves with, so naturally they had meant to kidnap a good-looking youngster—Miss Manwaring, in fact."

She nodded vigorous affirmation of the statement. "So I'm told, at least; so Walter tells me; and he ought to know; he claims to have been the moving spirit in the affair. When he found out his mistake, of course, he posted off after me to rectify the hideous error, and arrived just in time to effect a dramatic rescue. And then he had to confess... .

"The whole business," she went on, "from beginning to end, was very simple, childishly simple. In fact, ridiculous. And sickening. You're not going, Adele?" she interrupted herself as Mrs. Standish rose.

Without answer her niece moved haughtily too ward the door. Mrs. Gosnold nodded to Trego.

"Oh, yes, let her go. I'm sure I've no more use for her. But half a minute, Adele; the car will be ready to take you and Walter to the nine-thirty boat to-morrow morning."

There was no answer. The door closed behind Mrs. Standish, and her aunt calmly continued:

"It seems that Adele's notorious extravagance got her into hot water shortly after she divorced Standish and had only her private means to support her insane passion for clothes and ostentation in general. She went to money-lenders—usurers, in fact. And, of course, that only made it worse. Then Walter, who has never been overscrupulous, conceived the brilliant notion of squaring everything up for a new start by swindling the burglary-insurance people. Adele has always carried heavy insurance on her jewelry—almost the only sensible habit she ever contracted. And so they conspired, like the two near-sighted idiots they were... .

"On the afternoon of the day they were to start for the Island they gave all the servants a night off, and contrived to miss connection with the Sound steamer. Then they went to the Biltmore for dinner, and when it was dark Walter sneaked back home to burglarise the safe. I understand he made a very amateurish job of it. Into the bargain, he was observed. It seems that the servants had carelessly left the scuttle open to the roof, and Miss Manwaring, caught in a thunder-storm, had taken shelter in the house—which was quite the natural thing, and no blame to her. In addition, a real burglar presently jimmied his way in, caught Walter in the act of rifling his own safe, and forthwith assaulted him. Walter and the jewels were only saved by the intervention of Miss Manwaring, who very bravely pointed a pistol at the real burglar's head, and then, having aided Walter to turn the tables, ran away. So far, good; Walter booted the burglar out of the house, loaded up with the jewels, and left to rejoin Adele. But fate would have it that he should meet Miss Manwaring again in the Grand Central Station."

She paused for breath, then summed up with an amused smile: "There was a most embarrassing contretemps: a broken desk and empty safe at home to be accounted for, whether or not they attempted to swindle the insurance company; and if they did make the attempt—and remember, they were desperate for money—a witness to be taken care of. They couldn't let Miss Manwaring go and tell the story of her adventure promiscuously, as she had every right to if she chose, for if it got to the ears of the insurance people their plot would fail, and they were none too sure that they were not liable to be sent to jail for conspiracy with intent to defraud. So they cooked up a story to account for Miss Manwaring and brought her here, knowing that I had recently dismissed Miss Matring. And immediately, as was quite right and proper, everything began to go wrong.

"To begin with, the insurance people proved sceptical, largely through Walter's stupidity. It seems that certain evidences had been left in the house of Miss Manwaring's presence there with what we may call, I presume, Walter's permission, the fatal night. The servants who discovered the burglary noticed these evidences and mentioned them in their telegram. Walter hurried back to New York to hush the servants up. He wasn't successful, and the fact that he had endeavoured to cover something came to the attention of the police, and, inevitably, through them to the insurance company.

"Then Miss Manwaring turned out to be a young woman of uncommon character, less gullible than they had reckoned; also, I may say without undue self-conceit, they had underestimated me. I grew suspicious, and questioned Miss Manwaring; she was too honest to want to lie to me and too sensible to try.

"Meantime the need of money grew daily more urgent. They decided that

Walter must pawn the jewels in Boston. They could be redeemed piece by piece when money was more plentiful. But the jewels were here, and Walter in New York, and it would be insane for him to come here and get them and then take them to Boston. In his emergency Adele went Walter one better in the matter of stupidity. She took Mr. Lyttleton into her confidence—and, crowning blunder! took his advice. Mr. Lyttleton conceived a magnificently romantic scheme. Walter was to come to New Bedford, secretly hire a motor-boat, and be off the harbour here at a certain hour of night. Mr. Lyttleton was to leave the jewels in a designated spot at the foot of the cliffs. At an agreed signal between the yacht and Adele's window Walter was to come in, at dead of night, and get the jewels, return to the mainland, discharge his boat, go to Boston, pawn the jewels, and be here in good time the next day.

"Walter, notified of this arrangement by letter to New York, fell in with it heart and soul. More stupidity, you see. Worse yet, he put it into effect. The arrangement was actually carried out last night. And again their luck turned against them. It so happened that both Miss Manwaring and Mr. Trego were sleepless last night and observed certain details of the conspiracy; and to make matters worse, it was the very night chosen by the thief to steal *my* jewels.

"When that came out they were all in panic—Walter, Adele, and Mr. Lyttleton. They put their empty heads together to think what was best to be done to avert suspicion from themselves. Miss Manwaring was the real stumbling-block. She knew far too much, and had proved rather difficult to manage. Among them they evolved another brilliant scheme: Miss Manwaring must be kidnapped and hidden away in a safe place until the trouble had blown over. Miss Manwaring having ostensibly confessed her guilt by flight, suspicion of complicity in the theft would be diverted from Walter, Adele, and Lyttleton; though they had positively no hand in the thing, they lacked the courage of their innocence, and they argued that, when in their own good time they set the girl at liberty, she would be wanted by the police and would never again dare show her face where it might be recognised. Not only stupid, you see, but cold-bloodedly selfish as well.

"Walter undertook to manage the business. He hired a rascally chauffeur of his acquaintance and commandeered a closed car from my own garage, figuring that the kidnapping would be an accomplished fact long before the machine could be wanted, while its absence would never arouse comment on a fete night. He then induced Miss Manwaring to consent to meet him in a conveniently secluded spot near the gates. I overheard something, enough to lead me to suspect there was something wrong afoot, and therefore persuaded Miss Manwaring to lend me this costume of hers and went to meet Walter in her stead. Before I guessed what was up a bag was thrown over my head, my hands and feet were bound, and I was lifted into the body of the car and driven away at such speed that Walter, who found out his mistake almost immediately, was unable to overtake me before I arrived at the spot chosen for Miss Manwaring's prison—a deserted shooting-lodge on the South Shore."

"Meantime, when it was found that I had been kidnapped instead of the girl, and while Walter was going to fetch me and make what amends he could, Adele and Mr. Lyttleton lost their heads entirely. Adele rushed round looking for Miss Manwaring, and when finally she found her, endeavoured to induce her to run away on her own account. And Mr. Lyttleton (who, by the by, will be leaving with Adele and Walter in the morning) on his own behalf arranged to direct suspicion of the robbery to Miss Manwaring, induced Mr. Mason to exceed my instructions and open the envelopes in my absence, and led Mr. Mason to Miss Manwaring's room, where, to his own stupendous surprise, there was found hidden one of the rings that had been stolen."

"What makes you think he was so much surprised?" Mr. Trego cut in, who had turned in his chair to eye Mr. Lyttleton in a most unpleasantly truculent fashion.

"Because he didn't know it was there."

"But somebody must have made the plant," Trego argued. "There's no question, I take it, of Miss Manwaring's innocence?"

"None whatever!" Mrs. Gosnold affirmed.

"Then why not Lyttleton as well as another?"

"That," Mrs. Gosnold said slowly, indeed reluctantly, "brings me to the fact that no confession has been made, as I had hoped it might be. That is to say, the jewels have not been restored. I am sorry. I have done all I could to protect the thief."

"You know—?" Trego inquired.

"I saw the theft committed," said Mrs. Gosnold. "It was done not for gain, but for the sole purpose of securing Miss Manwaring's discharge—"

A short, sharp cry interrupted her, and in the momentary silence of astonishment that followed Mercedes Pride shut her eyes, sighed gently, slipped from her chair, and subsided to the floor in a dead faint.

CHAPTER XVIII

BREAKING JAIL

Within five minutes Sally was back behind the locked door of her bedchamber, alone with the glowing exaltation of complete exoneration and triumph over the machinations of her ill-wishers, alone with what should naturally have been tingling satisfaction in consciousness of having administered yet another and (it was to be hoped) a final stinging snub to that animal of a Trego.

Yet her gratification in the memory of the latter event was singularly vapid, flat, and savourless.

They had been the last to leave the boudoir where, with the help of her maid, Mrs. Gosnold was preoccupied with effort to restore her kinswoman—that hapless victim of her own malevolence.

The others had been only too glad to disperse, following that diversion which freed them from the open contempt of their hostess, Sally and Trego. Lyttleton, indeed, had not hesitated to show his spirit by taking to his heels down the corridor to his quarters when Trego betrayed an inclination to follow him. And it was this circumstance which had led to the discomfiture of Trego.

"A fine young specimen!" Trego commented with some disappointment, louring after the rapidly retreating figure. "But wait," he suggested ominously, "just wait till I catch him outside the house. I knew I did wrong to let him off so easy last night. But I'll make up for it, all right. Leave him to me!"

"I am not interested in your personal quarrels with Mr. Lyttleton," Sally told him frigidly. "Mine, if you please, I will settle for myself in my own way. When I desire your interference, I shall notify you. Till then—whatever the circumstances—I hope you will be good enough not to speak to me under any circumstances whatever."

With this she had left him dashed and staring.

Now, in retrospection, she was alternately sorry that she had said as much and that she had not said more. He had deserved either the cut direct and absolute, or he had deserved a thoroughgoing, whole-hearted exposition of his own despicable perfidy.

She could never forgive him—and, what was worse, she could never forgive herself for the smart of her wounded pride, when she recalled that shameful scene in the garden. She could not forgive herself for caring one way or the other. She could not forgive herself for admitting that she cared.

It was just this which rendered her position in Gosnold House positively untenable, however firmly it might seem to have been re-established by the events of the last half-hour.

It was just this which kept the girl from her pillow, buoyed by a feverish excitement.

She could never stay at Gosnold House and continue on terms of any sort with Trego and suffer the airs with which Mrs. Artemas would treat her vanquished rival in the man's affections, even though Sally had never been conscious of the rivalry nor in any way encouraged the putative prize.

It might seem ungrateful to Mrs. Gosnold; Sally couldn't help that, though she was sincerely sorry; the association simply must be discontinued.

And that, she declared in her solitude, was all there was about it.... .

By the time she had succeeded in composing a note which seemed sufficiently grateful in tone to excuse the pitiful inadequacy of her excuse for absconding—that she was "out of her element" on the Island, an outsider, a Nobody, and didn't "belong" and never could—the chill light of early dawn had rendered the electrics garish.

She read the note over with hypercritical sensitiveness to its defects, but decided that it must do. Besides, she had used the last sheet of note-paper in the rack on her desk; more was not obtainable without a trip to the living-room. Then in desperation she appended, under the sign of the venerable P. S., a prayer that this might prove acceptable in lieu of more gracious leave-taking, addressed the envelope to Mrs. Gosnold, and left it sticking conspicuously in the frame of her dressing-mirror.

Studiously she reduced her travelling gear to the simplest requisites; the hand-bag she took because she had a use for it, nothing less than to serve as a cover for the return of everything she wore.

She was determined to go out of this Island world, whose ether was too rare for her vulgar lungs, with no more than she had brought into it.

At length the laggard hands of the clock were close together on the figure 6.

She rose, let herself out of the room, and by way of that memorable side door issued forth into a morning as rarely beautiful as ever that blessed Island knew. It made renunciation doubly difficult. Yet Sally did not falter or once look back.

Her way to the village wharf was shortest by the beach. None saw her steal through the formal garden (with eyes averted from that one marble seat which was forever distinguished from all others in the world) and vanish over the lip of the cliff by way of its long, zigzag stairway. Few noticed her as she debouched from the beach into the village streets; her dress was inconspicuous, her demeanour even more than retiring.

Her hope was favoured in that on this earlier trip of the boat there were few passengers other than natives of the Island.

On the mainland she caught an accommodation train which wound a halting way through the morning and set her down in Providence late in the forenoon. Then ignorance of railroad travel made her choose another accommodation instead of an express which would have cost no more and landed her in New York an hour earlier.

Her flight was financed by a few dollars left over from her bridge winnings of the first day at Gosnold House after subsequent losses had been paid. Their sum no more than sufficed; when she had purchased a meagre lunch at the station counter in New Haven she was penniless again; but for the clothes she wore she landed in New York even as she had left it.

The city received her with a deafening roar that seemed of exultation that its prey had been delivered unto it again.

The heat was even more oppressive than that of the day on which she had left —or perhaps seemed so by contrast with the radiant coolness of the Island air.

Avoiding Park Avenue, she sought the place that she called home by way of Lexington.

She went slowly, wearily, lugging her half-empty hand-hag as if it were a heavy burden.

At length, leaving the avenue, she paused a few doors west of the corner, climbed the weather-bitten steps to the brownstone entrance, and addressed herself to those three long flights of naked stairs.

The studio door at the top was closed and locked. The card had been torn from the tacks that held it to the panel.

Puzzled and anxious, she stopped and turned up a corner of the worn fibre mat—and sighed with relief to find the key in its traditional hiding-place.

But when she let herself in, it was to a room tenanted solely by seven howling devils of desolation.

Only the decrepit furniture remained; it had not been worth cartage or storage; every personal belonging of the other two girls had disappeared; Mary Warden had not left so much as a sheet of music, Lucy Spade had overlooked not so much as a hopeless sketch.

Yet Sally had no cause for complaint; they had forsaken her less indifferently than she had them; one or the other had left a newspaper, now three days old, propped up where she could not fail to see it on the antiquated marble mantel-shelf. In separate columns on the page folded outermost two items were encircled with rings of crimson water-colour.

One, under the caption "News of Plays and Players," noted the departure for an opening in Atlantic City of the musical comedy company of whose chorus Mary Warden was a member.

The other, in the column headed "Marriages," announced tersely the nuptials of Lucy Spode and Samuel W. Meyerick. No details were given.

Forlornly Sally wandered to the windows and opened them to exchange the hot air of the studio for the hotter air of the back yards.

Then slowly she set about picking up the threads of her life.

Such clothing as she owned offered little variety for choice. She selected the least disreputable of two heavy, black winter skirts, a shirt-waist badly torn at the collar-band, her severely plain under-clothing, coarse black stockings, and shoes that had been discarded as not worth another visit to the cobbler's.

When these had been exchanged for the gifts of Mrs. Standish, Sally grimly packed the latter into the hand-bag and shut the latch upon them with a snap of despair.

Come evening, when it was dark enough, she would leave them at the door of the residence up the street, ring the bell, and run.

She sat out a long hour, hands listless in her lap, staring vacantly out at that well-hated vista of grimy back yards, drearily reviewing the history of the last five days. She felt as one who had dreamed a dream and was not yet sure that she had waked.

Later she roused to the call of hunger, and foraged in the larder, or what served the studio as such, turning up a broken carton of Uneeda Biscuit and half a packet of black tea. There was an egg, but she prudently refrained from testing it... .

It never entered her weary head to imagine that the feet that pounded heavily on the stairs were those of anybody but the janitor; she was wondering idly whether there were rent due, and if she would be turned out into the street that very night; and was thinking it did not much matter, when the footfalls stopped on the threshold of the studio and she looked up into the face of Mr. Trego.

Surprise and indignation smote her with speechlessness, but her eyes were eloquent enough as she started up—and almost overturned the rickety table at which she had been dining.

But he was crassly oblivious of her emotion. Removing his hat, he mopped his brow, sighed, and smiled winningly.

"Hello!" he said. "You certainly did give me a deuce of a hunt. I wormed it out of Mrs. Gosnold that you inhabited a studio somewhere on this block, and I suppose I must have climbed thirty times three flights of stairs in the last hour."

She demanded in a low, tense voice: "Why have you followed me here?"

"Well," he protested, "Mrs. Gosnold sent me—and if she hadn't, I would have come anyway. I told you last night that I loved you. I haven't changed since then. And now that you're in a fix, whether or not of your own contriving—well, it isn't my notion of love to let you pull out for yourself if you'll let me help. And that goes, even if you stick to it that you won't marry me."

"And Mrs. Artemas?" she inquired icily. "What does she think about your coming after me?"

He stared and laughed. "Oh, did you know about that? I hoped you didn't."

"I saw you with her in your arms."

"Yes," he agreed patiently. "She'd been laying for me for several weeks. I told you she was—don't you remember? Only, of course, I didn't name her. And last night, when I went back there looking for you, she cornered me; and while I was trying to be nice and explain I could never be anything more than a brother to her she began to blubber and threw herself into my arms and … What could a fellow do? I tried to make her behave, but before she would listen to reason those confounded people had to pop up. And, of course, she took advantage of that opening instanter. But—great Scott!—you didn't suppose I was going to be that sort of a gentleman and let her get away with it, did you? when I am so much in love with you I can hardly keep from grabbing you now! Not likely!"

She tried to answer him, but her traitorous voice broke, and before she could master it he had resumed.

"Mrs. Gosnold wants you back—sent me to say so—says she'll come after you if I fail to bring you."

"Oh, no!" she protested, trembling uncontrollably.

"You won't meet any of those folks. They're all going to-day. It's a new deal from a fresh deck, so to speak."

"No," she averred more steadily. "You told me I was foolish; you were right. I'm through with all that."

He came closer to her. "You needn't be," he said. "Don't damn Society just because you got in wrong at the first attempt. Try again. Let me try with you. I've got all the money there is, more or less. If you want a villa at Newport —"

"Oh, please, no! I tell you, I'm finished with all that forever."

"Well," he grinned fatuously, "what about a flat in Harlem?"

A little smile broke through her tears.

"Why must you go to such extremes?" she laughed brokenly. "Aren't there any more apartments to be had on Riverside Drive?"

THE END

www.ingramcontent.com/pod-product-compliance
Lightning Source LLC
Chambersburg PA
CBHW021231020726
47498CB00008B/2792